I0681171

DARK RESCUE

A FOREVER MAN NOVEL

BRIAN W. MATTHEWS

JOURNALSTONE
YOUR LINK TO ARTIST TALENT

Copyright 2018 © Brian W. Matthews

All rights reserved. No part of this book may be used or reproduced by any means, graphic, electronic, or mechanical, including photocopying, recording, taping or by any information storage retrieval system without the written permission of the publisher except in the case of brief quotations embodied in critical articles and reviews.

This is a work of fiction. All of the characters, names, incidents, organizations, and dialogue in this novel are either the products of the author's imagination or are used fictitiously.

JournalStone books may be ordered through booksellers or by contacting:
JournalStone
www.journalstone.com

The views expressed in this work are solely those of the authors and do not necessarily reflect the views of the publisher, and the publisher hereby disclaims any responsibility for them.

ISBN: 978-1-947654-21-1 (sc)
ISBN: 978-1-947654-22-8 (ebook)

JournalStone rev. date: March 16, 2018

Library of Congress Control Number: 2018936325

Printed in the United States of America

Cover Design: Chuck Killorin
Interior Layout: Jess Landry

Edited by: Vincenzo Bilof
Proofread by: Sean Leonard

DARK RESCUE

A FOREVER MAN NOVEL

For Robert and Michael
In a book about brothers, this one is for mine.

PART ONE: A WORLD ASUNDER

CHAPTER ONE

Gene Vincent mounted the steps to Celeste Florin's bungalow. She kept her doors locked, and the porch didn't have a bell. He pounded on the frame. No one answered.

He listened for Cheech. Celeste's bulldog wasn't barking, wasn't ramming his fireplug body against the door. Cheech always challenged visitors.

Celeste, the best waitress he'd ever had and a dear friend, hadn't shown for work. Her unexplained absence bothered him enough that he drove out here to investigate.

Not hearing Cheech, though—that set his teeth on edge.

He checked the rest of the house for signs of forced entry. The place was locked up tighter than an otter's pocket; not a thing out of place. Not that he expected anything different in a rustic burg like Kinsey. The local rag's crime blotter usually highlighted several weekend bar brawls and one or two cases of shoplifting. Not quite the Chicago crime scene he'd experienced years ago.

Still, Gene almost called Sten Billick, his friend and Kinsey's chief of police.

Movement drew his eye to an upper story window. A figure

moved in one of the rooms.

"Celeste," Gene shouted. "Hey, Celeste!"

The figure stopped. Shadows obscured its features. Gene could almost feel the person looking at him. Then the figure stepped away from the window.

All the saliva suddenly disappeared from Gene's mouth. The urge to run swept over him.

The front door opened. "What do you want?"

He recognized the voice: Celeste. She remained inside the house. He couldn't see her clearly, only a vague outline of her shape.

"You didn't show for work," he said. "I was worried, so I thought I'd come check on you."

"I can take care of myself."

"You sound horrible."

"And you sound like a nosy little *pendejo*."

Gene frowned. "Tell me what's wrong. Maybe I can help."

"I don't need help."

"Mind if I come in and look around?"

"I don't think so."

"Okay, then. Tell me one thing and I'll go. I won't bother you again. I promise."

"Fine. What?"

"Where's Cheech?"

"Who?"

"Cheech, your dog. Where is he?"

"Oh, him." Celeste glanced over her shoulder. "He's around somewhere."

"How could you forget your dog's name?"

"You asked, I answered. Now go."

"One more question."

"No more, *pendejo*. You're out of time."

"I'll call the police." Gene held up his phone. "You can talk to me, or you can talk to them."

Celeste hesitated, then said, "Be quick."

"What's my name?"

"More games? Go away. I don't have the time for them or you." She started to shut the door.

"That's the deal," he said. "Tell me my name or I call the police."

"Again with the *policia*. What is it with you? Did you sleep with the little whore? Is that why you're being such a *joda*? You fucked her, so now you think you love her?"

Gene tried to swallow but couldn't. His throat had become dust. "Come out where I can see you."

"I'm finished with you, *pendejo*."

"It's either me or the cops." Lifting his phone, Gene held a finger over the buttons. "Take your pick."

"Fine. If it will get rid of you." The door swung open and she stepped across the threshold.

Gene staggered. Someone, some *bastard*, had beaten Celeste Florin almost beyond recognition. Her dress hung in tatters around her battered body. Blood seeped from her nose, now clearly broken. The flesh around one eye had swollen to the point of closing.

"I'm getting you an ambulance," he said and dialed 911.

"Careful, little hero. Your cape is showing."

"Not a hero. A friend."

"No more time, *mi amigo*." She slid to the concrete porch. "You lost."

"Shit." He rattled off the address to the emergency operator and hung up. After mounting the steps, he stripped off his jacket and covered her with it.

"He made me lie to you," she said, her voice weak and shaking. "He has Cheech. Said he would kill him if you didn't leave. I'm sorry."

"Where is he?"

"Upstairs," she whispered, and closed her eyes.

Gene's fists clenched. Sten Billick would be here soon. Sten would arrest the son of a bitch who did this and toss his ass in jail. Sten would make sure the process happened smoothly and painlessly.

But in his mind, the abuse inflicted on Celeste demanded more than "smooth and painless."

Some debts must be paid in kind, and he would see this one paid in full.

✳✳✳

The inside of the house resembled a war zone. Overturned furniture. Picture frames shattered, the photos removed and torn. A broken wicker basket revealing skeins of yarn and knitting needles and a pair of scissors. Bloody handprints on the walls. His stomach turned at the sight of so much violence. Not since the events in Kinsey years ago had he seen such destruction.

Pausing long enough to listen at the base of a stairway leading to the upper rooms—he heard no footsteps, no creaking floorboards, no one moving—Gene hurried to the kitchen and found the same violence: an upended table, an old polaroid photograph, a pan of water on the stove, its handle wet with blood; more blood on the floor, a large red smear like a comma punctuating the struggle that had occurred.

Tearing his gaze from the violence, he found the block of knives on the counter. Crossing the room, he grabbed the biggest, baddest piece of cutlery in the block, a broad-bladed cleaver with enough heft to split open a skull.

Perfect.

The polaroid snagged his attention. It looked jarringly out of place on the counter, its edges curled and blackened: a photo of a man, dark haired and unshaven, a cigarette hanging from between his lips, his face turned away from the camera, as if disinterested in life or in the person taking the picture, or both.

Gene picked it up and fingered a charred edge. Clearly, someone tried to burn it.

The pan of water… a safe place to dump the photo once it'd been destroyed?

And who was the man in the photo?

Mysteries for later. He dropped the polaroid. It fluttered in the air like a feather, landed face-up on the linoleum—

—and within the photo, the strange man with the sepia-toned skin and the grainy stubble turned to face Gene.

Gene stared in horror as the man plucked the cigarette from his mouth. His lips peeled back, revealing a shock of crooked, yellowed teeth.

"You didn't tell me, *pendejo*." The man's voice wheezed like stale air escaping from a moldy accordion. "Did you love the little bitch?"

Gene stumbled back, slipped on the blood, landed next to the table. Pain ricocheted up his bad back.

The man in the photo laughed. "Stupid little hero can't keep his feet."

Heart racing, Gene dug his boots into the floor, tried to scoot away, but the blood made the tiles slick and his feet shot out and he kicked the table. It skidded, hit something solid, tumbled off to one side. Hidden behind the table was an animal, twisted and crushed almost flat, even its skull. Tufts of brown and white fur stuck out where ribs had punched through skin. One eye had burst into a goopy mess. Its jaw had been wrenched open, a coil of intestine pulled out through its mouth.

Cheech, Celeste's bulldog.

A rush of footsteps. Sudden, searing pain in his shoulder.

Gene twisted. Celeste brought the sewing scissors down again. The blades dug into his chest. A third blow laid open the skin on his neck.

"Celeste!" Gene cried out in alarm. "No!"

Celeste lifted the scissors. "You should have left, *pendejo*."

He didn't want to do it but she'd left him no choice. Arm raised to block her next blow, Gene buried the cleaver in the meaty part of her thigh. Skin and muscle unzipped, revealing a smooth contour of bone.

Screaming, she lunged at him, the blades poised to tear out his throat.

"Police! Freeze!"

Celeste screamed, her face red with rage. She brought the scissors down in a brutal, unforgiving arc.

Gunshots. Celeste jerked, blood spraying from holes in her chest. She tried again to advance, to attack. More gunshots. Her body flailed. She managed a weak, "*Pendejo*," before her eyes rolled up inside her head and she collapsed.

Sten Billick stepped into the kitchen. Face pale, a sheen of sweat on his brow, he kept his gun trained on Celeste Florin.

"Gene, what the hell's going on?"

||*

"Celeste told me there was someone in the house," Gene said. "Someone who was threatening her."

Sten Billick stood next to the hospital bed. He'd loosened the knot on his tie. "My men went through the place twice. Checked the attic, the crawl space, the rooms. They didn't find anybody."

"Celeste didn't kill Cheech. She loved that dog."

"Her wounds were consistent with an animal attack. Even a pet will put up a fight if it feels threatened."

A nurse entered the room, threaded a syringe to his IV line, and pumped him full of drugs. The warm glow of the narcotics washed over him and he liked it. He liked it perhaps a bit too much. Since the accident that had wrecked his back, he had struggled with opioid addition. Not always successfully either.

"Celeste wasn't a violent person," Gene said, somewhat mutely.

"Normally, I'd agree."

"She wasn't behaving like herself."

"She tried to kill you."

"It was more than that. Her speech pattern, the swearing… they weren't consistent with the Celeste I knew. It's like she was a different person."

Sten pulled a clear plastic evidence bag from his pocket. It contained the polaroid from the kitchen. The unshaven man once again looked away from the camera.

"We found a box of photos. All of the same man."

"Any idea who he is?"

Sten nodded. "We also found newspaper clippings. His name is Consuelo Pequin. Major low-life. Arrests for battery, sexual assault, armed robbery, resisting arrest, domestic violence. Died in a shootout with police back in the nineties. He left behind an ex-wife and three children, including a daughter." Sten lifted the bag. "Meet Celeste's father."

"That man moved." Gene jabbed a finger at the evidence bag. "He spoke to me."

"Any chance you imagined it?"

"He talked the same way Celeste did, the same speech pattern, the same tone." The same anger and disdain.

"The guy's been dead for almost twenty years."

"He even repeated the same words Celeste used."

"I don't believe in ghosts."

"What about monsters? Have you stopped believing in them?"

Sten's expression hardened. He had watched video of the attack on Kinsey's jail facility, where a monster called a Fek had torn the place apart and almost killed a man named Bart Owens. He had also conveniently erased the recording. "Different circumstances."

"Celeste's father spoke to me," Gene said. "Maybe he did the same thing to her. Maybe that's why she tried to burn the photo."

"It still doesn't explain why she attacked you, or killed her dog."

"Maybe her dad beat her as a kid, or sexually abused her. All of a sudden he's dead and she's free of him. Imagine the relief she must have felt. Now, years later, he starts talking to her. He's back in her life. All those horrible memories return. That could unhinge the strongest person."

"I might agree if she'd killed herself. But why kill Cheech, and then attack you? It doesn't fit."

It didn't. And with Celeste dead, they had no way to find out the truth. "What happens next?"

Sten put away the evidence bag. "I type up a report. Want me to include your statement about the photograph?"

That made Gene pause. As much as he believed in what he'd seen, police reports were public documents. Anyone could read them. Friends. Relatives. Customers.

"Nah," he said. "Skip that part."

Sten nodded. "I'll have the report ready by tomorrow. Stop by when you feel better and sign it. Barring something odd coming back on her autopsy, I think we can close the book on this one."

***

Laying in his own bed felt wonderful. Gene's body ached but the pain in his heart hurt more. Celeste had been more than an employee—she had been a close friend.

The polaroid. Consuelo Pequin had moved; he had talked.

Gene hadn't imagined it.

He dug into the pile of papers on his nightstand until he found an envelope with no return address. He removed the letter.

In case you change your mind.

The sender had written a phone number across the bottom.
The letter wasn't signed.
It didn't need to be.
He picked up his cell.

CHAPTER TWO

Izzy Morris paused at the entrance to Evelyn Lingard's room. Through the door she could smell the antiseptic housekeeping had used earlier. Work in a hospital and you get used to the bitter sting of ammonia.

She had been volunteering at Butterworth Hospital for almost two years, under the name Elizabeth Marzecki. A paid job was out of the question: providing the social security number of a presumably dead woman would out her immediately. But a woman needed a part of her life to call her own, even if it reflected too closely her day-to-day struggle.

Smoothing her uniform, Izzy forced a smile and pushed open the door.

A bed with fitted cotton sheets dominated the room. Evelyn Lingard's frail body lay on top of the mattress, a down-filled duvet brought from home tucked around her, a silk pillow, also from her home, under her head. A nasal cannula fed her oxygen delivered from a heavy, green metal tank.

Someone had taped an arc of get-well cards to the wall above the bed. Izzy read the names signed along the bottoms.

So many children, so many grandchildren. So much love.

Izzy wished she could say the same for herself.

A dinner tray, the food uneaten, sat on the bedside table. This marked the third day in a row Mrs. Lingard hadn't touched her supper. She had had her fill and was ready to slip away, content with the story of her life. Izzy prayed her passing would be pain-less and peaceful.

Outside the window, the late afternoon sun floated above Grand Rapids' skyline. Izzy raised the blinds to let in the warm evening glow. The light brought out the ruddier tones in Mrs. Lingard's thin, waxy skin and, for a moment, Izzy could almost imagine the woman was not dying.

The air compressor clamped to the foot of the bed rumbled to life. Mrs. Lingard's pressure relief pad hissed and creaked as it shifted her tiny body. The woman winced at the movement.

Izzy touched the woman's shoulder. "Mrs. Lingard?"

Evelyn Lingard moaned. Her right arm twitched. Her wispy eyebrows drew together, deepening the wrinkles on her forehead.

"Mrs. Lingard? Are you in pain?"

The woman's mouth opened. Her tongue emerged, stiff and dry, like an overcooked piece of brisket. "Nuh, nuh, nuh."

"You're thirsty? Sure, hold on." Izzy grabbed the water from the dinner tray, inserted a straw, and held it to Mrs. Lingard's lips. "Here you go."

Mrs. Lingard sucked weakly. Most of the water dribbled down her chin.

Izzy kept a pack of tissues in her pocket. She used one to blot Mrs. Lingard's chin. "Would you like more?"

Evelyn Lingard gave the barest shake of her head.

"That's all right, sweetie," Izzy said. "You go back to sleep."

***

Izzy visited two more patients before her shift ended.

Hospitals bustled with activity during shift change. Izzy joined a group of nurses riding the elevator to the parking garage, careful to keep her eyes down and conversations superficial. She stayed with them as long as possible before peeling off and heading for her car. Two small canisters dangled from her keyring, one in a smooth metal case and the other in a scuffed-up plastic case; she could tell one from the other by touch. The metal case held pepper spray and would drop a human in seconds. The latter contained a solution designed by Thomas, one of the cadre of Forever Men she had come to know and love, for times when the pepper spray wouldn't work. Or so he claimed. She'd not had a chance to test it.

She arrived at her car without incident. The drive home usually didn't take long, but tonight she had a stop to make.

The clerk didn't look up from her magazine when Izzy entered the drugstore. She made her way to the personal care section, where she loaded a carrier with cans of liquefied food, some baby wipes, and a bottle of shampoo. For good measure, she added two packages of adult diapers.

The supplies set her back fifty dollars. She paid cash. She always paid cash. Credit cards could be traced. Questions might arise. Difficult questions, ones to which she did not have good answers.

Such was life living under the radar.

She arrived home just past eight. Lights burned in the kitchen. Natalie sat at the table, eating leftover mac and cheese.

"Hey, sweetie," Izzy said. "Where's your brother?"

"I wish you wouldn't call him that," Natalie said, her voice sullen. "He's not my brother."

Izzy set her bag of supplies on the counter. "Really? We're going to have this discussion again?"

"Then don't bring him up," Natalie said. "Or better yet, let one of your friends take him. They can protect him just as well as you."

"You know we can't do that."

"You can. You just don't want to. You're obsessed with him."

"Kevin has more problems than you can imagine." Izzy picked a noodle off Natalie's plate and ate it. "He's special, and not always in good ways."

"He's special, all right. So special he's all you ever think about." Natalie shoved her dinner away. "I don't know why I'm eating. I'm not even hungry."

Izzy frowned. "Honey, look at me."

Natalie lifted her head. Her skin was pale, her expression tight. Wet eyes simmered inside tarry pits of thick, black liner. Goth chick going off the deep end.

"I thought so," Izzy said, and sat down. "What's wrong?"

"I don't know. The new Star Wars movie sucked? Bad cramps? Could be anything. Could be nothing."

"Holding it in will only make it worse."

"Good," Natalie whispered, and looked away. "Maybe that's what I need."

"Are you having nightmares?" Who wouldn't after being abducted by a monster?

Natalie shook her head. "No."

"How about Kevin? Did you guys have a fight?"

"He's been in his room all day. I haven't said a word to him."

"Then what is it? What's bugging you?"

"Drop it, Mom. You wouldn't understand."

Wouldn't understand? Her daughter must be kidding. "I chased that lunatic Darryl Webber through a forest to find you. I fought a monster to find you. I defied an entire town to find you. And then I gave up my life to keep you safe. Don't you dare tell me I wouldn't understand."

"This is different. You can't compare the two."

"You're right, I can't. Not if you keep your part a secret."

"Drop it, Mom. It'd only hurt you."

"Better me hurting than you."

"Fine." Natalie leaned in. "I want to see Dad."

Izzy suddenly had difficulty breathing. Old fears filled her, leaving no room for air.

Her father? She wanted to see *Stanley*?

"Oh, honey, I don't—" Izzy fumbled for the right words. "You know that can't happen. We'd be risking his life along with ours."

"I understand you don't love him anymore," Natalie said, "but I still do. I miss him, Mom. I miss him a lot. It's not fair we're kept apart." She wiped at her eyes, smearing her eyeliner, her face now as much a mess as her emotions. "He doesn't even know I'm alive."

"Natalie, if I didn't care about your father, I would take you to see him tomorrow. But think about what it would do to him."

Not to mention what it would do to her responsibilities here. "He thinks we're dead. He's had four years to move on with his life. What if he's found someone else, has a new family? What if he's happy?" An unexpected pang of regret stabbed at her heart at the thought of Stanley being with another woman. She thrust the pain aside and pushed on. "Now imagine us showing up on his doorstep. Not only would we potentially ruin his happiness, we'd have to deal with his anger at being lied to. In his eyes, he'll think I took you away—"

"You did!" Natalie said. "You took me away, and you never asked if I wanted to go!"

"He'll think I kept you from him," Izzy continued. "And I did. He'll call the police. Four years of work ruined, not to mention what it'll do to your father. Can't you see how cruel it would be? Stanley is a good man. I want him to be happy. He deserves to be happy. That's why seeing him is a bad idea. I know it's hard to accept, but it's the truth.

"Then there's Marbæs. She's out there, looking for Kevin, looking for us. Looking for Bartholomew. She could have someone watching Kinsey, waiting for us to make the very mistake you're contemplating. Do you remember what the Fek did to Jimmy Cain, to Katie's mom, to Chet Boardman? To you?" Izzy shuddered at the memory of the nightmare wolf-snake creature that had killed so many people she'd sworn to protect. "Monsters worse than the Fek exist. You know who Bartholomew is, who Philip and the others are. You know what they're doing for the world. Yet you want to risk drawing Marbæs and her ilk right to our doorstep." Her voice rose. "All because you want to see your father. Well, I'm sorry, Natalie. It sucks, but we're dealing with bigger problems than you missing your dad."

Izzy forced herself to stop. Natalie's request had touched off a storm inside her, one that threatened to rage out of control. She sympathized with her daughter's plight, but with Katie and Philip gone, and the other Forever Men on the way, Izzy didn't need another complication. As much as it hurt her to do so, she couldn't give her daughter what she wanted.

"I'll never see him again?" Natalie asked.

"Sweetie, I don't know. Never's a long time." Izzy grabbed the plate of mac and cheese and dumped the food down the drain. "Do me a favor, check on Kevin. He had schoolwork he should have finished by now." She put the plate in the dishwasher. "I'm fixing sloppy joes for dinner. Since you didn't finish your meal, you can join us later. First I have to go downstairs. I won't be long."

"You ever get tired of being a hard-ass?" Natalie said.

Izzy picked up the bag of supplies and headed for the stairs. "Every minute of the day."

***

The basement smelled faintly of antiseptic, similar to Mrs. Lingard's room at the hospital but less intense. Death and decay had no foothold here.

Several lamps brightened the room. Most of the furniture had been cleared out, put into storage at a nearby facility. She had kept the wall hangings, a set of comfortable chairs, and a bookcase filled with works from Chaucer and St. Augustine to the more contemporary books of Graham Greene and Joseph Conrad. Philip had insisted on the former.

"History is filled with hope," he had told her. He hadn't smiled since the events in Dearborn, two weeks ago. "The books have a place here, where hope is needed most."

She approached the bed in the middle of the room. Bartholomew Owens lay on it with his eyes closed. He wore a hospital gown Izzy had taken from work. A nasogastric tube had been inserted through one nostril. She had watched the procedure at work, and it had taken her a few tries before she got it right. Luckily the old man was next to impossible to injure.

"I'm here, Bartholomew," she said, unsure if he could hear her. It didn't matter. He had done much for the world, had helped so many people. She wasn't going to let him go through this crisis thinking he was alone. "I'm here."

She shook her head. To have someone seemingly indestructible laid so low terrified her; to have him dependent upon others for his basic care filled her with sorrow.

She busied herself putting away the supplies. At the wash basin she opened a can of liquid food and used a large syringe to draw some out. She rolled the syringe in her hands to warm Bartholomew's dinner.

After pushing the food through the nasogastric tube, she waited a few minutes and checked Bartholomew's diaper. True to form, his bowels had evacuated after his feeding. She used a baby wipe to clean him, and more to wash his skin. She put a new diaper on him. Unlike with normal men, she didn't have to worry about bed sores. His ability to heal himself hadn't diminished with his condition.

Finished with his feeding and bathing, Izzy looked at the man who had saved her life, at his expressionless brown face. His eyes didn't move under their lids.

"We'll find you," she said, and lightly touched the teardrop-shaped mark under his left eye. She knew what it symbolized, and how much Bartholomew had sacrificed to bear it. "Wherever you've gone, we'll find you. I promise."

She needed to start dinner, to care for the others living under her roof. She started up the stairs but stopped when her phone buzzed. She checked the display.

Her eyes widened when she saw the caller's name.

CHAPTER THREE

Izzy whipped together the sloppy joes in no time.

"Natalie, Kevin," she called out. "Dinner."

Footsteps pounded down the hallway and Kevin burst into the kitchen wearing pajama bottoms and a Grand Rapids Griffins shirt. He must have been working on his art project: he'd somehow gotten blue paint on his cheek, a mark that looked eerily similar to the teardrop on Bart Owens's face.

"Dinner!" he said, giggling, and took his place at the table. "Go joe, go!"

Izzy sighed. Kevin's von Kliner's syndrome, an unusual (some might say *supernatural*) variant of autism, intruded into his life in so many ways. Even though he was twelve years old, often he spoke and behaved like a child. His maturity had improved over the years, but not enough for her, and it wrung her heart. Only during his times of clarity, when his condition either receded or thinned, did she see him as he should have been.

More often than not, those times left her feeling exhilarated, and profoundly frightened.

"Yes, I get it," she said. "You love sloppy joes. Go fix yourself a sandwich."

Kevin approached the stove. A smile spread across his pudgy face as he glopped cooked hamburger onto a bun. "More," he said, and heaped another spoonful onto the bun. By the time he got to the third helping, the juices had soaked into the bread and the sandwich disintegrated under its own weight.

Kevin scowled at the mess on the floor. The corners of his mouth turned down. His lower lip quivered.

"Sorry," he said. "I'm sorry, Mom."

Izzy grabbed a paper towel and cleaned the mess. "It's all right, honey. You just got excited. Go get another bun. Two helpings this time, no more."

"No, Mom. I mean it. I'm sorry."

The change in Kevin's voice, the unexpected logic of his words, caught her attention. Kevin's eyes had taken on an uncommon clarity, a piercing focus she knew would not last. She also knew to listen when these episodes came over Kevin.

"Sorry for what, Kevin?"

Kevin hesitated. "For what's going to happen." He picked up a bun and began loading it with meat. His movements had become slow and precise, like his words. "You have to go away. It's the only way to save Bartholomew, to save the rest of us. You can try other solutions, but they won't work. You'll just be wasting your time." He squirted mustard on the sandwich and set the other piece of the bun on top. "The journey won't be easy, but you have to go. You have to take the chance. There's no other way." He took a bite. Yellow-tinged juice dripped down his chin. He twitched, and then giggled. Izzy's heart sank. She was losing him. "Only, the answer you're looking for, it isn't where you think it is." He giggled harder this time, as if he had just told the world's funniest joke. His time with her was almost over. "I feel sorry for you, for all of you. Most of all, I feel sorry for Matthew."

Izzy sat back on her haunches, the paper towel damp in her hand. Matthew? She couldn't recall Kevin ever having a conversation with the reticent Forever Man. She wasn't sure he even knew Matthew existed. "Why do you feel sorry for him?"

Her question had come too late. The clarity in Kevin's gaze slipped away like quicksilver. He wandered over to the table and began to eat.

She stood, wrung the paper towel out in the sink, and tossed it in the trash. Like Kevin, she worried about Matthew, so her son's sentiment didn't surprise her. Except...Kevin couldn't know of Matthew's troubles, even if they had spoken. Matthew himself never broached the subject. Not that this mattered, she supposed; circumstances like reality didn't always apply to Kevin.

In an effort to get back on track, she opened a bag of chips and poured some onto Kevin's plate. He crammed several into his mouth.

A door slammed, and moments later Natalie made her typical grand appearance. Dressed in black jeans and a black shirt, her black hair combed, her black eyeliner reapplied, she looked ready for more than dinner.

"Going somewhere?" Izzy asked.

"The mall. I need space." Natalie fished around in her purse and pulled out her car keys. "Don't wait up for me."

Izzy snatched the keys from her daughter's hand. "You know the rules. What time will you be back?"

"Give me those!" Natalie reached for the keys.

Izzy slapped her hand away. Kevin flinched at the violence but didn't say anything. He rarely commented on their altercations.

"What time?" Izzy said.

"Jesus, you never give up. The mall closes at ten. How about eleven?"

"An hour to drive back home?"

"I might hang out. Is that a problem? Is it against your rules?"

"I almost lost you once," Izzy said. "I put these precautions in place to help prevent that from happening again." She dropped the keys in Natalie's outstretched hand. "Eleven o'clock. You have your phone?"

"In my purse."

"And Thomas's spray?"

"The same," Natalie said, her words snapping like firecrackers. "Are you through with the interrogation?"

Izzy bit back a sharp retort. Natalie had adopted a disturbing nonchalance about what happened to her; a gauzy barrier, transparent yet impenetrable. Bring up her abduction and the gruesome murder of Jimmy Cain and Natalie immediately changed the subject; ask about her time spent with the Fek and its sociopathic master, Darryl Webber, and she paled. But at the same time, she insisted she remembered none of it.

Izzy knew better. The incidents of four years ago had affected her daughter, had likely warped her view of herself and the world. Natalie fluttered like a rag caught in a windstorm, anchored only by her steadfast refusal to address her fears.

The last part worried Izzy the most: if Natalie were to open up, if she were to become unburdened, and therefore unanchored, what would happen?

Would she lose her little girl all over again?

"Just be careful, okay?" Izzy said. "Call me if there's any trouble. And don't forget, we have company coming tomorrow. I'll need your help."

Natalie started for the door. "Fine, wake me early. I'll do what I can."

"Bye-bye, Nat." Kevin flapped his hands in the air.

Natalie gave him a withering look and stormed out of the house.

Smiling, Kevin made himself another sloppy joe. "She loves me," he said.

Izzy joined him at the stove, picked up a bun, and made her own dinner.

"Yes, she does," she said softly. "I just hope she remembers it one day."

***

Natalie wandered the aisles of one of the mall's many clothing stores.

Nothing appealed to her. The shirts looked like human skins, the pants like straight razors. She chose a black tag hat with a heavy chain and spikes and set it on her head. It looked like shit. She took it off and tossed it aside.

An entire store of goth wear and she couldn't find a single thing she liked.

She was about to leave when someone walked up to her.

He looked young, about her age, with unevenly trimmed hair brushed over the left part his face, intense eyes, and sculpted lips. Studs pierced his eyebrows and nose. Red hoops stretched his earlobes wide enough she could stick her tongue through the holes.

He held out the hat she had tried on. "This looked good on you. You should buy it."

"Not my style. Besides, look at the price. I don't have the cash for that."

"Okay, then." He dropped the hat and kicked it under a rack of coats. "All gone."

Natalie couldn't help but laugh. "What's your name, funny guy?"

"Sean."

"Natalie."

"Does Natalie have a last name?"

"Marzecki. Yours?"

"Leyton."

He reached out and touched her face. "You're beautiful, you know."

An image flashed through Natalie's mind—Darryl Webber, his coarse hand stroking her hair—and she flinched. "Don't do that."

He lowered his hand. "Sorry. Didn't mean to upset you."

"Malls are filled with creeps."

"I'm harmless, really."

"Maybe you are, maybe you aren't. Point is, I don't know for sure."

"Then find out. It'd be worth your time."

"You certainly don't lack for self-confidence," Natalie said.

Sean smiled. "Let's hang for a while, get something to eat, catch a movie. I get the feeling you don't have many friends."

"I have plenty of friends." Old defenses kicked in, and the lie flowed as smooth as melted chocolate off her tongue. "I don't need more."

"I've been there," Sean said, fingering a button on his jacket. "Alone in my own world. I know how it feels. I'm asking for a chance, Natalie. That's all, just a chance."

"A chance for what?"

"To be something I think you don't have many of—a friend."

Natalie's breath caught in her throat. She did feel alone, and terribly lonely. Despite her mother, despite Bartholomew and Philip and the others, despite the recent reappearance (and subsequent disappearance) of Katie Bethel, she had no close friends, no one who could understand what had been done to her.

She really could use another friend.

But her mother had trained her to be cautious, to take nothing and no one for granted, to keep her guard up and her pretense going. She had been told, time and again, how secrecy would keep her alive.

She didn't know Sean Leyton. She wasn't sure if he was even human.

She did possess a way to find out, though.

"I'll hang with you," she said. "But only under one condition."

"Fair enough. Name it."

Natalie removed two tiny canisters from her purse and showed them to Sean. "This one here," she said, pointing to the canister with the smooth metal casing, "contains pepper spray, so don't get any funny ideas. This other one"—she held up the canister in the scruffy plastic casing—"is harmless, but I want to spray you with it anyway."

Sean reached out to the canister but stopped short of actually touching it. "What's inside it?"

"Water, but just for fun, let's say it's *holy* water. Are you a vampire? Are you worried you'll melt?"

His expression hardened. "Seriously, you want to spray me with water?"

"Just a spritz. Is a wet face too high a price to pay to get what you want?"

"What I wanted was a friend, not some bullshit hazing ritual."

Anger clouded Sean's features. She couldn't blame him: her request was way out of line. But she had to be sure. She wouldn't let herself be hurt again.

"I understand what this must look like," she said. "But I have my reasons. It's the only condition I have. Take it or leave it."

"How do I know it's not acid in that thing? I don't want my face to melt off."

"Attack you in the middle of a store, with a dozen or more witnesses?"

"Stranger things have happened."

"It's not acid," she said. "I'm not going to stand here all night. Do we have a deal?"

"You're asking a lot, Natalie. Especially since I just met you."

"So that's a no?"

Sean hesitated. He stared at the canisters as if they were venomous snakes. After a few moments, he shook his head. "Sorry, but I'll pass."

"I guess it was a bigger deal than I thought." She put the canisters away. "You seem like a nice person, Sean. I'm sorry we didn't get to be friends."

She left the store. Sean didn't chase after her, saying he'd changed his mind. That he didn't hurt a little.

She'd parked her car two lots over. The temperature had fallen, making the walk brisk. Her breath flowed white from between her lips.

She had passed a midnight blue sedan with rust eating away at the fenders when the car suddenly beeped and the headlights flashed. Startled, she spun around.

Sean Leyton walked toward her, car keys in his hand.

"My ride." He pointed to the sedan.

Natalie tried to bring her racing heart under control. "Thanks for the warning."

"That's the second time I startled you. Not the best way to impress a lady."

"Whatever. Just don't do it again." That's when Natalie realized she was alone with Sean in the parking lot: no cars nearby, nobody coming out of the mall. Her hand dove into her purse as she searched for her canisters.

"Damn, girl," Sean said. "You have some serious trust issues. What were you, kidnapped as a child?"

Natalie jerked her head up. "Yes, asshole. I was. And I almost died." He'd made her mad, which only angered her more. She hated showing weakness. "Leave me alone, Sean. Go find someone else to make fun of."

Sean approached her. His smugness evaporated under the heat of her embarrassment. "Hey, I didn't know, or I wouldn't have said anything. I can be a jerk sometimes, but I'm not big on intentionally hurting people. If you'd only told me from the get go, I'd have been less worried about your odd little request." When he was close enough to touch her, he put his hands on her shoulders and gently squeezed. "I can't imagine what you went through. My mom and dad, they used to go nuts if I was late for anything. We'd get into shouting matches. They thought some pervert had taken me. I thought they were being stupid. Guess I didn't understand them either."

"It happened years ago," Natalie said, regretting her harshness. "I should be over it by now, not taking it out on strangers."

"I can't see how anyone gets over something like that." He released her. "You told me what happened to you, which is probably the bravest thing I've seen someone do. At least I can try and do the same." He stood straighter. "Go ahead. Hit me with your water."

Natalie tried to smile but couldn't seem to work the proper facial muscles. "You're sweet, but no. It was a stupid request."

"You didn't think so in the mall."

"I was wrong."

"If a little water helps us get past this, I'm all for it. It'll take what, two seconds?" He closed his eyes. "Come on, get it over with."

"You really mean it? You'd do this for me?"

He nodded stiffly. His face had lost some of its color, and sweat dampened his upper lip. He may be going along with her request, but he was still afraid.

"I promise it's harmless," Natalie said. "I wouldn't intentionally hurt anyone either."

"Just make sure you have the right canister."

"Okay, here we go." Her heart pounding, Natalie grabbed the canister filled with Thomas's solution. What it contained she didn't completely understand, but Thomas assured her it would not hurt a human. She hoped he was right.

She pressed down on the release valve. The canister emitted a slight hiss of escaping air and a fine mist shot out. It coated Sean's nose and chin like a glistening mask; she tried to avoid his eyes, just in case.

Seconds passed and nothing happened. Sean finally opened his eyes. "That was it?"

"I guess," Natalie said with no small amount of relief. "The whole thing seems kind of silly now, doesn't it?"

"Maybe a little." Sean used his sleeve to wipe dry his face. "So, when do we get to hang?"

Natalie smiled inwardly. She found his self-confidence attractive. "My schedule's pretty much open. How about you?"

"How about Saturday? That good for you?"

"Yep." She gave him her cell number. "Text me and we can work out a place to meet."

"Great. See you then." Sean hesitated, then gave her an awkward hug. "Take care of yourself, Natalie."

She watched him climb into his car and drive away.

As Natalie walked toward her car, her black gloom lifted a little. The day hadn't been a total bust after all.

***

Izzy's fingers worked the laptop's mouse, clicking on report after report.

"...incidents of extreme violence have risen dramatically..."

"...a woman wielding a large knife savagely attacked a young boy standing at a bus stop, screaming that he had ruined her marriage. According to the boy's parents, they had only recently moved into the area and had never encountered the woman before..."

"...in Grayling, a nine-year-old girl stole her parents' pickup and purposefully drove it into an ambulance transporting a critically ill man to Munson Hospital in Traverse City. The man died as a result of the collision. The girl, by all accounts an excellent student and aspiring soccer player, appeared intoxicated, somehow managed to operate a stick *shift, and used language not commonly known to one so young…"*

"…in a grotesque display of self-mutilation, Father Geoffrey Callahan of Christ the King Catholic Church, located just outside of Seattle, was found with strips of flesh cut from his face and stomach. The ribbons of skin, removed with a knife clutched in the priest's hand, were found nailed to the crucifix hanging behind the altar. Church officials have declined comment…"

"…police reports say that Farley Whetting, a local restaurateur, brutally murdered his wife and young daughter, then went on a killing spree, shooting several people in his restaurant before running out of ammunition and being tackled by a customer. During the shooting, Mr. Whetting, according to witnesses, went on about how his brother had come back from the dead and told him horrific things would happen if he didn't…"

Sighing, Izzy closed her laptop. "It's started."

CHAPTER FOUR

The next morning broke bright and clear, with a pale sun pinned to a cobalt sky.

Izzy started the day tending to Bartholomew Owens. She made sure he was fed and cleaned, then flexed his arms and legs to keep the joints limber. The old man may heal miraculously fast, but she wasn't sure if that applied to muscular atrophy from disuse, and she didn't know how long his condition would last.

Besides, she wanted to do everything in her power to help.

She woke Natalie around eight and had her start scrubbing the bathrooms. To Kevin she assigned the simple task of picking up off the floor anything that didn't belong there. He hummed as he strolled the house, dropping anything he picked up in a large, black garbage bag.

Later all three sat at the dining room table, eating a meal of eggs and toast and jam.

"What time are they supposed to get here?" Natalie said. She'd stabbed her egg with a fork and was busy smearing the yolk around her plate.

"Not sure," Izzy said. She had heard from two and knew to expect them this afternoon. When Thomas and Matthew might appear was anyone's guess. "No later than nightfall, I'd expect."

"Then why do you keep looking at your watch?"

Izzy cheeks grew warm. "Well, I, um—"

The doorbell rang.

"You two stay here." Izzy rose to get the door but paused first at a kitchen drawer. She pulled it open to reveal her old concealed carry pistol, a standard .38 revolver. She picked it up. It felt familiar in her hand. She almost smiled.

The doorbell rang again.

She hurried down the hallway.

When she bought the house, the front door had been a flimsy, piece-of-shit hollow core that wouldn't have stopped a determined cat. She'd quickly replaced it with one made of sturdy oak, complete with a brass peephole.

She peered through the fisheye lens. Gene Vincent peered back.

Slipping the gun into her pocket, she flipped the deadbolts and opened the door.

Gene didn't smile. He didn't scowl, like he had the last time they'd seen one another, not ten days ago. He didn't do anything. He just stood there, hands folded casually in front of him like a parish priest who'd forgotten how to say a proper greeting.

She noticed a few more crow's feet gathered at the corners of his eyes, and his hair had gone gray at the temples; facts which, for reasons she couldn't put into words, made her feel lonely.

"Hey," she said. "Thanks for coming."

"Izzy." The word sounded clumsy on his lips. "Are you going to let me in?"

"What? Oh, sure." She stepped aside. "Sorry."

Gene Vincent stepped across the threshold and reentered her life.

***

Izzy paused at the entrance to the kitchen. "Natalie."

Her daughter looked up from her eggs. "What?"

"Honey, we have a visitor."

"Now? But I thought you said—"

Gene Vincent stepped into the kitchen. "Hey, Nat."

Natalie stared for a moment. Then, with a squeal loud enough to shake the walls, she jumped up and hugged him. "Uncle Gene, what're you doing here?"

Gene hugged her back. "It's complicated. But to keep it short and sweet, I'm here to help."

"Help?" Natalie turned to Izzy. "You knew he was coming?"

"We talked last night," Izzy said. "I didn't tell you because I wasn't sure he would show. No sense getting your hopes up for what might be nothing."

"Talked? You mean, you called him?"

"No, sweetie. He called me."

Natalie seemed to puzzle this over. "You switch phones every few months. Whatever number he had when we left wouldn't have been good."

Izzy took a seat next to Kevin. The boy had finished his eggs and now eyed their newcomer with a measure of suspicion. She ran her fingers through his tangled hair. "It's okay, Kevin. You haven't seen Mr. Vincent in a long time, but he's a friend. I asked him to help." Her next words were for Natalie. "Yes, he called me. Remember when I went away a few days ago? Well, I went to see your Uncle Gene."

"Wait—you went to Kinsey?" Natalie said, her disbelief raw and wounding.

Izzy braced herself for the upcoming explosion. "I felt the need outweighed the risks."

"You went home *and you didn't take me?*"

"Someone needed to watch Kevin."

"Are you kidding me?" Natalie's face had gone scarlet. "I ask to go see Dad, you refuse, and all the while, you'd already been back? For fuck's sake, Mom!"

Gene, who had been watching the exchange, suddenly stepped into the fray. He put his body between Izzy and Natalie. "Who said you could talk to your mom like that?"

"Uncle Gene, you don't understand—"

"I understand enough to know you don't talk to your mom like that. She went through hell to save you and refused to give up. If she had, you'd have been lost for good. I thought you'd be more appreciative. You're alive because of her."

"You call this living?" Natalie said. "Hiding from the world, never going to school, never getting a job. And don't get me started on friends. I live my life in a box, Uncle Gene, a box filled with… well, very strange people."

"Natalie, that's enough," Izzy said. "He hasn't seen us since the forest. He doesn't know what you're talking about."

"What does she mean by strange people?" Gene asked.

"Later," Izzy said. "You need to rest before we tackle that one."

"Strange," Kevin said, his voice crowing like a magpie. "I'm strange."

"Hush, Kevin. Don't talk about yourself like that." Izzy turned to face Natalie. "With Bartholomew out of the picture, I knew we would need help. We have to save him *and* we have to keep a lid on the chaos that's about to start. When I went to see Gene, he turned down my request for help, not that I blame him. But I also sent him a letter with my phone number, in case he changed his mind."

Gene sat at the table, his movements stiff and deliberate. "Bartholomew? You mean Owens?"

"Yes," Izzy said. Bartholomew Owens, the man who four years ago entered their lives and changed their world forever.

Gene nodded and shifted his attention back to his goddaughter. "Nat, seeing your dad would be a bad idea. It took him a year to recover from his heart attack and the belief that his wife and daughter were dead. During that time he stayed home and barely kept the pharmacy running. He hired an assistant and eventually sold the store to her. He still lives in Kinsey, comfortably, but he's alone. I think he prefers it that way. I think he's finally content, if not precisely happy."

Across the table, Izzy kept her expression neutral. Sadness for Stanley's loneliness warred with the profound relief she felt at knowing he'd survived. They had walked through a crumbling marriage together, and while she didn't love him anymore, she certainly didn't hate him. She'd learned too much from Bartholomew to hate anymore.

No, a better gift would have been hearing how he had remarried, how he enjoyed a newer, happier life. But she had gotten what she'd gotten, what she had suspected, an emotional *fait accompli*, and felt content.

"Thank you, Gene," she said, her voice barely above a whisper. "I never wanted him to be hurt."

Natalie rose, rinsed her plate, and jammed it into the dishwasher. "You have a funny way of showing compassion, keeping a father away from his daughter. Don't you wonder how Dad would feel if he knew I was alive, if he could see me again? It might be enough to shake him out of his isolation and bring some joy back into his life. I think it's arrogant for you to make this decision for him. And worse, for you to make it for me."

Natalie turned on her heels and left.

Gene watched her go. "When did she get so mouthy?"

"She's been through a lot." Izzy took a moment to gather her thoughts. "She's changed, Gene. She's darker, more depressed. I don't know what to do, other than let her work out whatever she's going through and be there when she needs me."

Kevin unexpectedly reached over and gave her a hug, his innocent face pressed hard against her shoulder. "Don't be sad. Nat will be okay." Then he turned and cast a curious eye at Gene. "Who're you?"

"Mr. Vincent," Gene said. "Mrs. Morris introduced me—"

"Marzecki," Izzy said, cutting him off. "Elizabeth Marzecki. We don't go by Morris anymore. We're supposed to be dead, remember?"

"Seems I've got a lot of catching up to do." Gene laid a hand on Kevin's shoulder. "I'm a friend, Kevin. I knew you a long time ago."

Kevin's slender brows drew together. "Friends till the end?"

"Absolutely," Gene said. "Friends until the end."

"Good," was the boy's only reply.

"Off to your room," Izzy told Kevin. "Mr. Vincent and I need some time alone. We have a lot to discuss."

"Okey doke," Kevin said, and bounded out of the room. "Bye."

"Interesting crew you've got here," Gene said. "I suppose Owens is somewhere nearby."

Izzy took Gene's hand and brought him to his feet. "I've got something to show you. Afterwards, we can talk."

"Will it take long?"

"Given the history we have to cover, it'll take a while."

**

Gene raised a trembling hand. "Hold on. Let's stop right here. I need a minute, okay?"

While Izzy waited, her face lined with worry, Gene tried to process everything he had heard. Two-thousand-year-old men, mythical figures emerging from the mists of history to walk the world, protecting mankind from an ancient evil intent on damning the souls of humanity.

His gaze drifted to Owens. The old man lay on a hospital bed, unconscious, completely dependent on Izzy for his care. A sight incongruent with the Owens he'd met years ago: a man profoundly old, who could heal at an amazing rate, and who had the uncanny ability to inflict pain. A man who had destroyed a monster. But an immortal, one of twelve men who helped change the course of civilization? How could such a thing be possible?

"Tell me again about this Veil thing?" he said.

"A young man named Miles Knight was tricked into putting on the Crown of Thorns," Izzy replied. "He thought he was saving the world, but all he did was sacrifice his life to a false end, and for the first time in history, a living man entered Heaven. The Veil is the barrier that keeps the living and the dead apart. When Miles put on the Crown, he weakened the Veil. It's out of balance."

"Heaven and Hell. Those places really exist?"

"I've come to believe. It wasn't an easy process."

"You said Katie Bethel is part of this."

Katie Bethel. Along with Izzy, the second of Kinsey's residents to take up Bartholomew's cause. And in doing so, she had rediscovered her purpose in life, a life that had been scarred by the suicide of her father and the murder of her mother. Izzy had come to love Katie almost as much as she did Natalie and Kevin.

She nodded. "She became Bartholomew's helper, though that's not the right word. Protégé might be better, except she'll never have the same abilities as Bartholomew. She's been traveling the world with him."

"Where is she now?"

"She left with Philip. From what I gather, they're looking for something that will help Bartholomew."

"Philip," Gene said, and shook his head in disbelief. "These Forever Men—how many are there?"

"Six."

"And Judas Iscariot? What's his part in this?" He couldn't believe he'd actually said that name. The Great Betrayer, believed to have died by his own hand millennia ago.

"No one knows. That he still lived only recently became known to them."

Gene had a sudden hankering for a painkiller; not the over-the-counter crap but the real deal. Something that would throw a warm opioid blanket over his jittery nerves...

"I can't keep up with all this," he said. "What you've said is hard enough to believe without laying impossibilities down, one after the other."

"We don't have the time to go easy. Events will start moving faster and faster. If you want to help, I need to bring you up to speed."

"All I'm asking for is a few minutes."

"Take more than a few, but not too many." Izzy smiled, though it didn't last long. "Why are you here? You seemed pretty firm the other week: no more superhero stuff. Something serious must have happened to change your mind."

An image of Celeste Florin popped into Gene's head. Not from the last time he'd seen her, bloodied and deranged and wielding scissors, but before, when she'd been happy and content with her life. It made his heart ache to think of all that potential gone.

He told Izzy what happened. He didn't leave out any details. He told her about the dog, Cheech. The photograph of Celeste's father that had moved and spoke to him. He told her about Celeste's attempt at murdering him, how she had acted like she was someone else, and how Sten Billick had been forced to kill her.

"Sten." Izzy said the name with fondness. "How is he?"

"The city made him chief after you disappeared. He's a heck of a cop. The town's lucky to have him."

"He's one of the people I miss the most." She shook her head, as if the motion would clear away the past. "You said Celeste acted like someone else. In what way?"

"How she spoke, how she carried herself. Even if she'd gone mad, she would still sound like Celeste. Use the same speech pattern, some of the same mannerisms. People don't change that much. But yeah, it was like talking to someone else." Gene considered. "The person in the photograph—her father. She talked like him, like a man, as impossible as that seems."

"Not when you consider the Veil being damaged. It could have been her father. You said he died years ago."

He grew cold. "Her father came back and what, possessed her?"

"The dead can only pass the Veil as spirits, and they can only act in our world by possessing a body."

"That's what we're up against? Real-life, spin-your-head-around-and-spit-out-pea-soup shit?"

"It'll be far worse than that." Izzy looked at her watch. "The others will be arriving soon. We need to decide how to best help Bartholomew and stop what will be a global epidemic of violence. You'll be part of the discussion."

Fear fluttered in his chest. "What have you gotten me into?"

Her expression never changed. "The struggle to save humanity. Don't worry, you get used to it."

***

Izzy spent the afternoon preparing for her visitors. Gene helped, though more than his goddaughter, Natalie. Kevin, oddly, kept to himself—he remained in his bedroom playing Connect Four with an imaginary friend named Doug.

She called for a lunch break just as Gene finished setting up cots in the spare rooms. The three of them gathered in the kitchen. Kevin still hadn't emerged from his room.

"Thanks for the help." She handed Gene a plate of leftover sloppy joes and chips. "How's your back holding up?"

Gene half-shrugged. "Twinges here and there. Nothing I can't

46

handle." Despite his assertions, he pulled a small container of pills from his pocket. "Over the counter stuff," he said, and dry swallowed two. "Nice place you've got here, big but not obvious. Plenty of room for guests. How'd you decide on it?"

Natalie, who had been picking at her lunch, rolled her eyes. "It wasn't my idea. Nobody ever asks my opinion."

"Even if this were a normal situation," Izzy said, pointing at her daughter with a fork, "your opinion, while noted, would not have mattered much. But it isn't a normal situation. People are searching for us, they want to kill us. Miss one trap or surprise attack and someone could die." No longer feeling hungry, she set her fork on the plate. "I suggest you drop the attitude. The world isn't here to serve you, it's the other way around. Given who we're living with, I thought you would've learned that by now."

Natalie's face turned bright pink. "It's not a lesson. It's a rule! Follow this or else, do that or else. Tell me, Mom—what's the 'or else'? What happens if I stop listening? What are you going to do if I decide to live my own life?"

"Nat—" Gene said, a rebuke forming on his lips.

"It's all right, Gene. She's got a point." Izzy took a moment to calm herself. This argument was as old as their exile from the world at large: the debate about choice. Izzy cherished free will, the ability to live the way you wanted as long as you didn't hurt anyone. Most cops she knew felt the same way.

Natalie waited for her to reply. The thick black mascara, lips dark as tar, the anger burning in her eyes—Izzy barely recognized her own daughter beneath all the rage and makeup. Natalie's defiant behavior reflected more than a young woman's convoluted transition into adulthood. And at twenty-two years old, an adult she was. Izzy needed to treat her like one.

"If you decide to leave," she told Natalie. "If you decide to live your own life, I won't stop you. I won't have Philip find you, or have Thomas build something to keep you here. You'll be truly on your own. You can live your own life. Get a job. Pay bills. Get married and have your own kids. You'll have your freedom, but it'll come at a price."

"Let me guess. You'll never speak to me again?"

Gene stirred in his seat. Izzy put a restraining hand on his arm. She didn't need his temper complicating the situation.

"I'll always talk to you," she said. "You're my daughter. I couldn't abandon you any more than I could cut off one of my arms. And I'd always take you back."

"Then what's the price I'm supposed to pay?"

"The price isn't mine," Izzy said. "It's yours. By leaving, you'll be exposing yourself. You'll bring danger with you wherever you go. Your friends, your husband." She paused. "Your children. You'll make them targets for the rest of their lives."

"You're talking about Marbæs," Natalie said.

"I'm pretty sure I know who Philip and Thomas are," Gene said. "But who's Marbæs?"

"Someone you don't want to meet," Izzy said.

"Think Sauron with a bad attitude," Natalie added with a smirk.

"Don't turn this into a joke," Izzy said. "We've worked too hard, sacrificed too much, for you to take that kind of attitude."

"She hasn't found us, Mom. Maybe she isn't even looking. Have you thought of that?"

Izzy shook her head. Had her daughter learned nothing over the years? "The threat is real. Marbæs will kill you if she finds you. Or worse, she'll force you to tell her where we are, and then she'll kill all of us. All because you didn't want to take any of this seriously. I don't say this often, Nat, but you disappoint me. I thought you cared more about us."

Natalie's cheeks burned. Izzy's words had stoked a fire inside the girl. "I care about me," Natalie said. "I care about my life—or the lack of one—and I care about my future. I care that I might die childless and alone and lonely. And the funny part is, she doesn't even want me. She wants Kevin. I'm suffering because of him."

Gene stirred in his seat. "If this Marbæs found Kevin, wouldn't she kill him too?"

"Most likely," Izzy said.

"We don't know that," Natalie countered. "She tried to kidnap him once, maybe she'd keep him alive."

"That would be worse, and you know it." To Gene, she said, "Marbæs is...different. She can get into your head, make you see things, hear things. Your life would be a nightmare. Most people would rather die than go through that."

"You'd condemn a child to that kind of existence?" he said to Natalie. "A little kid?"

"He's not my brother," she replied. "I don't owe him anything."

Izzy sat there, speechless. When had her daughter grown so callous?

Fortunately, Gene had words to spare. "Tell you what. Go ahead and leave, start building that life you so desperately want, find that husband." His expression hardened. "Willingly let a child be tortured? Now there's an attractive quality in a wife. I'm sure plenty of men would love to marry a woman like you. I wonder if there's a dating site for spoiled princesses who care about nothing but themselves?" He snapped his fingers. "Wait, I know. I'll create one. I'll call it heartlessbitches dot com"

Natalie flinched under the barrage of words. "Uncle Gene—"

"Shut up, I'm not done with you." Gene laid his hands flat on the table. It looked as if he were trying to keep from jumping out of his chair. "You remember Ms. Flores, my waitress? Yes? Well, guess what? She's *dead*." Gene said the word like it was a knife through his heart. "Sten Billick shot her while she was trying to kill me, and that's after she slaughtered her dog. Either she'd gone insane or was possessed or something. I don't know. But if this Marbæs lady has anything to do with what happened to Celeste, then she's major trouble." Gene sat back, a look of disgust on his face. "And you want to send Kevin to her so he can live out his life the way Celeste might have, insane and thirsting for blood and death. There's nothing approaching decency in that kind of thinking, that kind of cruelty. Hearing you talk like that makes me sick to my stomach."

Natalie's face grew more and more pale as Gene chewed into her. Izzy felt sorry for her daughter but knew Nat needed to hear this from someone other than her mom.

Natalie, her lips a thin, angry slash across her bone-white face, rose to her feet. She looked so small in her baggy black coat, so frail, that Izzy ached for the little girl she once knew.

"You don't know anything," Natalie said. "You come back into my life after years of being gone and expect to tell me how to be-have? How to live? You have no idea what my life is like or what I have to deal with every day. If you knew, you'd be more consider-ate. But that's beside the point. You're not here for me." Her eyes travelled to Izzy. "You want her." They looped back to Gene. "And she wants you. You're not fooling anyone. I've known it for years. You want to help her save Bartholomew, go ahead. Just leave me out of it. I didn't ask for any of this, and I don't want it." She stood straighter, as if her words had given her the strength to stand up to his rebuke. "I'm sorry about Ms. Flores. I really am. She was a sweet lady, but I've come to learn the world's a hard place, and hard places require harder attitudes if you're going to survive. And I will survive. I don't care about monsters and madmen. I care about me."

Having said her piece, Natalie abruptly left. Izzy half-expected to see a trail of smoke drifting behind her, Nat was so angry.

"Jesus," Gene whispered. "What the hell was that?"

"She's the reason I drink." Izzy shook her head. "She's also the reason I keep doing what I'm doing. She was tortured, and that affected her. But she's also a good person. I know it. She's lost, is all. She needs someone in her corner, someone to fight for her. If I don't do it, no one will."

"She might not agree."

"I might force it down her throat." A mother's instinct is to protect her children, to give them a better quality of life than she had. But this...Natalie's hostility was alien to her, something she didn't understand. It left her feeling cold. "I won't let my daughter turn into a tool for Marbæs."

"What if you can't stop it?"

Izzy gave him a level look. "Then I'll die trying."

∗

Gene spent the next hour helping Izzy finalize the preparations for her guests.

Just after noon, he heard a low rumble coming from outside the house. It grew louder until he recognized the unmistakable growl of motorcycles.

"Time to start the party," Izzy said, and headed for the porch. Gene trailed behind.

"Who are we waiting for?" Gene asked.

She frowned at him. "You don't understand by now?"

"I mean who, as in, which ones."

"Just wait. It'll only be a second."

True enough, from around the corner at the end of the street two motorcycles turned and accelerated. The riders wore leather jackets, jeans, and well-sprung biker boots. Helmets covered their heads. One wore a pair of sunglasses, the other sported goggles similar to ones worn by World War II aviators. Both had unlit cigars sticking out from the corners of their mouths.

Their grins could be seen from a block away.

The bikers slowed as they approached the house and turned as one into the driveway.

"You ready for this?" she said.

Gene shrugged. "I don't have much choice."

"Come on, let me introduce you."

They approached the newcomers. One, the man wearing the aviator goggles, paused to light his cigar. He removed his helmet, revealing charcoal hair with a shock of gray flowing from his forehead along his right temple, his neatly trimmed beard barely more than whiskers. Something about the man seemed familiar to Gene, and when the Forever Man removed the goggles, Gene abruptly stopped.

"You've got to be kidding." He turned to Izzy. "Please tell me that's not who I think it is."

Izzy smiled. "Gene, meet John Willenby. John, this is Gene Vincent, a friend of mine from the old days."

John Willenby rested his helmet on the Harley's seat. His handsome face pinched into a frown. "Great, another name to remember."

"John Willenby," Gene said weakly. "You mean the guy who wrote *Sufferance* and *The Passage to Avalon* and *Tears in the Era of Joy*? The same guy who won a Pulitzer for *Famine and Frustration*?"

The other newcomer, his large frame filling every inch of his leather jacket, laughed. He had removed his helmet and glasses.

His gray hair was bushy on top and cut close on the sides, and he sported big, bold mutton chop sideburns.

"Imagine that, another fan," he said to John. "Try not to let it go to your head."

John Willenby shot the man a withering look.

"Behave," Izzy told the burly biker with a playful slap on the shoulder. "Gene, this is James Conwell."

James extended a hand. "Happy to meet you."

Bewildered, Gene shook the man's hand. "I thought you guys kept a low profile. I remember Owens going to lengths to remain behind the scenes." He nodded to John. "Yet your face has been on the cover of all the magazines."

James laughed again. "It's only because he's the best-looking of the bunch, and the one most comfortable with a public image. Put Matthew or Philip or Thomas in front of a camera and they practically faint. And Bartholomew…" The man's expression grew somber. "Well, Bartholomew puts up with so much already. And he definitely needs to stay 'behind the scenes.'"

"I have a public image," John said, "because I'm the least threatening to our enemies."

"No," James said. "That would be Matthew."

"We don't know that," John countered. "We don't know that at all."

James stowed his unlit cigar in the motorcycle's saddlebag. "Believe what you want. It wouldn't be the first time you were wrong."

"You're not going to smoke that?" Gene asked, pointing to the cigar.

"Haven't you read the surgeon general's warning?" James said. "They cause cancer."

"But—?"

James shot Izzy a questioning look. "How much does he know?"

"Most of it," she said.

John looked alarmed. "You told him?"

"He's had first-hand experience," Izzy said. "Gene helped me in Kinsey with Webber and the Fek."

"I heard about that," James said, and Gene thought he detected a measure of respect in the man's voice. "I understand you did well."

"Do me a favor and keep the story to yourself," John said sourly. "I don't need to hear it again. It'll only upset me."

A lump of unease formed in the middle of Gene's chest as he struggled to understand the dynamic between the two men. They were so far apart in personality, even with the strong family resemblance...

"You're brothers, aren't you?"

The two men nodded in unison.

"And you." Gene pointed to John. "You mentioned getting upset."

Izzy stepped forward. "Remember how I told you Bartholomew was the Protector, and Philip the Finder? Well, John is the Historian. He remembers everything he's seen or heard. Two thousand years of memories, none of which he can forget. They get overwhelming, almost to the point of being painful."

Gene felt the lump in his chest grow. "And you?" he said to James.

"I work for Doctors Without Borders," James said. "I save people caught in the savagery of war."

"The Healer," Gene whispered.

"Thomas is the Maker," Izzy added. "He can craft just about anything."

"And Matthew?" he said. "What's his role?"

John bristled at the words. James suddenly looked uncomfortable.

"Later," Izzy told him. "For now, let's go inside. These two will want to see Bartholomew."

CHAPTER FIVE

The visit lasted longer than Gene expected.

James and John lingered next to Owens, their faces expression-less. Izzy remained off to one side, biting the nail of her thumb. Gene couldn't remember her having done that before.

"What have you been doing for him?" James asked. He hadn't laid a hand on Owens, hadn't performed even a rudimentary examination. All he'd done was pull the blanket up until it covered the old man from the neck down.

"Exactly what you told me," Izzy replied. "Feed him three times a day through the tube. Bathe him. Do limb exercises as often as I can. Keep his skin moisturized. I keep checking for lesions, even though I know better."

"What's wrong with him?" Gene asked. "Izzy wasn't too specific."

John sat in the room's only chair. He'd shed his leather jacket and heavy shirt in favor of a light pullover. He held a pen in his hand and clicked it repeatedly.

"That's because no one really knows," he said. "Bartholomew is physically unharmed —there's no obvious threat to his body—but he won't wake up. It's like he's in a coma."

Gene had been thinking along the same lines. "Could it be as simple as that—a coma?"

"Comas most often result from trauma." As if making a point, James pulled a pen light from his jacket and shined it in Owens's eyes. "Blows to the head and such. Bartholomew didn't experience any of that. Philip witnessed everything. All Judas did was kiss Bartholomew's cheek." He returned the pen light to his jacket pocket. "There's no evidence of brain damage."

John made a rude noise. "Any physical trauma would have healed by now."

"Still and all," James said, "harm has been done. We need to figure out how to heal him."

Gene approached the bed. Despite four years having passed, Owens hadn't changed. He had the same smooth black skin, the same short hair, the same teardrop-shaped tattoo under his left eye. Bart Owens lacked any sign of having aged.

"Remember when we first met him," he said to Izzy. "We thought he was an ex-con because of the tattoo."

"Please don't start telling a story," John said, his pen clicking away. "You're going to fill my head with unnecessary information."

James rolled his eyes but refrained from commenting. Gene didn't know which brother was older, though at this point that particular fact seemed irrelevant. James deferred to John, despite the latter Forever Man's irascible attitude.

"It's not a tattoo." Izzy approached the bed. "It's a mark of some kind, a reflection of the birthright they share."

John rolled up a shirt sleeve, revealing a flowing mark that resembled an old-fashioned quill. James lifted his shirt. He had a mark, vaguely heart-shaped, located on his chest slightly left of his breastbone.

"Each mark reflects their role," Izzy said. "A heart for the Healer, a quill for the Historian."

"And Owens's teardrop?" Gene asked.

John rose from his chair and started pacing. "Bartholomew feels the pain of his ability. It's a constant annoyance for him, and it makes him sad." He shot an irritated look at Izzy. "Does he know about Bartholomew's skills?"

"I was there when he saved our asses from a monster." Gene

allowed a trace of anger to bleed into his voice. John's attitude had gotten to him. "And if you have questions about me, you can address them to me."

John's lower lip puffed out. To Gene, the man looked more like a petulant child than a world-famous author. "Forget not to whom you speak, young man."

James put a hand on his brother's shoulder. "That's enough. You're better than that."

John shrugged off his brother's hand. "He keeps telling me new things. You know how that affects me."

"I do," James said. "And you know that he's an Innocent. We're here for him, not the other way around." James put his hand back on his brother's shoulder, this time squeezing hard enough to keep it there. "Like Bartholomew, you are burdened. I cannot heal him of his burden, nor can I heal you of yours. It is what you both have to bear." His grip hardened. "I won't allow you to take your frustrations out on him."

John winced and ducked away from his brother. "All right, all right. You've made your point. I'll go easy on him." He jabbed his pen at Gene as if it were a dagger. "You don't know how my life has been, and it's unfair to judge you on information you lack. But please remember, everything you say is locked up here." He tapped his head with his free hand. "Can you imagine the information already in there? All that I have seen, all that I have heard?" Anguish made his eyes looked hooded. "Like Bartholomew, I long for the day I will be free from my duties. I wish to be a normal man again, and finally go to my reward."

Gene watched the interplay between the brothers. Apparently, he'd been wrong about James. He didn't defer to his brother; he tolerated him. And he bore that tolerance out of guilt.

I cannot heal him of his burden, nor can I heal you of yours.

Gene squirmed a little. Guilt also burned inside of him. He hadn't saved Celeste. Ignore the fact he didn't understand what was going on, or that he wouldn't have known what to do to stop a possession; he hadn't saved her.

He felt for the vial of pills in his pocket, shame now mixing with his guilt. He had also failed Izzy. He had lied to her. His pills weren't over-the-counter painkillers. They were something far stronger. Before leaving Kinsey, he made sure to pack his stash, a collection of narcotics he had harvested from different pharmacies, Stanley's included. He had tried conventional treatments like exercise and meditation, but nothing helped. Against his better judgment, he turned to narcotics. Drugs were the only way to control the pain, to keep him from losing his mind from the constant, unending dagger thrusts.

Could James heal his back? Could he truly be pain-free for the rest of his life?

But that would mean confessing to his falsehood—his back hurt far worse than he'd let on—and also admitting to his addiction. He didn't think he could do that. He felt too ashamed.

He moved away from the bed. He needed space, whether figurative or literal. His emotions had bunched up, knotting in his chest like a fist.

"Gene?"

Izzy stood next to him. He could smell her perfume—the subtle scent of rosewater, simple and honest, like her.

You loved her once yet you're lying to her, letting her down again.

More shame; more guilt.

He hung his head and fought back the tears.

"Gene?" Izzy repeated his name. Hearing her say it made his head hurt.

"I'm here."

She moved closer, so close he could feel the heat from her skin. His heart raced.

"What's wrong?" she whispered. "I can tell something's bothering you."

He snorted. It wasn't a rude sound, but an exasperated one.

Oh yes, something was definitely wrong.

He just realized his problem: he'd never fallen out of love with Izzy Morris.

"Are you going to tell me what's the matter?" Izzy asked.

"Too much to take in," he said, his voice low. "I'm feeling overwhelmed, like I've been thrown in the middle of the ocean with lead weights on my feet and I'm expected to swim for shore. It's a losing battle." He frowned at the floor. "How do you do it? How do you cope with all of...?" He waved his hands at the clutch of Forever Men.

"I've had years to process it," she said. "In the beginning, accepting who they were wasn't easy. I felt angry and confused and lost. Except for Nat and Kevin, I'd left behind everyone who mattered to me. I had no one to turn to, no one to express those feelings to. For a while I became depressed. I even started drinking too much. But that wasn't going to help anyone. I still had Kevin to raise. And Natalie." She shrugged. "Nat has her own issues, and I'm not sure how much I can help. So, I forced myself to address these feelings, to admit I felt scared. You've seen only one of the horrors from the other side, the Fek. There are other, more dangerous ones. They're after us. They're after Kevin. I'm on guard all the time. But I cope. I have no other choice."

"Owens didn't help? He dragged you into this."

"He didn't force me into anything. I made my decision based on what was at risk. I'm a cop, Gene. I protect. It's what I've done my entire adult life. When he offered me the chance to be a cop on a much larger scale, how could I say no?"

"He could have acted as a sounding board, given you perspective on what your life would be like."

"He doesn't have time to play counselor."

"What about the others?" Again, he gestured toward James and John. "You have at least six other people who could help you."

"They all have jobs. Babysitting isn't one of *them*."

"And Katie Bethel? What about her?"

"She has her own life to live, her own direction to find."

Gene grew quiet. He missed the outgoing girl. "You said she was off somewhere with one of them."

"Philip. They went to try and find a way to help Bartholomew."

John walked up. He'd put his pen away but now kept his hands stuffed in his pockets. The man must possess a tremendous amount of nervous energy.

"Are you caught up?" he asked. "Or are we going too fast for you?"

"Are you always this arrogant," Gene replied with tone sharp as a shark's tooth, "or is it just for me?"

"I'm pretty much this way all the time," John admitted. "Don't expect an apology, either. You know how old people get set in their ways? Imagine how it is for us."

Gene hesitated, then realized John had just made a joke. Some of the tension slipped from his shoulders. "Have you decided what's wrong with Owens?"

John nodded, and James took the opportunity to join them. "Your coma theory wasn't all that far off. Bartholomew isn't physically hurt; that's not the reason he won't wake."

"Then what is it?" Gene asked.

James's expression turned grim. "He won't wake because he's not there anymore."

The sound of chimes floated down the stairs.

"The others are here," Izzy said.

***

People filled the living room almost to capacity. Izzy stood near the doorway to the kitchen, James and John in chairs near a bay window, and the two newcomers on the sofa.

Thomas, the oldest-looking of the Forever Men (well, the oldest-looking of the ones Gene had met), resembled a wizened gnome from an epic fantasy novel: short and balding with a large, hooked nose and a bushy mustache.

Seated next to Thomas, Matthew possessed handsome features, rough-hewn, as if they had been carved in expressionless stone; the man barely smiled. And his eyes—they held so much sadness Gene wanted to hug him and tell him everything would be all right. Matthew hadn't said a word since his arrival, and his demeanor suggested he wouldn't say anything until time ended.

Dressed in black, Natalie sat cross-legged on the floor. Some of her perpetual scowl had softened in the presence of the Forever Men. They'd apparently had some sort of positive impact on her.

Kevin, strangely, had been instructed to stay in his room.

"Has anyone heard from Philip?" Thomas asked. The man had rolled up his sleeves the way a construction worker would before tackling a big job. His mark, a chisel-like stain on his left forearm, looked like blood on his skin.

"Not since he and Katie left," said Izzy. "Six days ago."

60

Thomas grunted. "And we don't know where they went?"

"He didn't exactly broadcast his travel plans," John said, his pen clicking away. "Safer that way."

"Did he say how long he might be gone?" James asked, his bulk making the sofa sag.

Izzy shook her head.

"Why did Katie go with him?" Thomas said.

"Because she wanted to go." Natalie looked at the others. "Before she left, she told me she needed to go with Philip. Not because Philip needed her, but because she owed it to Bartholomew."

"What do you think?" Gene asked Matthew, hoping to draw the recalcitrant Forever Man into the conversation. "Surely you must have an opinion."

Those sad eyes fixed on him. They were a bruised green color, like a field of fresh-cut grass, and they held such self-reproach Gene couldn't imagine anyone faulting him more than he faulted himself. What could possibly make a man loathe himself so?

"Any opinions I have," Matthew said, "I shall keep to myself. I have no business being here, save for my misguided fraternity with these other fine gentlemen. I cannot help either Bartholomew or our mission. I am, ultimately, useless."

"But you're a Forever Man," Gene argued. "Your opinion matters."

"Only to the likes of you, it seems," Matthew replied. "And that's hardly reason enough to motivate me."

John abandoned his pen clicking for pacing. His expression looked animated, even eager, as if he couldn't wait to begin whatever it was they were supposed to do. Gene wondered if the man's nervous energy had to do with the span of memories clogging his head, if they acted as a fuel for his brain.

"They went somewhere," John said. "To retrieve something, if I had to guess. The two went to get something."

"Why not tell us?" Thomas's frown wrinkled his face even more deeply. "Why the secrecy?"

A new voice intruded on their discussion. "To keep any of you from following."

Gene turned. An older man stood behind him with a stiff, white beard and sea-foam eyes. Ugly bruises marred his cheek and neck. He carried Katie Bethel in his arms, her head tilted back, her eyes closed. On her chest rested a plain wooden cube, the surface polished to a high sheen. It seemed to glow in the light.

"Help her, James," Philip said, his voice cracking.

Thomas and Matthew jumped from the couch. Philip laid his charge on it, then took the cube from her.

James examined Katie. Grim-faced, he said, "She's alive, but these wounds...What happened?"

"We went looking for this." Philip held out the cube.

"What is it?" Gene asked.

Thomas approached Philip. Gingerly, almost reverently, he took the cube. "I made this," Thomas said. "A long time ago. I never thought I'd see it again."

"Retrieving it wasn't easy," Philip said, and patted at the purple splotches on his arms. "I've got the bruises to prove it."

Philip had a certain gregariousness about him Gene found endearing. Similar to Owens, he might come to like this Forever Man.

"But why?" Thomas said. "It simply stores things. A gimmick really, made while I was bored. What use could it be to us?"

Katie moaned and lifted a hand to shade her eyes. "Bright...too bright."

"Give yourself a few minutes to adjust to the light," James told her. "How do you feel?"

"Better than I expected," the girl replied, and threw a weary glance at Thomas. "Philip said—insisted—that the cube was important."

"That's right. Bartholomew's life depends on it," Philip said. "I know where he is, and I think I know how to save him."

Gene noticed that John had stopped pacing, that the author now stared at Philip and Thomas. Kneeling next to the sofa, James stopped working on Katie. Even Matthew seemed to take an interest.

"You'd better tell us what happened," Thomas said. "And what the cube has to do with this."

Philip nodded at Katie. "It's her story to tell. Without her, we may have never recovered the cube."

Katie swallowed, her face pale, and began to talk.

CHAPTER SIX

Katie shrugged into her jacket. Philip had woken her minutes earlier and told her to meet him in the basement, where Bartholomew lay unconscious.

Since the events in Dearborn, her life had felt incomplete, adrift. She had become accustomed to Bartholomew taking charge. He would decide where they went and what they did. She would simply follow his lead and absorb every facet of the lessons he taught. He had become like a father, far different (and far better) than the real father she barely remembered, the man who had killed himself and left his only child behind to deal with a dysfunctional, alcoholic mother.

But now Bartholomew was gone, and she missed him dearly. She'd come to love the old man; him and the rest of the Forever Men. They had to find a way to bring Bartholomew back. Without him, Marbæs would likely win. Without him, her life would have no purpose.

Slipping on her sneakers, she left the room and headed downstairs.

Philip stood next to the hospital bed. Bartholomew lay on it, eyes closed, his chest gently rising and falling beneath the covers.

As she approached the bed, Philip took one of Bartholomew's hands in his: an oddly tender gesture, and one she was not used to seeing two men share.

"I have an idea, old friend," Philip said, his eyes never leaving Bartholomew. "One I think may help you. Everyone else is at a loss. That leaves me, and I owe you." He licked his lips. "I'm going away. If I succeed, I won't be gone long. If I fail...well, no one lives forever."

"What are you talking about?" Katie said as she approached Philip. "Where are you going?"

"Don't you mean, where are *we* going? Or have you changed your mind about helping?"

She didn't hesitate. "Tell me what you need."

Philip nodded. "This will be dangerous. I wasn't kidding when I said I might not return."

"*We* might not return," she clarified, then thought for a moment. "If we don't succeed, what are his chances of recovering?"

"Somewhere between zero and not a damned chance."

"Then if we fail, I don't want to come back." Katie took Bartholomew's hand from Philip. The old man's skin was warm and dry. If she didn't know better, she'd have assumed he was sleeping. "He's like a father to me. I would do anything for him."

"Most of us feel the same," Philip said.

Katie pressed the tip of her index finger onto Bartholomew's wrist. She searched until she felt his pulse, strong and regular.

"How long can he go on like this?" What she meant was, how long before he starts to die?

"We've never run into something like this before. It could be weeks. It could be years. For all I know, as long as someone keeps caring for him, he could stay like this forever."

A movie played out in Katie's mind, one where Izzy grew older and grayer as she fed and bathed Bartholomew. Her body aged, became frail, and eventually failed. Then someone else would take over. Perhaps Katie, now old and her face seamed with wrinkles. All the while, Bartholomew remained unchanged.

How many generations of caretakers would tend to the old

man before one simply forgot to keep feeding him, or went about his business and through denial or whatever psychological mechanism, pretended that the undying man in the basement didn't really exist? He would eventually become a commodity, a burden: one easier forgotten than remembered.

And then Bartholomew would die. Not on the terms he had chosen, but because he had become a nuisance.

Something inside her bristled. She wouldn't let that happen. Bartholomew had done too much for the world to see him slip away, an unimportant houseguest that never left, never aged.

She brought Bartholomew's hand to her lips, kissed it, and gently rested it on the bed.

"You better tell me what you've got planned," she whispered.

***

The night sky sang to darkness, the moon a stitch of white binding the stars to a promise.

Katie followed Philip along a gravel path until they came to a tall fence. Age had weakened the structure, the chain links sagging here and there. At other spots, rust had eaten it away completely. Still, it looked formidable. A large, heavy chain with a sturdy padlock sealed the entrance.

Pleased she had remembered to bring a flashlight, Katie flipped it on and directed the beam at a sign wired to the fence.

HARBOR VIEW COPPER MINE
!!CAUTION!!
DO NOT ENTER

Katie frowned at Philip. "An abandoned mine?"

"Privacy," Philip said. "There's a weakened area of the fence off to the east."

With Philip's guidance, they located a span of chain-link that had collapsed under the unforgiving fury of Michigan's winters.

They slipped through and approached the mine. Katie used her flashlight to look around.

A sinewy complex of metal scaffolding led to a sprawling complex of brick-and wood-sided buildings, their windows boarded over and decorated in spots with colorful graffiti. A tall chimney rose from the center, the brick shaft climbing so high she couldn't find the top with her light.

"The smelting facility," Philip said. "That metal structure carried copper ore to the smelter. Back in the 1880s, you could see the smoke rising from that stack from miles away."

"You worked here?"

"Of course not, I like my comforts too much. Thomas worked here. He likes to make things, and the mine provided him with the raw materials he needed to work his craft. I would visit him on occasion."

Beyond the smelting complex, rail tracks led off into the distance. Mining carts gathered at one end like giant tortoises, great beasts who hadn't moved in years. Rust had corroded them so badly the wheel assemblies had collapsed.

"The mine must be that way," she said, moving the beam along the tracks.

Philip nodded. "The entrance is sealed with concrete."

"You intend to enter the mine?"

"We aren't here to admire the scenery."

"Thomas worked here," Katie said. "He made something, didn't he? And he left it in the mine?"

Grinning, Philip headed for the tracks. "Bartholomew always said you were smart."

They walked almost a mile before they reached the entrance: a hole in the broad face of a hill. Wood beams shored up the sides. A narrow roof, more a rocky overhang, protected it from the weather. As expected, a heavy concrete slab plugged the hole completely. The metal rails disappeared into the concrete. It had been poured and not simply set in place. The blockage was seamless. Katie couldn't find a gap large enough for a spider to squeeze through.

Philip approached the entrance, placed his hand on the impenetrable barrier, and closed his eyes.

Katie waited, keeping time with the troubled beating of her heart.

Soon Philip opened his eyes and turned to Katie.

"I found a way in."

***

Scrub brush had grown over the mine's airshaft, providing a thick tangle of camouflage. If they hadn't known for sure the location, they never would have found it.

Katie cleared the vegetation, revealing a hole about the size of a large man. She shot her light down it. "It appears clear," she said. "Not that I can see far."

Philip put his feet into the shaft. "How good are you in tight spaces?"

"I've never suffered from claustrophobia."

"This might challenge you." He held out his hand, and she gave him the flashlight. "I'll go first. Wait until you hear me call out before you follow."

"What if it goes straight down?"

"Then I'll reach the end faster, won't I?"

"Not funny. Not funny at all."

"No, I suppose not." He shone the light into the shaft. "I expect there'll be debris in there, something to slow my descent. And I can use my hands and feet to grip the walls for control. It shouldn't be too difficult." He swung the flashlight in her direction. "You sure you can do this?"

"I'll be fine," she said, ignoring the ball of ice that had formed in her chest. While not claustrophobic, she had never liked heights, and the airshaft seemed like it went a long way down.

Philip slid half his body into the shaft. "Be careful, and take your time. You won't be able to help if you break your leg."

Katie watched him edge his way into the shaft. His feet and hands did help slow his descent. He hadn't gone far when he called for her to follow.

Smaller than Philip, she had to stretch her arms and legs to touch the stone sides. Gravel dug into her back as she scooted into the airshaft.

The air stank of dirt and mold, and she wondered if water had collected somewhere in the mine.

Swallowing hard, she started after Philip.

Katie pressed harder against the sides to keep from sliding uncontrollably downward. Sweat broke out across her skin. A dull burn flared across her shoulders.

The angle of the shaft gradually steepened.

"How are you holding up?" Philip called to her.

"Fine," she said, teeth clenched. "Keep going."

She continued her descent. She could feel her weight bearing down on her aching feet. Soon she was practically vertical.

Her arms and legs trembled from the strain. She could feel them weakening.

She wasn't going to make it.

Philip suddenly shouted. "I'm in the mine! Katie, can you hear me?"

She tried to ease her way downward, but her sweat-slicked palms couldn't find purchase, and she began to slide.

She drove her feet hard against the walls of the shaft. Bits of dirt and stone flew up into her face. Her fingers clawed at the earth.

Her slide became a free fall and she cried out.

A light flashed in the distance. "Katie," Philip shouted. "*KA-TIE!*"

With all the effort she could muster, Katie dug in with her heels. The impact hurt her knees. One ankle twisted.

The shaft suddenly opened up. Philip stood below her, his arms up. The flashlight lay next to him on the ground.

"Roll when I push you!" he yelled.

She broke free of the airshaft and fell on him. Stronger than he looked, Philip absorbed some of her fall with his arms, then pushed her. She hit the ground awkwardly but managed to tuck and roll. Pain shot up her leg from her ankle. Her head smacked hard against the stony ground. She rolled and rolled and eventually came to a stop.

Clouds of dirt settled around her. She hurt so much she wanted to cry.

Philip picked up the flashlight and ran over to her. "Are you all right?"

She coughed. "My ankle. I think I might have broken it."

"Let me see." He gently lifted her pant leg. Strong fingers probed her ankle. She tried not to wince. "I don't think it's broken, but you probably sprained it well and good. Here, let me help you up."

She stood, keeping weight off her injured ankle. With one arm slung over Philip's shoulder, she took a moment to assess her physical condition.

With each breath she felt a sharp, stabbing pain in her side, though not severe enough to suggest a broken rib, and her head hurt. The rest of her seemed uninjured.

"I think I'll be fine," she told Philip. "That was scary."

"What about your ankle? Will you be able to walk?"

Good question. She put weight on it. Pain shot up her leg, but not enough to keep her from walking. "I'll be good."

"We don't have much farther to go." He shone the light down the mine shaft. Rough dirt walls faded into darkness where the beam ended. "What I need is that way."

"How far?"

Philip set off down the shaft. "As far as it is."

They walked for a long time. Philip paused occasionally, mostly at intersections, and proceeded down other shafts. There seemed no rhyme or reason to his choices, but Katie understood: Philip followed his own internal compass, one that rarely failed.

They came to a wide intersection where several shafts met. Rail tracks emerged from each tunnel to converge at a central mechanism with a rusty metal switch. She could tell the switch allowed cars to change tracks. Oil lamps hung from hooks embedded into the walls, their fuel wells long empty.

Katie removed a lamp from its hook. The wick was missing. Probably taken by rats to make a nest. "Didn't the miners worry about explosions? I heard mines and flames didn't mix."

"You're talking about coal mines," Philip said. "Here it's just copper, and copper doesn't burn."

She replaced the lamp. "Are we close to whatever you're looking for?"

"The ward is that way." He gestured to the far right-hand tunnel.

They walked on, their footsteps kicking up dust. Philip went first, flashlight in hand; Katie limped behind him. The tunnel led them ever downward. Soon the air took on a gritty quality.

"Didn't they have ventilation this far down?" she asked.

"Not enough without power to run the air pumps. Luckily we won't be here much longer."

They stopped in front of an unassuming rock wall. Philip directed the flashlight at the stone and moved it around, as if searching for something. He fixed the beam on a piece of wall about chest high from the ground and covered in dirt.

"Here," he said, pointing. "Do you see that?"

Katie used her hand to brush away the dirt. Beneath she found marks on the rock. Someone had scored the surface with a sharp implement. They weren't random marks, either. They formed a crude shape.

A chisel.

"Thomas," she said.

Philip nodded. "I could have found it easily enough, but he put the mark there in case one of the others came. They would know when they found the correct spot." He handed her the flashlight. "Hold this for a moment."

She took it and shone the light on the chisel shape. "What do you do now?"

Philip pressed his hand firmly against the stone, his palm covering the crudely hewn chisel.

Seconds passed. Katie sensed the tension building in her uncle.

Philip pushed his shoulder forward, giving the wall a useless shove. His eyes narrowed to points. Then his lips started moving. He appeared to be talking, but she couldn't hear any words.

"You sense something," she said.

Sweating, Philip continued his silent incantation, his lips twisting as they formed the obscure words.

Alarmed, she grabbed his arm. "What's wrong?"

Philip suddenly staggered as if struck by a powerful blow. He turned to face her, his eyes wide with fear.

"This isn't Thomas's carving," he whispered. "*This isn't his carving!*"

Katie stiffened. She heard a noise coming from the darkness, far away but approaching rapidly. A scratching, like claws scrambling over rock. Soon she could make out harsh breathing, a rhythmic panting, growing louder and louder. Fear raced through her. For the first time since she'd been a little girl, her bowels threatened to let loose.

Then she heard the howl, an eerie two-toned wail like the cry of a tortured soul.

She'd heard that howl before.

Four years ago.

In Kinsey.

The hairs along her arms rose in terrified waves.

It can't be! It's dead! Izzy killed it!

She remembered what Bartholomew had told her.

There was another.

A Fek.

"You know what that thing is," she said. "You know we can't outrun it."

Philip searched the wall, hands flying over the stone. "It has to be nearby. I felt it. I'm not wrong." His voice climbed to a shout. "Help me or we're dead!"

Tucking the flashlight under her arm, Katie wiped at the dirt.

The sounds of the Fek—the mad scrambling of its claws, that godawful howl—thundered in the narrow chamber.

Philip shifted away from her, his hands brushing away dirt in a frantic attempt to find Thomas's carving.

She did likewise, moving in the opposite direction.

The Fek's howling—

Screaming, the damned thing was screaming.

—pummeled her senses.

She didn't want to die down here, where no one would find her. Desperate, she flailed at the wall. The flashlight's beam danced mad circles on the stone.

Dirt. So much dirt. Her lungs labored to draw air.

The Fek let out a series of harsh barks. Katie thought she heard a voice in those dreadful yips, a familiar voice.

Jack Sallinen, Kinsey's heartless banker. The man who had orchestrated the events that led to so many deaths. The man who had become the new Fek after he'd consumed the dead body of

Darryl Webber.

She didn't want to see Jack Sallinen's eyes staring at her from within that nightmare beast's skull.

Philip let out a cry. "I found it!"

With dirt and darkness settling around them, Katie rushed to his side. Gray powder coated Philip's face, but he was grinning.

"There!" He pointed to a spot on the wall. "It's there!"

Katie trained the light on the spot he'd indicated. She saw it: markings that formed a chisel. It looked just like the other one they'd found.

"Hurry," she said. "That thing's almost here."

Philip lifted his hand to place it on the wall.

Hurry, Katie urged silently. Her heart hammered in her chest. *Hurry!*

A roar came from the tunnel directly opposite them. The Fek emerged from the darkness, claws digging into the rocky ground, its powerful, lupine body covered in spots with snake-like scales. The thick muscles of its shoulders bunched and flexed as it hurtled toward them, jaws open, lips peeled back.

Then she saw its eyes, bright blue, the same color of Jack Sallinen's, a man who should have died four years ago, a man condemned to live as a monster, and she felt her blood run cold.

They had run out of time.

The Fek hit Philip and sent him sprawling and then pounced on him. Philip grabbed the monster, tried to keep its claws away from his face. The Fek thrust its ugly head forward, jaws snapping in an attempt to tear out Philip's throat.

Katie dropped the flashlight and leapt onto the monster's back. Arms around its throat, she tried to strangle the thing. She had seen Bartholomew do the same once, at the Kinsey police station.

She needed to wrench its head away from Philip or he would die, but the creature was strong. Powerful muscles corded its neck and shoulders; they formed a protective sheath around its vulnerable areas. With a desperate cry, she jerked upward as hard as she could.

Her scream distracted the Fek, giving Philip a chance to attack. He dug his thumbs under the Fek's jaw, between the long bones that formed its snout. Philip's shoulders bunched as he pressed his attack.

The Fek coughed, a sound too human for a monster, and reared back.

If Katie had not clung to its neck, she would have been dislodged. As it was, she locked her fists together and lifted with all her might. She tilted her head back, her lips peeled back into a grimace. Her shoulders ached from the strain.

The Fek's neck arched, exposing its throat.

Philip cocked a fist and drove it into the creature's neck.

Have a windpipe, Katie prayed. *Dear God, please have a windpipe.*

The Fek's cough turned into a hacking gag. It shuddered and twisted violently, coiling like a serpent, bringing its head around to face Katie.

Those blue eyes, brimming with insanity and hatred, widened momentarily, almost as if it had recognized her. Then its powerful jaws clamped down on her shoulder and threw her from its back.

She landed several feet away and hobbled up to find her footing. Philip did the only thing he could—he drove his fists over and over into the monster's throat.

The Fek, driven by whatever warped intelligence remained of the two men it had once been, roared and launched itself at the only thing that might give the two humans the advantage.

The flashlight.

The monster snatched it up in his jaws and threw it against the rock wall.

The bulb shattered, plunging them into darkness.

***

Katie heard the Fek scream, not in pain but in joy.

Mad, ebullient joy.

"Katie!" Philip said. "The Fek. You need to stop it while I get us out of here."

But I can't see! she wanted to scream. *How can I stop it when I can't see?*

She shook off her panic. That was the old Katie, the girl who hadn't been trained by the most inspiring man she had met, the girl who hadn't been trained to save Innocents from the evils of the world.

The Veil had been weakened. The dead had returned to the world. People possessed by spirits were killing Innocents. And it would only get worse.

They needed Bartholomew.

They needed to restore the Veil.

If she and Philip failed, that would never happen.

Millions of Innocents could die.

Marbæs would win.

Judas Iscariot would win.

She couldn't let that happen.

"I can do this," she whispered. She closed her eyes and listened.

The Fek moved. She heard its claws scrape along the floor.

Philip posed the greater threat to the creature. It would attack him first.

Moving her head back and forth, using her ears to triangulate, she determined the monster's location—

—and charged.

Her feet falling almost soundlessly on the ground, she spread her arms wide. When she collided with the monster, she wrapped her arms around it, then her legs. Jaws clenched tightly, she twisted, she thrashed, she pulled. She did everything she could think of to keep the Fek away from Philip.

She felt powerful muscles flex under her, but Katie only gripped it tighter. It smashed its body against the rock wall. Katie grunted but held on. It shook its shaggy coat, yipped and snapped, but couldn't dislodge its attacker.

The Fek howled in frustration and doubled its efforts.

Katie felt her arms slip. The Fek again bashed her against the wall. She slipped a little more.

Her energy almost spent, Katie understood she wouldn't last much longer.

Then, in the middle of the darkness, she saw a light, faint but clear. It illuminated part of the wall.

Philip stood in front of the light, his hand covering Thomas's mark.

The light came from his hand.

The Fek once again howled, this time in surprise and rage.

Katie could see it now. She clung to its back, her face near the monster's. Its eyes rolled wildly in their sockets. Its jaws snapped angrily at the air.

They weren't far from Philip. The light from his hand grew. It spread across the wall's surface like a ripple in a pond. Where the light touched the rock, the wall faded and a hole opened up.

With an enraged cry, the Fek turned to attack. If it reached Philip, it would keep him from finishing what he'd come here to do, something that could save them.

She'd fought one of these creatures before. She knew she couldn't kill it, but she could damn well hurt it. Last time, she'd shoved a burning flare into its eye. She didn't have a flare this time, but she did have something nearly as good.

She shifted her clenched fists closer to the monster's face, thrust out her thumbs, and drove them into the Fek's eyes.

The orbs ruptured with a wet, popping sound. Oily fluid spilled over her hands. Swallowing back the bile rising in her throat, she pushed her thumbs farther into the monster's skull. Maybe if she pierced its brain—

The Fek screamed, rose onto its hind quarters, almost standing erect, and shuddered so powerfully that Katie finally lost her grip and fell from the creature's back.

Philip hadn't moved. The light from his hand now encompassed part of the wall roughly the shape of a large door. It shimmered, as if the stone had turned to water. Beyond it Katie saw another tunnel.

"Go through the ward," Philip shouted. "Get to the other side."

She didn't need to be told twice. The pain of her injured ankle a distant annoyance, she lurched forward, practically *fell* forward. Her body hit the ward, shoulder first. A bitter cold sliced through her as she passed into the other tunnel. She felt a slight tugging, a pulling at her insides, as she forced her way through the ward.

Soon she was on the other side.

She turned to face Philip.

He slowly pushed his way through the ward. Behind him,

the Fek raged, lashing out blindly in an attempt to find them. A clawed foot raked the air and hit Philip in the back.

Having located at least one of its prey, the Fek launched itself at Philip. Its jaws snagged his shirt, narrowly missing his arm.

Philip pushed his way through the ward. The Fek pulled at him, stopped his advance. Philip stretched out his hand. Katie took it and pulled.

The man fell forward, followed by the Fek.

As soon as Philip passed through the ward, the shimmering boundary winked out of existence.

The Fek had been partway through when the rock wall returned and cut through its flesh. Its grizzled head fell to the ground, blood seeping from the severed end. The rest remained back in the copper mine.

"It's dead," Katie said, her voice ragged. "It has to be. Nothing could survive that."

"Are you all right?" Philip asked. With the ward extinguished, darkness had once again taken them.

"My ankle still hurts, but otherwise I'm okay." She paused to catch her breath. "What do we do now? We can't see."

"This tunnel isn't long," Philip said. "Just follow me."

Katie followed the sound of his voice. Not much time had passed before Philip called for a halt.

"Let's see if I can't make us some light," he said.

Katie waited patiently. It wasn't easy. The oppressive darkness hung like a yolk around her shoulders.

She was about to ask Philip about the light when it appeared. Similar to the ward-light, it shimmered faintly.

She could finally see.

A niche had been carved into the wall where the tunnel ended. In the niche sat a plain wooden cube, roughly two feet by two feet. It had no markings, no carvings.

The light came from the cube.

Philip removed it.

"What is it?" Katie said.

"A container. Thomas made it so that anything can be safely stored within it."

Katie frowned. "But there's no lid. How do you put something inside it?"

"It's not that kind of container," Philip replied, smiling.

"Then what does it hold?"

He held it out to her. "Anything a Forever Man puts into it."

Katie accepted the cube. When it came in contact with her skin, she felt a stabbing pain in her head. White light flashed behind her eyes, and she felt a push, like a hand on the back of her skull.

She had enough time to become aware of something new inside her, some space she could neither define nor identify. And in that space, a face emerged.

Oh God, no.

Another blackness claimed her, and she saw no more.

PART TWO:
BROKEN JOURNEYS

CHAPTER SEVEN

Izzy listened to Katie's story. "The other Fek," she said. "I thought I'd buried it under tons of rock." In that cave in Kinsey, where she had killed, and in killing, she'd been changed.

"Creatures like that don't die easily." Philip sat in a chair, a glass of water in his hand. James had attended to the worst of his wounds; the rest would quickly fade. "It survived somehow, not that I'm surprised. But here's what puzzles me—how did it get in that mine?"

"It had to be put there by the same person who made the false ward," Thomas said. The gnome-like man held the cube in his lap. "It was a trap, meant to snare at least one of us."

"Few people know how to make that ward," James said. "Knowing what we now know, I can think of a suspect."

"I saw him," Katie whispered. "Just before everything went black. I saw his face."

Izzy stepped forward. "Whose face?"

"Judas. I saw his face in my mind." She looked away. "He was laughing at me."

John nodded. "Judas set this in motion. He did this to Bartholomew. He'd also guess we would try to heal our brother, so he set a trap. And if Philip is right, he knew we'd need the cube, that we would come for it. It was genius."

"But he failed," Gene said. "We have the cube."

"Perhaps not," Thomas said. "If Judas could make a false ward, he could have also trapped the cube."

"Can you tell if the cube's been altered?" Matthew said. The ruggedly handsome man hadn't said a word in almost an hour.

Thomas's eyebrows climbed his forehead. He must have been as surprised as Izzy that Matthew had spoken. Turning his attention to the cube, Thomas's strong fingers caressed the surface, touching all the sides. It didn't take long. "Doesn't seem different. I can still put things in it and take them out again."

"Prove it," Matthew said.

"Natalie," Thomas said. "Do you have a pen or something?"

Natalie reached into her clutch, pulled out a mascara pencil, and handed it to Thomas.

"Thank you, dear." Holding the pencil in one hand and resting his other hand on the cube, Thomas stared at the mascara pencil.

While Izzy wasn't astonished at what happened next, it still impressed her.

The pencil winked out of existence.

Gene, on the other hand, took a surprised step forward. "Hey, where'd it go?"

"It's in here." Thomas shook the cube. The faint rattle of the pencil could be heard bouncing around inside.

"Wait," Gene said. "How do I know it didn't rattle like that before?"

Thomas gave him a level stare, then set the cube on his lap and held out his palm. Seconds later, the mascara pencil appeared in his hand. After returning it to Natalie, he lifted the cube and shook it.

No rattling.

"Satisfied?" he said.

Izzy touched Gene's arm. "They get nothing out of lying to us."

"Right," Gene said. "I'm just not used to seeing the impossible happen."

"You saw what Thomas did," Matthew said. "He put the pencil

in the cube, and then he removed it. Why use a word like 'impossible'?"

"Because he didn't put it in," Gene said, pointing to the cube. "It disappeared. How can you say he did anything?"

Matthew pursed his lips. "You don't believe him."

"I don't know what to believe," Gene said. "That's the problem. Nothing makes sense. I'm a stranger to everything I used to know."

"If that's the case," Matthew said, "you understand my dilemma better than most."

Natalie stirred from her spot on the floor. "Mom, can I go to my room?"

Izzy shook her head. Natalie had yet to learn that there was more to living than loud music, black eyeliner, and a lousy attitude. "We're not done yet."

"But what's this got to do with me?"

"You live in this house, and you're part of this family. Trust me when I say it concerns you."

Natalie grimaced but remained silent. Izzy didn't think her daughter's silence would last for long.

"You said you know what happened to Bartholomew," she said to Philip. "That you know where he is."

Philip looked uncomfortable. "You ready for this?" he asked John.

John tapped the pen against the side of his head. It was a trivial gesture, but his expression was anything but trivial. "It will all be up here."

"First of all," Philip said, "we know where he is, at least his physical body. It's lying downstairs and has been for weeks. But we all agree that what's missing is his consciousness, what makes him who he is. His memories, his emotions. Everything that made him a human. What's left behind is nothing more than an organism— a biologically sophisticated one, but an organism nonetheless. He eats and he shits. That's about it."

"Crude," James said. "But accurate."

"His soul," Izzy said. "You think he's missing his soul."

Philip nodded. "That's the assumption I'm working off of."

"But you know where he is?" James asked. He had finished with

Katie, who now sat upright, her expression intense.

"I might know where to look," Philip said. "It's why Katie and I retrieved the cube."

Thomas sat up straighter. "You mean to put our brother's soul in the cube."

"And bring it back to his body," Philip finished. "It's the only chance Bartholomew has."

"I see two problems," John said. "Though I like your thinking."

Philip crossed his arms and waited.

"One," John said. This time, instead of clicking his pen, he twirled it between two fingers. "If we succeed in obtaining Bartholomew's soul, how do we get it back inside his body? Second, this is clearly what Judas intended. He'll have set a trap, the same way he did with the cube." He caught the pen in his fist. "He means to kill as many of us as possible."

"He must know how hard it is to kill one of us," Philip countered, "let alone several. And again, to what purpose? He's lived all this time without revealing himself. He could have finished out his years with no one the wiser." His stance softened some. "He has nothing to fear from us. He did what he did, for whatever the reason. He did what he had to do."

"When you think of it," James said, "his treachery set everything in motion. Without him, none of us would likely be sitting here now."

"I think my slightly sluggish brother is onto something," John said with a quick grin.

Thomas scoffed. "Right, so now he's a hero?"

"Judas may not be a hero," John said, "but he was certainly essential. His act changed the world, moved it in an entirely different direction."

Izzy had been trying to take all of this in. Treachery. Fate. The intertwining of the two. But one thing still stood out to her.

"Why now?" she asked. "What does he get from acting now after centuries of anonymous and safe isolation?"

The answer came from the person she least expected.

"Marbæs," Natalie said. Her daughter spoke softly, as if afraid of drawing attention to herself. "Maybe he's doing this because of her."

John turned to her in surprise. "What makes you say that?"

Natalie squirmed under the man's hawk-like gaze. "He's lived as long as you. We know how each of you became...like you are. But how did it happen to him? My guess is it was Marbæs. Maybe she's calling in a favor. You know, I made you immortal and now you have to do this.'" She seemed to fumble for something else to say and finally settled on, "I know, it sounds stupid. Forget I said anything."

"No," Izzy said, smiling. "That wasn't stupid at all. You've pointed out something important. I'm proud of you, honey." She turned her attention to the others. "What do you think? Could it be Marbæs?"

Philip and James looked uncomfortably at one another. Thomas rubbed at his temple, while John's eyes burned with interest. Only Matthew looked as implacable as granite as he sat with his hands in his lap.

John finally broke the silence. "It's a good theory, but I don't think it works. Marbæs can do a lot, but I seriously doubt she can confer onto Judas what was forced on us."

"It was not forced," James said. "We willingly accepted it."

John spun to face his brother. Spots of red burned in his cheeks. "That was before I understood how long this would take. No sane man would agree to this...this torture."

"But agree we did," Thomas said, siding with James. "There's no sense rehashing what we've discussed for hundreds of years. Either get over it or leave. We can do this without you."

"You don't understand," John said. "I believe in what we're doing. I want us to succeed. But what I want more is for it to end!" He looked away, but not before Izzy saw the wetness in his eyes. "Don't any of you get tired?"

James rose and pulled his brother into an embrace. The other man accepted it.

Philip cleared his throat. "I happen to agree with John. Marbæs likely wasn't involved in Judas's existence. It seems beyond her abilities, which means someone or something else intervened." He let his statement linger. "The question of Judas will have to remain a mystery for now."

Gene, who had been quietly watching the interplay, looked

up. "You said you know where Owens's soul is," he said to Philip. "Where is it?"

His expression grim, Philip said, "Not a place you'd like to visit."

***

Natalie's phone buzzed. Her heartbeat quickened when she checked the display.

"Mom. Please, can I go? I really need to take this."

"Who is it?" her mom asked.

Natalie clutched the phone tighter. "Mom, please?"

"Who, Nat?"

Blood rushed to her face. "It—it's a boy."

Her phone buzzed in her hand. She gave her mother another pleading look.

Her mom hesitated. "Go," she finally said. "But you and I will talk later. And you can't go out until then."

Natalie surged to her feet. "Thanks, Mom!" she said, and rushed out of the room.

"Remember, don't leave the house!"

Nat brought the phone to her ear. "Hello?"

"Hey," Sean Leyton replied. "I almost hung up. Is this a bad time?"

"No, no. It's fine. Just let me get to my room."

Natalie raced up the stairs, bounded into her room, and leapt onto her bed. "I was wondering if I'd hear from you again."

"Been busy. Working the late shift's a bitch. End up sleeping all day. But the bank I'll make will help me snag this new video game." He hesitated. "You play Xbox?"

"Oh—yeah, sure. Got one in my room." Natalie glanced at the tiny television sitting on her dresser. It was the only piece of electronics she owned. "Which game?"

"*Duskers*. You heard of it?"

She had. The zombie apocalypse shoot-em-up was the hottest game on the market. She felt a stab of jealousy. She had zero chance of ever owning it.

"Sure," she said glumly. "Everyone's talking about it."

"You sound funny. Something wrong?"

Natalie forced herself to smile, even if Sean couldn't see it. "I'm good. Just not much going on. Kinda bored, if you want to know the truth."

"Anything I can help with?"

"Are you free later?" she asked.

"I don't work again for two days. That's why I called."

"Got anything specific planned?"

"Just hoping to see you."

"You know that little diner across from city hall?"

"Sure. Tagliata's."

"Meet me there."

"All right. When?"

She smiled. "How about dinner tonight?"

||*

Sean Leyton hit the END button and tossed the phone on the table between a half-consumed sandwich and a cup of coffee, now cold.

"Man, that's one weird chick." He looked at the man seated across from him. "The first time we met, she sprayed water on me, like I was a disobedient cat."

The man's eyes narrowed. "Water, you say?"

"Yeah, it was weird. How do you know her?"

"I don't," the man replied. With his swarthy skin and black hair, Sean thought he looked foreign. Middle Eastern, maybe? He did have an accent, but it wasn't one Sean could place.

"I don't get your interest in her," Sean said. "What is she, a local celebrity or something? Or are you a creeper, got a thing for younger women?"

"My interest in her is of no concern to you. I only need you to get close to her, earn her trust. Such a request shouldn't be too difficult for a handsome lad like you."

Sean felt pinpricks run along his skin. This man—Jonathan Whitlock, if he'd told Sean his real name—made him feel uneasy. And the comment about him being a "handsome lad" only made his uneasiness intensify.

"Say I succeed—what am I supposed to do then?"

Jonathan Whitlock reached for his briefcase. It was large, made of plush leather with heavy brass locks, and looked expensive as hell. Sean's dad owned one like it, though not as fancy. Whitlock withdrew an object from the case and handed it to Sean.

Circular in shape, it was about six inches across, the narrow rim constructed of some dark, lightweight material Sean couldn't identify.

Like the guy's accent, he thought uncomfortably.

Inside the circle were more circles, smaller and evenly spaced, made of the same dark material. Those smaller circles were attached to the rim of the larger one. Black threads were woven in a complex pattern among the rings. Thin strips of leather had been tied to the rim.

He looked up at Whitlock. "A dreamcatcher?"

"Of sorts," Whitlock said with a bemused grin.

"Don't play games with me. Either it is or it isn't."

"How should I put this?" Whitlock thought for a moment. "Okay, let's say you're generally correct but precisely wrong. That's as much detail as you're going to get."

Sean scowled. He didn't like being talked down to. Fuck the reward, the old dude had better watch his mouth or he'd have to find someone else to help him.

He returned his attention to the dreamcatcher. It seemed to have no weight; holding it was like holding a bubble while standing on the surface of the moon. Curious, he tilted it in his hand, allowing the light streaming in from his window to wash over the dreamcatcher's many interlocking circles. They twinkled in the glow of the sun, but in different colors, like prisms scattering light. As his eyes followed the flashes, Sean felt an itch form inside his head, an unpleasant scratching beneath his skull. Small at first, like tiny hornets skittering about, the sensation quickly intensified, swelled, expanded, until it felt like a whole nest of them had set up shop inside his head.

Then the stinging began...oh God, when *that* began—

Sean dropped the dreamcatcher and clapped his hands to the sides of his head, his eyes leaking tears, his mouth dropping open in a silent scream.

Whitlock quickly snatched up the dreamcatcher and dropped

it into his briefcase. His bemused grin fractured in a hundred places. He now looked royally pissed.

"Don't do that again." Whitlock spoke slowly, as if he were addressing an imbecile. "Ever."

Sean dropped his hands into his lap. With the dreamcatcher out of sight, the hornets had fled the nest or flown the coop or whatever it was that hornets do, leaving his head empty and numb. *"What the hell was that?"*

"Keep your voice down," Whitlock snapped. "I'm supposed to be giving you guitar lessons. Start shouting and we'll have more trouble than either of us wants."

A guitar case rested at the foot of his bed. Whitlock had brought it with him. Inside was a 1960 Gibson Les Paul Standard with a washed cherry top and original PAF pickups. Sean's own guitar, a cheap Squire his wealthy parents had gotten him for his birthday, sat untouched in the corner of his bedroom. He was almost embarrassed to plug it into his amp, it sounded so awful. What he really needed was a good axe, an EPS Limited or a Jackson SL1. Then his playing wouldn't sound so goddamn lame.

Whitlock's voice dragged him from his thoughts. "You're thinking about your reward."

Sean wiped at his eyes. Whatever the dreamcatcher had done to him now seemed a faraway memory.

"I can have any guitar I want?" he asked. "No matter the cost?"

"It has to be available for sale. I won't be party to theft."

Sean's fingers itched at the thought of playing a real axe, one worthy of James Hetfield or Slash. "All I have to do is get close to her? I don't have to, you know, hurt her or anything?"

Whitlock shook his head. "You will do no harm to her. In fact, if you do, our deal is off. Is that clear?"

"Cozy up to Natalie, skip the violence. Sounds easy. Heck, I'm almost there now."

Whitlock help up a cautioning finger. "You will have to do more than get close to her, though."

Sean's elation drained out of him. He knew it had sounded too easy. "You never said anything about doing more."

"What I have in mind won't take much effort. Trust me, getting close to the girl will be the hard part."

I'd have a better chance than you, you old creeper. "What do you want me to do?"

"You are to hide this in her house." Whitlock retrieved the dreamcatcher. When Sean averted his eyes, he added, "You don't have to look away, just don't stare at it."

"Fine." Sean took the dreamcatcher, holding it between two fingers. "Where do I hide it?"

"Preferably the living room, but anywhere on the first floor should work."

"That's it? Nothing else?"

"Nothing else."

Sean relaxed some. "And this won't hurt Natalie?"

"Not at all."

He had a sudden thought. "Or me?"

"Of course not. I'm not into hurting children."

Sean bristled. "I'm twenty-two, dude. Don't call me a child."

"Sorry, that was an unfortunate choice of words."

Sean glared at Whitlock. "Just put the dreamcatcher in her house," he said. "Then I'm done, and I get my guitar?"

Whitlock hesitated for just a moment, then said, "Yes. Place it in her house and you are done. The guitar will be yours." He glanced at the cluttered room. "One more thing: don't leave the dreamcatcher in here. I doubt you'll ever find it again."

Sean bristled. "Keep the opinion to yourself," he muttered, then, louder, "I guess we have a deal."

Whitlock caressed the scar around his neck. Sean swore it looked like a rope burn, like the man had tried to hang himself. Too bad he didn't succeed.

"We do, indeed," Whitlock said, and picked up his Les Paul. "Now, we'd better get on with your lesson or your parents will start to wonder what we're doing in here."

Sean reluctantly plugged in his Squire.

To get his hands on a real axe, he'd do practically anything.

***

Gene watched his goddaughter bolt out of the room. Having never had children of his own, he wasn't accustomed to their hot tin mood swings.

"Boys?" he said to Izzy with a raised eyebrow.

"She's twenty-two. An interest in boys is healthy. It's just..."

"What?"

Izzy seemed to struggle with a reply. That was another new aspect of her personality, one that bothered Gene more than the worrying and fingernail biting. The Elizabeth Morris he remembered would've let it rip and to hell with the consequences; her opinions were as solid as her police work, and often just as fair. To see such a strong woman battle with herself somehow made him feel even smaller, like he should be more worried, more frightened.

If they were going to live through this crisis, they would need the old Izzy back.

"Maybe Stanley was right after all," he said. It hurt him to say the words, but he needed to do this, he needed to shock her back into reality. "I can't believe I'm saying this, but maybe he was right."

Izzy's head snapped up. "Right about what?"

"You're more style than substance."

"He said that?" Her cheeks flushed crimson. "About me? Stanley said that about *me*?"

Gene nodded. "We would talk on occasion, after we thought you were dead." It was easy to sound bitter at this point; she had fooled him into thinking she was dead. "Mostly, we would talk about you. Part of the grieving process, I suppose. It sounds almost poetic now, or it would if you hadn't lied to us."

"You know why I did it. I don't see any point in—"

"Going over it again? No, neither do I." Gene rested his back against the wall and crossed his arms over his chest. He had to hold himself together, almost physically, to keep his emotions from flying apart. "One day—maybe a year or so after your supposed death—we ran into each other. I'd finished up at the bar, and I guess he'd closed up shop at the pharmacy. This was before he sold it. Anyway, I walked out of the IGA with a couple bags of groceries when he turned the corner and almost ran smack into me. He apologized...and then he smiled. I hadn't seen him smile in a long time. The sight took me back a ways, to when you and he and I were all friends, and something like warmth spread through me. I smiled back, and we'd got to talking.

"He touched on the problems you two were having. The fights, the uncomfortable silences, the days filled with tension so thick he could 'hardly breathe,' as he put it. He blamed you, of course. He felt you were more into the roles you played than being Izzy Morris."

He scratched at the whiskers on his cheek. "I didn't believe him, and I told him so. He was parceling out his arguments to fit his thinking. I told him he couldn't realistically expect you or anyone else to be the same person in each situation. You were as strong on the inside as you presented to the world. It wasn't your fault he couldn't see it." He paused, then shrugged. "That pissed him off. He told me my memory was failing, or that I was remembering you in a better light. He also refused to take any responsibility for what happened to your relationship. That's Stanley for you."

Izzy shook her head. "But I—"

"Don't interrupt. You're going to hear what I have to say." When Izzy reluctantly quieted, Gene continued. "Now here you are, four years later, and imagine my surprise when I see that Stanley was right. I'm seeing your substance for the first time, or at least allowing myself to see it. Insecure. Hesitant. Uncertain of what to do or say. You're nothing like the Izzy I once knew." The Izzy he'd loved—and still loves. "Without the role of cop or wife, you're stuck with being a mom, and with a twenty-something-year-old kid, even that has its limits. What I'm seeing now is the plain vanilla Elizabeth Morris, and it shocks the hell out of me."

He stopped there. He had to. He'd hurt her. He could tell by her silence. He only hoped it had been enough. He didn't think he could bring himself to do that to her again.

Izzy refused to look at him. Her eyes remained locked on the floor.

As Izzy chewed on what he had said, he finally noticed the Forever Men. They stared at him. Philip looked upset, almost angry, as if Gene had just told his mother to piss up a rope. Thomas hugged his cube tighter to his chest, his weathered face pinched in disapproval. James and John traded uncertain glances. Only Matthew remained expressionless, as if he hadn't heard Gene's sharp words, or hadn't cared much about what he'd said.

Gene ignored them—what argument or excuse could he use for his behavior that they hadn't heard time and again over their long years? Instead, he focused on Izzy.

She kept staring at the floor, fists clenched, the muscles of her jaw flexing and flexing. "You're right," she finally said, her voice wound so tightly it almost hummed. "And you're wrong. So damned wrong."

"Then explain it to me." *Tell me it's okay to be afraid.*

"It's true," she said. "I'm not the same person you knew back in Kinsey." She hesitated, licked her lips, and pushed on. "You didn't see me during those four years. Yes, I'm not a cop anymore. Yes, I'm not a wife anymore. But I'm still a mother, and not just to Natalie, but to Kevin. I fought for them. I took shit from others for them. I gave up my life for them. I did it all, and I did it by myself. And what do you do—you show up and judge me, after the fact?" She shook her head. "I won't allow that. I've worked too hard to be treated this poorly."

He wasn't about to let her off that easily. If they were going to survive this, she needed to be large and in charge. "What about the uncertainty, the hesitation?"

"Because the situation is new," she said. "The Veil's weakness and Bartholomew's unconsciousness happened two weeks ago. I became a round-the-clock caregiver two weeks ago. I'm still trying to process what happened and how to fix it. I don't have a magic eight-ball that I can shake and get the answers to everything. You have to give me time. I'm only one person." Her words trailed off, her anger unspooling like fishing line. "I'm only one person."

Gene pushed himself off the wall, grabbed her shoulders, and held them. "Well, you can start by realizing you're not alone. I'm here to help, for as long as it takes. And stop being so damned indecisive. Trust yourself like you used to. This whole situation is new, and weird as hell, but look who we have on our side." He nodded to the others in the room. "How can we fail with their help?"

John started clicking his pen, realized what he was doing, and stopped. "Having us here doesn't guarantee we'll succeed," he said. "The other side has plenty of assets, most of which you haven't seen, and I dearly hope you never do."

Philip, his anger still as bright as a newly minted penny, stepped forward. "What we need to attempt will not be easy."

Matthew looked up with a queer hunger in his eyes, and John's expression grew rabid. James stuffed his hands into his pockets, a look of discomfort on his handsome face.

Thomas simply rolled his eyes. "Aren't you being a little overdramatic?" he said to Philip. "You said it yourself—we're a lot tougher than we look, especially when we're together."

"We're down one, and an important one at that," Philip countered. "Bartholomew is the Protector. Without him, we have little in the way of defending ourselves—"

Katie, who had taken a place on the couch next to Thomas, sat up straighter. "Tell that to the Fek we just killed."

"I remember that thing," Gene said. "The damage it did to Owens. We thought it had killed him."

"I agree with Katie," Izzy said. "We're still formidable."

"But I still haven't told you where we're going," Philip said grimly. "Where I think Bartholomew's soul is."

No one spoke for a moment, then Gene said, "Okay, I asked it already, but I'll ask it again. Where?"

"Judas must have had this planned for some time," Philip replied. "The Crown, manipulating the weakening of the Veil, encountering Bartholomew after so much time had passed. To have so many pieces fall into place at the right time is almost a miracle." His gaze bounced from person to person. "With the Veil weakened, Judas somehow was able to send Bartholomew's soul to the one place he could never have done so before, and the one place no one would want to go."

"Enough!" Thomas snapped, his knuckles white as he gripped his cube. "Enough with the drama! Tell us where our brother is!"

"Topheth," Philip said. "We have to travel to Topheth."

"No," John whispered. The man's face had gone a deathly pale, his innate confidence seemingly shaken to the core. "Impossible. No one can get there."

Tears stood in James's eyes, and he wiped at them with his hand. "All those children...their bodies burned...their screams drowned out by the drumbeats."

"*It will break him.*" Setting his precious cube aside, Thomas dropped his head into his hands and wept. "It will break him."

Only Matthew remained silent. Gene noted the reticent Forever Man looked distressed, almost resigned, the way someone would look when told he'd been hired to do a job he really didn't want.

"I don't get it," Gene said, puzzled. Izzy and Katie wore the same confused expressions. "Where's Topheth? I've never heard of it."

"I'm not surprised." Philip rubbed worriedly at his beard. "It's a place of sacrifice. Children were burned to death there, untold numbers of them, their screams covered up by the beating of countless drums. It's also known as the Valley of Slaughter."

"That doesn't sound good," Gene said.

"The Middle East," Izzy said. "It has to be there. So much history happened in that region. I'm guessing Israel or Egypt."

"Or Iraq," Katie said. "It used to be called Mesopotamia. Lots of history associated with it, too." She bit her lip. "How will we possibly get there?"

"It's worse than that," Thomas said. "Far worse."

"Topheth isn't a place on Earth," James said.

John nodded, his shock of gray hair seemingly aflame with fear. "No plane or boat can take us there."

A cold stone had formed in the pit of Gene's stomach. "Wait. What are we talking about if we're not talking about a place on Earth?"

"Topheth," Philip said, "exists in Hell."

***

The guy has got to be kidding, Gene thought. It's some kind of sick joke.

But in his heart, he knew it wasn't. The reactions of the Forever Men had been too real, too full of fear.

Philip's words burned into him.

Topheth exists in Hell.

To save Owens, they must travel to the realm of the condemned.

"Let's think about this for a moment," John said. The color had come back to his face, and he had recovered some of his self-assurance. "Why there? What does Judas get from sending Bartholomew's soul to Topheth?"

"Prior to the Veil being weakened," Philip said, "going there would have been impossible, so what Miles did with the Crown was a precursor to this whole scheme."

"Right," John said. "He opened the way for us to recover Bartholomew's soul." His eyes clenched shut. "My head is spinning. Too much new information."

"Which means," Philip said, "he wants us to make the attempt."

"That makes sense given what I saw in the mine," Katie said. She had stood and was now testing her healed ankle. "When I touched the cube, I saw Judas laughing at me."

Thomas shook his head in frustration. "If he'd altered the cube, I should be able to sense some residue of his interference."

Izzy stirred. "He must get something out of this, or he wouldn't be going to so much trouble."

"We're forgetting one other thing," Katie said, and looked at Philip. "Remember how Bartholomew didn't put up a struggle? He and Judas stood calmly talking at the side of the road, and then Judas kissed his cheek. Bartholomew let him do it. It's almost as if he'd agreed with whatever Judas had planned."

John made a rude noise. "They hadn't spoken in millennia. What could Bartholomew possibly know of Judas's plans or purposes?"

"'Trust me,'" Gene blurted out. He had been thinking how this sounded like a game—a dangerous one, but a game nonetheless— and his mind had turned to Truth or Dare, one he'd played as a kid. You really had to trust the people who joined you in the game or you could find yourself doing something embarrassing, something you would spend the rest of your life trying to forget. "Maybe that's what Judas told Owens: Trust me."

"Not with his reputation," Thomas said. "None of us trusts him."

"You didn't know he was still alive until recently," Gene countered. "You've had no interactions, no conversations. Nothing. And how do you know what Owens was feeling? Maybe his views had changed over time. The fact remains that Owens agreed with whatever Judas had planned. I haven't known the man as long as any of you, but I learned quickly to trust him. Maybe you should consider doing the same."

"Gene's right," Izzy said, staring at him with what looked like pride. "Bartholomew has earned our trust over and over. For whatever reason, if he let Judas do this to him, I'm willing to risk it was for a good reason. And if Philip believes he knows how to get Bartholomew's soul back, then we should make the attempt." She opened a screen on her cell phone and held it out to the others. "As soon as possible, because it's not getting any prettier out there."

Gene craned his neck to look at the display. It showed a news report. A frazzled woman, her hair a tangled net on her head, talked into the camera while periodically glancing over her shoulder. The cameraman panned the shot right and focused on what had gotten the reporter so riled.

A house burned uncontrollably. But instead of running away from the flames, a large man with a bald head and tattoos on his meaty arms wrestled with police. Gene gasped in horror as the man broke free, wheeled away from the flames, and grabbed a woman huddled near a police car. An officer challenged him, but the guy gave him a straight-arm worthy of an NFL linebacker and sent the cops windmilling backwards. The tattooed maniac dragged his captive toward the burning house.

The other cops pulled their weapons. One fired, the round plowing into the bald man's leg. Whatever pain he felt didn't seem to register. He dragged the screaming woman until he got close enough to the fire. Then he threw her into the flames.

Apparently not satisfied, the bald man howled and raked at his cheeks with his fingers. Blood trickled from the gashes as he ran into the fire. His skin blistered, then blackened. His clothes burst into flames.

His hands searched until the found the burning woman. As if he knew he was on camera, he turned to the reporter, lifted the woman, and bit into her neck. His jaws worked, his teeth rending her flesh.

That's when someone—likely the program director back in the

studio—cut the feed. Izzy's cell display faded to black.

Gene pointed a trembling finger to the phone. "That's happening around the country?"

"All around the world," Izzy said, and put away her phone. "It's the same situation you saw with Celeste Florin. The damned are crossing the Veil. They're possessing people, and then using them. It's devastating, and as long as the Veil is weakened, these kinds of tragedies will continue. The violence will get worse and worse."

"Marbæs," John said. "This is her plan. She's getting Innocents to kill Innocents, and she doesn't have to lift a finger to encourage it."

"I don't get it," James said. "That would mean Judas is colluding with Marbæs. He acted to weaken the Veil so she could unleash this brutality. And he removed Bartholomew from the picture, the one man best equipped to stop either of them. Yet he also gave us a way to recover Bartholomew's soul, to put it back into his body, which should revive him. Bartholomew would be back in action, which thwarts what Marbæs is doing. He seems to be working for and against either side."

A thought occurred to Gene. "You mean, like a double agent?"

"Exactly," James said. "What if he's working for neither side and both at the same time?"

"That would fit," Izzy said. "Like you said, we know practically nothing about him. But his actions haven't been consistently for one side. He seems to be helping and hindering at the same time."

Katie said, "It fits with his history."

"He betrayed our master," Philip said, "which ironically led to the deaths of both, or so we thought. But without that betrayal, nothing might have changed. He both hindered and helped change the course of civilization."

Thomas's thumb caressed his cube. "And what if that dichotomy followed him into his extended existence?"

"'Extended existence,'" John said, his mouth twisting. "And I thought I had a way with words."

James gestured for his brother to be quiet. "Let's not get caught up in that argument again."

"Pardon my ignorance," Gene said. This discussion had gone

way over his head. These people shared a history, they had a common frame of reference, and he was the newcomer. He felt like a dead autumn leaf being blown in different directions by several strong gusts of wind. "What does any of this have do with helping Owens?"

That brought the others up short. After some puzzled looks, Philip was the first to respond. "To better predict what dangers we may face, we need to understand what we are up against. Judas started this, he gave us a way to rescue Bartholomew, and yet he is still trying to prevent us from succeeding."

Thomas tapped the cube. "He likely sent the Fek to watch this."

"But he failed," Gene said. "He gained nothing."

Matthew looked at Gene. "What makes you think he failed?"

Gene frowned. "We went over this. We have the cube. We can save Owens."

"You're quick to ascribe success and failure, young man," Matthew said, giving Gene a wan smile. "Perhaps too quick."

"Matthew is right," Izzy said, "What if, by retrieving the cube, we ensured our failure?"

"Thomas proved the cube works," Gene insisted, growing more frustrated with the convoluted reasoning. "It has to help."

"Your statement makes perfect sense," Matthew said. "But Judas is subtle. What seems the most obvious is also often the most treacherous. We cannot trust our former brother."

"No one trusts him," John said. "We've already established that."

"Then why the talk of traveling to Topheth?" Matthew asked. "If that's what Judas wants us to do, does it make sense to go?"

Philip rounded on the other Forever Man. His eyes were wide with surprise. "You mean leave Bartholomew there?"

Matthew looked as implacable as ever. "That is precisely what I mean."

***

Gene gaped at Matthew. The reserved Forever Man had taken him by surprise.

Apparently, he wasn't alone.

Philip, who Gene could tell was closest with Owens, seemed to swell with anger to the point of exploding. "Condemn a brother to eternal torment? That's your suggestion?" He blew great puffs of air from between his lips. "How can you even entertain such a thought?"

"I find nothing about this entertaining," Matthew said. "I abhor the thought of leaving Bartholomew there. But we have to think about our mission, why we are here in the first place. We were entrusted with a great responsibility, one that all of humanity counts on, even if they don't know about it. And we've been at it for almost two thousand years." He held up at hand to John, who had opened his mouth to speak. "Please, spare me your diatribes. Frankly, I've had my fill of them." It was the strongest rebuke Gene had heard in his limited time with the man.

John, normally nonplussed, blinked, and then frowned, and then, to everyone's surprise, nodded for Matthew to continue.

"Thank you," Matthew said. "Now, as I was saying, we have a mission to complete. We accepted it. We have a responsibility to keep at it. Let's not mince words. We know about our longevity, our resistance to aging and disease. What we have never broached, at least not openly, is the possibility one of us may die." Matthew interlaced his fingers over his knee. "We will die, one day. No power can prevent that. When that day arrives, when the last of us passes on to our reward, hopefully we will have finished our work, and humanity doesn't have to worry about the evils of Marbæs and her ilk. I don't know when that will happen, but I know it isn't here yet. *We are not done.* And in two millennia, we have yet to suffer a loss. None of us has come close to dying. Until today, that is. We have to accept it, and we have to move forward. The Veil is weakened, the world is falling apart, and we're talking about abandoning our responsibilities. Right now, when we are needed the most." Matthew looked away. "As painful as this sounds, we need to ask if we are acting in the best interests of the Innocents, or our own."

No one spoke for a moment. Then Katie stepped up to Matthew and slapped the Forever Man hard enough to snap his head back.

"Never," she said through clenched teeth, "have I been more

ashamed at being one of you than I am at this moment."

Matthew rubbed at his cheek. His gray eyes held no reproach, only his ubiquitous sorrow. "Forgive me, Katie, but for all you have done, specifically with Bartholomew, you are not one of us. You do not carry the same onus. That means you have no say in this. My brothers and I will decide on a course of action. It's what we have done, and what we will continue to do, long after you are dead. I hope you understand."

"I do *not* understand!" Katie said. "After everything Bartholomew has done for you"—she gestured around the room—"for all of you, I don't understand how you could live knowing you condemned him, you left him to suffer for the rest of time. All he ever wanted, all he ever spoke about, was being reunited with Inanna, to be back in the arms of his wife. That desire was so strong it kept him going, long after he wanted to quit." Except for Philip, the other Forever Men looked shocked at her words. "Yes, he had his moments, his doubts. But he kept going. And now you want to deprive him of his only remaining hope. I can't believe you would be so cruel." She turned her back on Matthew and went to stand next to Philip.

"For one man's life, we put all of humanity at risk," Matthew said, refusing to budge. "Who here thinks that is a good idea?"

"I know you're right," Philip said, a blush creeping up from the collar of his shirt. "I've already considered the consequences. But I tell you now, I will not abandon my friend. I will go after him, even if it means going alone. Nothing you or anyone else can say will change that."

Thomas cleared his throat. "Bartholomew is my brother, and he is my friend. I would move the earth to help him. But the point Matthew makes is compelling. We have a duty, one we chose to uphold no matter what. To abandon it now is unacceptable, perhaps even unforgivable. It comes down to the life of one man versus the lives of millions." His voice sharpened. "I think Bartholomew would say the same, if he were able: 'Leave me behind and help the Innocents.' He was the Protector. His first instinct would be to protect. It is too risky to go after him." His mouth turned down at the corners. "Make no mistake. What I've said will haunt me for the rest of my life."

"As it should," James said, his brow knitted into a disapproving frown. "You talk of missions and Innocents. Weren't we once one of them? Have we sacrificed so much that we are no longer human?" He jabbed a finger at Matthew. "Were it an Innocent banished to Topheth and we had a chance to save him, would you make the same choice, in light of our mission? Well, I say Bartholomew is now an Innocent. He is a man again, and his soul is lost. I say our mission demands we make the attempt. To do less is to become what we have fought against for so long. To do less is to become another Marbæs."

Gene could tell that the Healer's words had had an effect on Matthew. The Forever Man's face had paled, and his aged skin now appeared taut, as if it had been pulled tight against his skull. But his eyes remained defiant, and Gene thought James had not made enough headway with Matthew.

Gene performed a quick tally. The score was even: Philip and James advocating a rescue attempt, Thomas and Matthew arguing against.

All eyes turned to John, the only Forever Man yet to speak on the matter.

John, the Historian, the man responsible for remembering everything that had happened to the Forever Men (and for the entire world, as far as Gene could tell) didn't immediately speak. He gazed at his pen, an unusually somber expression on his face, and Gene suddenly realized the pen meant more to John than its use as a simple writing implement: it was a symbol, both of his faith and his role. It marked who he was as indelibly as the quill-shaped tattoo on his forearm. He seemed to carry it with him at all times.

As much as the man griped about what had been done to him, about what he had been asked to sacrifice, John remained as committed as the others at what they had set out to accomplish.

An uneasy lump formed in Gene's throat. Owens's life likely depended on a man more committed to a purpose than a person.

John finally raised his head. "I'm sorry," John whispered. His attention was fixed on Philip, but Gene got the impression the man was talking more to himself than to the other Forever Men. "After all these years, all that we've given up..." He brushed back his hair, and his voice firmed. "We can't risk failing now, even if it means saving Bartholomew. Were we to die, it would render everything we did, all our successes, for naught. The Innocents would be left defenseless. And as much as I hate to say this, we very well may still have more time in front of us than behind. We can't abandon them to Marbæs's will. James is right, but for the wrong reason. We cannot become that which we have fought for so long. The Innocents *must* come first." He moved to stand in front of the window. He looked out at the world, the one they were tasked to protect. "The Innocents must come first." Then, in a hushed tone, he added, "May God have mercy on my soul."

Gene swallowed hard at the lump in his throat. He couldn't believe it. They had chosen to let Owens die.

"It's decided then," Matthew said. "We will stay and do what we can to protect the Innocents."

"No, it has *not* been decided," Katie said, her face a mask of fury. She jabbed a finger at Matthew. "I've worked side-by-side with Bartholomew, and with Philip, for too long to be ignored. I've risked my life to help your cause. That makes me one of you, no matter what you say. Which means I get a vote. And I vote we make the attempt to save Bartholomew."

"We have a tie," Philip said. Apparently he wasn't going to allow any debate about Katie's status among them. Gene secretly cheered him on.

Izzy chose that moment to step into the center of the room. "If Katie has a vote in this," she said, "then so do I. As Bartholomew's friend, as the person who has been taking care of his body, as someone who loves him as much as the rest of you, I vote we make the attempt. I vote we save Bartholomew."

Lips pressed into a thin line, she turned and fixed her gaze on Gene. He could see the familiar determination burning behind her eyes, the iron will of the woman he had grown to love.

The old Izzy was back.

He gave her an elated smile. His elation didn't last long, though. Philip broke it when he shot Gene an inquiring look.

"Yo, new guy," Philip said. "How do you feel about going to Hell?"

CHAPTER EIGHT

The sleek sedan pulled into the parking spot, the door opened, and Judas Iscariot stepped out. The day was clear and bright. Smiling, he fed several coins into the meter.

People hurried past him in either direction, either chasing their shadows or fleeing from them. Even though he stood in the middle of the sidewalk, blocking the path of just about everyone, they all gave him a wide berth. And if they'd bothered to pay attention, they would have felt a bitter chill as they passed the man in the three-piece suit, a chill incongruent with the weather, one that clutched at their bones and reminded them of the deepest night of the darkest winter. One that hinted at betrayal, and murder, and suicide.

The building he sought was a brisk five-minute walk. He took his time. The weather really was splendid.

When he reached his destination—the sign proudly displayed the name MABEL STEARS AND ASSOCIATES, PLLC in the window—he pulled open the door and entered.

A pretty young secretary sat behind a desk covered with neat stacks of papers. Judas noted a small leather folio on a corner of her desk containing the business cards she kept as contacts for her job.

At the sound of the door, she turned from her computer screen and smiled. "Can I help—"

Her smiled faltered. Judas knew the woman, and knew that she didn't like him, but he didn't care in the least. "Elise," he said. "It's a pleasure to see you again."

"Mr. Whitlock," she returned. "I—I wasn't expecting you."

"I didn't have time to make an appointment," he said. "If you would be so kind as to announce me?"

"Do we have to go over this again, Mr. Whitlock? No one sees—"

"Never mind." He brushed past her and entered a short hallway with doors on either side and one at the end. "I'll just pop in."

She hurried after him. "Wait! You can't just—"

"Oh, yes I can."

"I'll get fired!"

"Wouldn't that be a pity." He turned to face her. "With you being almost two months behind on your rent. What would happen then? You'll soon lose your apartment, I'd imagine. And then where will you go? Move back in with poor mommy and daddy, septuagenarians who barely get by on their social security checks? Would you really put them through that? Are you that selfish?"

Elise Summers paled. "How can you possibly—"

"Then there's the baby," Judas continued, firing harsh realities at her the way a sniper fires rounds at unsuspecting targets. "Your indiscriminate little love child. The snow will be flying by the time she arrives, mewling and shitting through her diapers and generally being a pain in the ass. How will you afford formula, clothes, the aforementioned diapers? You think baby-daddy will provide for her? He fled the coop, as we say, didn't he? Left town, made like a banana and split. He's gone, Elise. And he's never coming back. You're on your own, sweetie."

Elise's hand shot to her mouth. "That's not possible. No one knows about the baby."

"Without this job, you'll never make it. You'll be without a place to stay, forced to live on welfare and food stamps and whatever money your parents send you, if they send you anything." He

smiled coldly. "Maybe you'll be forced to blow a guy or ten just to get by. Maybe you'd even let your precious little girl watch, teach her the harsh realities about surviving in this cruel world."

The color returned to her cheeks, high and hard and glowing like coals. "You bastard," she whispered. "You fucking bastard!"

"Exactly," he replied, and approached her desk. He took his hand and swiped the papers onto the ground. "Pack up your shit. If you're still here when I'm done, you'll have more to worry about than your impending unemployment."

Weeping, Elise Summers bent to pick up the papers. While she was distracted, Judas slipped a business card from his pocket and placed it along with the other cards she kept in her contact folio. It contained the number of an employment agency, one in which he retained a controlling interest. He would make a brief phone call, let them know poor Elise Summers would likely be calling, and to find her a better paying job.

"Take only what's yours," he added with brutal finality. "And good luck with your miserable, sad sack of a life."

He turned his back on the woman.

Help and hinder.

It was his curse, and his blessing.

He approached the door at the end of the hallway.

***

Judas Iscariot collapsed into the overstuffed chair, bruised, blood flowing freely from a wide cut at the corner of his mouth. His jaw ached as if it were on fire. His breath came in rapid, shallow gasps; it hurt far too much to draw more air than that. Perhaps he had a broken rib. He hadn't thought that possible before today.

He swallowed back the pain.

He had endured worse.

A few feet away, Marbæs glared at him with eyes as yellow as disease. Gone were her dusky, slightly Asian features. Her delicate skin had thickened until it resembled the hide of a prehistoric beast. Her face had elongated, her cheekbones now swept out in severe ridges, giving her a reptilian look. Her fingers ended in long, sharp talons.

"You were supposed to prevent them from retrieving the cube," she said. He knew her anger; he could feel it in every ache and throb of his pummeled body. "*Prevent them*. And now they have it. They have the means by which they can save Bartholomew." She made a visible effort to restrain herself, for which Judas was extremely grateful. "I should kill you for this failure."

Judas removed a handkerchief from his jacket pocket and dabbed at his mouth. He knew going in that this meeting would be difficult. Marbæs demanded perfection. She met any mistake, any deviation from her exact instructions, with severe punishment. And he had, from her perspective, failed.

A fact which should not have surprised her; she understood his nature.

He forced his eyes to meet hers, and when they did, he thought he caught of glimpse of something else, something elusive, like a hint of something vast lurking beneath a perilous sea.

Was it fear he'd seen?

Could it be Marbæs was actually afraid? It was certainly something to keep in mind.

"You didn't make me do this," he said, straightening his tie. Blood had ruined his handkerchief. He had nowhere to put it, so he stuffed it back into his pocket. "I am not subject to your demands, like your other pets. I follow my own path." He paused. "No matter what I do, no matter who my efforts help, there needs to be a chance of failure for each side. It's central to my nature. I set the trap in the mine, but I also set another, and another, and still another. I worked this particular problem from two directions. Just because one effort failed doesn't mean the others will. You need to be patient. You have gotten far, farther than I suspect even you thought possible." And much farther than I am comfortable with, he added silently. "Let's see how this plays out before you start threatening death."

She kept her baleful gaze on him for moments longer. Then her shoulders bunched, and Judas thought with a mixture of glee and trepidation: This is it, I'm finally going to die. But instead of resuming her attack, Marbæs turned away. Breathing a little easier, he watched as her talons retracted, becoming docile, fleshy fingertips. The bones of her skull shifted beneath her skin, which had

BRIAN W. MATTHEWS

already started thinning. Moments later, when she turned back to face him, she once again wore her human mask.

There was a large desk in the room, the surface speckled with drops of Judas's blood. Marbæs took a seat behind it.

I'm out of danger, Judas thought, at least for the moment. He didn't know if she could kill him. No one knew who made him, not even he did. This gave him reason to think it might be impossible to kill him. Still, he didn't want to risk being proved wrong on that theory.

Marbæs hit the intercom button on her phone. When her secretary didn't answer, she gave him a quizzical look.

"I'm afraid poor Elise quit," he said. "Something about moving on to a better position."

"I suppose you had a hand in that decision?"

Judas waved off her question. "Your original plan worked. The Veil is weakened. Even if Bartholomew's soul is retrieved, what could he possibly do? Nothing can repair the damage that has been done." Judas kept his expression carefully neutral. If she caught even a whiff of what he and Bartholomew had arranged...

"It's not simply the Veil," she said. "I want Bartholomew to suffer."

"He is suffering."

"Has time ended?"

Judas frowned. "Of course not."

"Then he hasn't suffered long enough." Marbæs looked at her phone. "I was going to have Elise bring us coffee."

"I can do without if you can."

Apparently, she could. Settling back in her chair, she said, "You spoke of traps. Explain yourself."

"Rest assured, I have your best interests in mind."

"As well as the Forever Men's?"

He shrugged. There was no sense denying it. "Both you and they can either succeed or fail. I guarantee nothing."

"You helped me accomplish the Veil's weakening. What did you do for them?"

"I prefer to keep my own secrets, thank you."

"The Veil will stay weakened?"

That got his attention. "You know of a way to repair it?"

Marbæs didn't immediately reply. Eyes fixed on his, she tapped a fingernail on her desk. Each lacquered strike made a sharp, unsettling sound, like small bones snapping.

Judas's heartbeat quickened, and his skin grew clammy. This is it. This is where everything could fall apart. He'd spoken of the potential for failure; he and Marbæs had just reached one of those necessary points.

"Repaired?" she finally said. "No, not by any means I am aware."

He forced a smile. It felt like it would crack his face. "Then accept your victory. The damned are returning to this world. Forget about Bartholomew and the others. From this point on, you can't lose."

Her finger stopped tapping, and she matched him, smile for smile. "Judas?" she asked politely.

Now his heart hammered in his chest. She rarely called him by his given name. "Yes?"

"Why are you sweating?"

"It's warm in here," he said, surprised the words had come out as smoothly as they did. "And I'm wearing this suit. Besides, physical violence does that to me; it makes me perspire. Your fault, really."

She leaned forward in her chair. "You're hiding something, aren't you?"

He swallowed back his panic. If he lost it now, she would surely try to kill him.

"As I told you," he said, "I have many secrets. Yes, some are hidden from you. Some do not even relate to you. To secure my continued assistance, it is a condition you will have to accept. If, however, it is too much to ask..."

If events were not so critical, he would just as soon be rid of her. But he could not afford that luxury; theirs were intertwined fates, like the raw hemp that is woven together to craft a hangman's noose.

Her eyes did not leave his, and Judas suddenly wished for that coffee. It would give him something to focus on other than her unloving stare.

Finally she released him, shifted her eyes away from his wounded face, and crossed her arms over her chest. "You once told me you don't like me," she said. "I cannot help but wonder if that dislike clouds your nature. I wonder if you are not inclined to help one side more than the other. And if that were proved true...well, there are few places on this world where you could hide from me."

"And I cannot help but wonder why you are so focused on threatening me. It seems, I don't know, almost desperate. Are *you* hiding something from *me*?"

He was taking a terrible chance by confronting her; her wrath was a dagger at the heart of everyone she knew. But her questions had become too intuitive; she was coming perilously close to the truth, and the only way he knew to deflect her involved challenging her ego.

Her hands clenched, gripping her elbows. "Others have overstepped themselves," she said. "None have lived."

"Then I will be the first," he said cheerfully and rose from the chair. It was time to end this casualty of a meeting. If he stayed any longer, he might lose his nerve and start screaming. "I have done as you requested. The Forever Men cannot succeed. Thanks to me, Thomas's ridiculous cube will fail them, and they will return to this world in despair, if they return at all."

"You had better be right," Marbæs said. A dark malevolence smoldered in her eyes.

"Always a dear." Blowing her a kiss, Judas spun on his heels and left, hoping beyond hope she didn't kill him before he made it through the door.

***

Natalie lifted her cream soda and clinked glasses with her date.

Sean Leyton smiled at her from across the booth, his longish black hair uncharacteristically brushed back from his eyes. She liked his eyes; they possessed a slightly dangerous smolder, accentuated by the black eyeliner and that wry twist of a grin which gave him the "I don't give a fuck, I'll do what I want" attitude she found so attractive.

"How'd you escape?" he said after sipping at his cola. "When I called, I got the impression you were housebound."

"It's not that bad. I'm not a prisoner." She arranged and rearranged her knife and fork around her plate as if they were satellites. Her burger and fries, which she had been so eager to consume, sat untouched. "I can come and go as I please. It's just, with her company and all, my mom likes to have me around to help."

Sean snatched one of her fries and nibbled at it. He'd finished his mac and cheese so fast she wondered if he had even chewed. "Sounds like slave labor to me. Thirteenth Amendment shit. Maybe she needs to reread the Constitution."

She smiled at him, impressed. "Somebody paid attention in government class."

The smolder she had so admired in his eyes became a quiet seething. "I'm not stupid, you know."

"I'm sorry," she said. "I wasn't trying to insult you."

Eager to fill the gap of her embarrassment, she took a bite of her hamburger. It had grown cold, but she ate it anyway.

Sean pulled out his phone and stared at the screen. She choked down another mouthful of cold, ground flesh.

At last Sean put down his phone. "I'm sorry," he said. "The kids in school used to make fun of me. They thought I was retarded or something because of the way I looked." He fingered the silver stud in his lower lip. "I should learn to let it go. No sense other people paying the price for what a handful of ignorant snots did years ago."

"Did you go to college? You sound like you did." Indeed, his vocabulary seemed a lot more sophisticated.

He looked uncomfortable. "For a couple semesters. The education system and I didn't see eye-to-eye on a few things."

"But you did well?"

"A little better than average. Nothing great, but I didn't flunk out, if that's what you think."

He'd just handed her a second rebuke in as many minutes. She set down her burger. "Is there something wrong? I feel like I'm standing in front of a firing squad and waiting for the next bullet to hit."

She could see darkness swimming behind his eyes, and the corners of his mouth pulled down enough that his smile disappeared. His change in mood was so abrupt she wondered if she had done something terribly wrong.

She needed to steady her nerves, to keep from falling to pieces and making matters worse. Pulling air into her lungs, she held her breath for a heartbeat or two, and slowly let it out. Better. She felt better. More centered.

Still, when she picked up a french fry and brought it to her mouth, her hand trembled.

Sean must have sensed her discomfort. The danger that had clouded his expression cleared like thunderheads blown away after a summer storm. His twist of a smile returned.

"It's not you," he said. "I've had lots of stupid stuff on my mind recently. Stupid job, stupid parents. Stupid expectations people put on me without even asking if I want them." He grabbed another fry. "I don't know why life forces us to conform or be cast out. What if conforming results in a pointless existence? You fade into the background of everyday bullshit and eventually disappear, left wearing Dockers and drinking Starbucks and wondering where all the excitement went? It's not the life for me. I want more. There has to be some fun out there, something new and edgy that makes your heart beat. Because what's the alternative?" He jabbed the fry at her. "Death by stagnation."

He had recaptured her attention. His words, spoken with such passion, poured into the void of her own stagnant existence. But she also knew he was wrong: Life on its own could be pleasant, fulfilling. The alternative, as he envisioned it, could be deadly. Monsters roamed the world. She had encountered them.

She pushed her plate away. "If I hear you right, the world is supposed to challenge you, not the other way around. I'm not sure I buy that reasoning. It's too convenient. It lets you shift blame onto others if your life doesn't work out. You don't have to take responsibility for anything. How are you supposed to grow that way?"

He seemed to consider her words. "Maybe I'm not being clear enough. I don't expect the world to come to me, to entertain me. It's my responsibility to make the life I want. It's just...I'm not cut out to be stuck behind a desk, staring at a computer screen until my eyes bleed, just because someone says I should. There has to be something different out there, places where I'll feel challenged. What I disagree with is conforming to society's expectations. I prefer to set my own." His brows drew together into a frown. "Does that make sense?"

She thought it did, and told him so. She also knew where he might find that challenge, if she could muster enough courage to tell him. *Monsters and madmen roamed the world.* She didn't think she could tell him, or even that she should, but the compulsion to share was strong. To not live alone with her secret...

"Natalie?"

"What?"

"You got real quiet. Is something wrong?"

"You asked if you were making sense. Well, I get it. Create the life you want and to hell with what other people think. But what are you doing to reach that goal? Have you considered what you're going to do next?"

Sean suddenly looked uncomfortable. "Well, this may sound dumb, but I'd like to be a musician. I play guitar, just not that well. I also know the competition is almost impossible to overcome. So many people releasing music on their own. It's hard to stand out, get noticed."

"I think that's great! Do you have a band yet?"

"Only a couple friends who also play. But what I really need is a new axe—guitar, I mean. The one I have is terrible. It sounds thin. If I had something better, something with more punch, I bet I'd get farther. And I really need to get farther. I'm living for this dream. I've put so much into it, so many hours of practice." His shoulders slumped. "If I fail, I'm back looking at desk jobs, or working food service for the rest of my life. It'd strangle me. I'd die on the vine."

Natalie's heart went out for him. She understood his pain. Her life was going nowhere. She didn't even have any good prospects. All because of her mother and the bubble she had forced them into.

"Isn't a good guitar expensive?" she asked.

His discomfort seemed to deepen. "Yeah, but I've got a line on one. Shouldn't cost me an arm and a leg."

She smiled. "Then you're partway there. Good for you."

Sean shook himself, as if he wanted to shrug off this conversation. "When do I get to meet your mom? And what about your dad? You never talk about him."

Her mom and dad. A cold discomfort crept up on her like the shadow of a mugger. How could she possibly explain them to a man lacking experience with the supernatural? "My parents are separated," she finally said. At least it was sort of the truth. "For a few years now. I haven't seen my dad in a while. I'd like to but it's... complicated."

"Not an uncommon story," he said. "And your mom?"

Thoughts of her dad filled her so much that she'd lost the thread of the conversation. "What about her?"

He smiled. "You know, when do I get to meet her?"

Her mom. The former police chief and current lieutenant in a supernatural war. If she thought explaining her dad was tricky, having Sean meet Izzy Morris would be like throwing him head-first into a cement mixer.

"That's not a good idea," she said.

"Why? You think she won't like me?"

"It's not that. She has company." Oh boy, does she. "I don't think she'd appreciate the intrusion."

He shrugged. "You said she needed your help. What if I offered my services? Think that would do it? I can be charming when I want to."

Natalie twisted her fingers together. This was getting worse, not better. "She's sort of strict. Careful about who she lets in the house. I think we should wait—"

"For what? Permission? Is that how you live your life, conforming to rules and expectations set by someone else? I thought you were better than that, stronger than that."

I am, she thought, but didn't say. Her mother wasn't a subject for idle conversation. Then again, she didn't want to offend Sean. She liked his eyes, after all.

"You don't understand," she said. "She's...formidable."

"Formidable in what way?"

Natalie couldn't tell him the truth; Izzy Morris still possessed a cop's instincts. Her mother insisted they never talk about their past. It was too dangerous. But maybe this time she had an out.

"She's from a cop family," she said. Not entirely a lie, but not entirely the truth. "Growing up, she had to stick up for herself surrounded by my macho uncles. She doesn't take shit from anyone."

"It's my looks," he said. "She doesn't like guys with piercings. She'll think I'm some kind of gang-banger or low-life druggie." He began removing his studs and rings, dropping them onto the table like loose teeth. "I'll take them off. How about that?"

"Sean, no!"

He finished removing his piercings, at least the ones she could see. "There, now I'm presentable," he said, his tone bitter and chaffing. "I'm *conforming*."

He didn't understand. This wasn't what she'd meant. He was taking it too far. "It's not your appearance. Believe me, it's not."

"Then what is it?"

I can't tell you, she wanted to say, because if I did, your life might be in danger.

But no, she couldn't say that either. Her answer begged even bigger, more lethal questions. She tried to gather her thoughts, but her feelings crowded her thinking. She couldn't come up with a single intelligent thing to say.

She'd waited too long. Scooping up his hardware, he stuffed them into his pocket. Then he signaled the waitress. "I can't be with someone who is ashamed of me," he said. "Go if you want. I'll cover the check."

Fear choked her. She was going to lose him. "No, don't go! I apologize. It really isn't about how you look. I'm sorry I gave you that impression." The waitress set the check on the table and walked away. "Please," Natalie said. "Don't give up on me."

He threw a few bills on the table and stood. "Some things can't be fixed. Have a good life, Nat."

She panicked. He was going to walk away. She'd never see him again.

The words came out of her mouth before she could stop them.

"Okay, you can come over! But just for a few minutes. And if my mom tells you to leave, you do it. Refusing her is not a way to win her approval."

Sean halted, his face an inscrutable mask. She couldn't tell if he was relieved or excited.

But then he smiled and offered his hand.

CHAPTER NINE

Everyone gathered around Bartholomew's bed.

We look like a bunch of mourners saying goodbye to a loved one, Izzy thought.

The basement felt too warm despite the chill in the air outside. April headed out like a lamb, with a temperate climate and the barest hint of the summer heat that would rapidly approach.

She blotted her forehead with her sleeve. Maybe the severity of their visit had kindled an emotional furnace in her. Either that, or the stark fear of what they would soon attempt burned through her good senses.

Topheth. They had to travel to Hell to save Bartholomew.

She could see the Forever Men surviving the attempt, but how could ordinary humans hope to return alive? They didn't possess the considerable resources Philip and the others possessed: the rapid healing, the preternatural strength. An evil place like Topheth could strip Izzy, Gene, or Katie of both life and soul.

Bartholomew's face remained expressionless. His eyes didn't move beneath their lids. At least he wasn't dreaming. What would a soul trapped in Hell dream about? Her mind shied away from the possibilities.

A sliver of memory came to her, rising from her subconscious like vomit from a sour stomach, a snatch of bitter conversation between her and Stanley, one of their perpetual arguments about her role in their lives:

Which person will I see today, Izzy? Wife, mother, or cop?

And now she was facing yet another role: supernatural rescuer.

It was too much. For the first time in years, she felt pulled in too many directions. How was she expected to accomplish all this? Who had thrust her into this crazy juxtaposition of demands?

Another snatch of memory, this time more recent:

I'm seeing your substance for the first time, Gene had told her not two hours ago, *and it shocks the hell out of me.*

Maybe she needed to stop trying to conform to the roles others see her taking and focus on her, on what she felt was right.

Either way, that was a thought for later. She had other priorities at hand, ones that demanded her complete attention.

Her gaze wandered from Bartholomew to Philip. Despite his fierce determination—his forehead was a clenched fist, daring anyone to challenge his authority—Philip spoke with the equanimity of a seasoned general before he led his troops into a hopeless battle.

"We know what must be done," he said. "The only thing to decide now is who will make the attempt and who will remain behind."

"Remain behind?" Gene blurted out. "I thought we were all going?"

John, his voice liquid with sarcasm, said, "If we all travel to Topheth, who will watch—no, who will *guard*—Bartholomew's body? It would be a damn fine joke if we returned with his soul only to find his body gone or destroyed. We are hard to kill, Mr. Vincent, but not impossible to kill."

James nodded his agreement. "Someone will need to feed him, too. We don't know how long this will take. He could die from hunger or thirst."

"And we can't forget about Kevin and Natalie," Izzy said. "While Nat can take care of herself, someone will have to watch over Kevin. He's too important to risk being left alone."

A flush of embarrassment crept up Gene's neck to color his cheeks. "Okay. I get your point. I'll keep quiet."

"It's not that," she told him. "We need everyone's input. Keep speaking up." She shot John an irritated grimace. "Some of us like to rub their superiority in the noses of others."

The Historian returned her look with a wide, insolent grin.

"Okay, people," Thomas said. "Enough of that nonsense. We have a decision to make. Who stays behind?"

"I'm not staying behind," Katie said. "Don't even suggest it."

"I wouldn't dream of it." Matthew rubbed the spot on his cheek where she had slapped him. "The strength of your convictions is painfully obvious."

"I wouldn't either," Izzy said. "I know how close you and Owens are."

"But I *am* that bold," Philip said. "I'm against anyone going but me."

Katie's mouth dropped open in surprise. James adopted an expression of muted surprise. Everyone else frowned. Except Matthew, that is; he remained nonplussed, as if he had expected Philip's declaration.

Then everyone began to talk at once.

"Let me explain," Philip said into the growing uproar but was quickly drowned out.

Izzy raised her hands. "Like I told Gene, we all have opinions," she said in a voice loud enough to be heard. "Let's hear them before we start reacting. No one will benefit if we fling accusations around. Agreed?"

Katie nodded. "I'm willing to listen, but I don't care what they have to stay. I will not be left behind."

"I alone can find Bartholomew." Philip stood ramrod straight, as if all his energies were focused on what he was about to say and he had little left over for nuances like stance or expression. "I'm also his oldest friend. Those two facts mean I'm going. I also feel that one person can succeed where many might fail. None of us has been to Topheth. We don't know what to expect. It might be easier for a single person to move about without being seen than several. Third, I can't see your skills helping where I am going—"

"Where *we* are going," Katie cut in.

"Katie," Izzy said softly. "Please."

Katie's lips pressed into a thin, reproachful line across her face and turned away.

"Your skills," Philip said, trying hard to ignore Katie's rejection but failing, "your *individual* skills, would not likely prove useful to me. While military strategy isn't my expertise, I know that you take with you only those individuals who can materially contribute to your success. Since none of you increases the odds of success, I think you should stay here." He looked at Matthew. "You were the one talking about our mission, and how we can't abandon it when the Innocents need us the most. If I alone go, that leaves the rest of you to help protect them."

"I can find a few flaws in your argument," James said. The Healer ticked up three fingers and counted them off. "One, you might get hurt, and I could heal you more rapidly. That improves your chances of success. Two, you may die. In that case, we would need someone else to take up the cause or all of this discussion and work will be for naught. That improves our odds of success." He ticked down his third finger. "Finally, you're not Peter. You don't get to make all the decisions. No one would argue your right to go, but that doesn't mean you get to decide for the rest of us. We should all have a say."

"We did," Matthew said quietly. His expression grew troubled, as if he'd thought of something unpleasant. "Earlier."

"This is such bullshit," Katie said. Her eyes glittered like hot gems. "I owe Bartholomew my life, and I won't be left behind when he needs me the most. End of story."

Thomas cleared his throat. "I, for one, will not go, and for two very good reasons."

"And they are?" John asked.

"A device of my creation will deliver you to Topheth," Thomas said. "I will be the only one who possesses the skill to operate it. If I go and end up killed, there will be no one who can bring you back. You do not want to risk being stuck in Topheth forever."

John nodded appreciatively. Philip looked like a man wanting to argue the fate of stars. Matthew's eyes filled with a strange sort of sorrow, but he didn't offer up a response.

"And your second?" James asked.

"The Veil," Thomas replied. "It needs to be repaired, and I hope to find a way to accomplish that."

Izzy felt a thrill run through her. "You think it can be fixed?"

"Possibly," Thomas said with a shrug. "We have to at least try. And if Philip succeeds in bringing Bartholomew back, I want to have a plan in place. The longer we wait, the worse it will get for the Innocents."

"It's not like a hole in the wall," Matthew said. His sorrow seemed to have deepened with Thomas's proclamation. "You cannot fix something that lacks physical form."

"A hole doesn't have a physical form," Thomas said. "The wall does. Maybe there's something I can devise that will shore up the area around the weakness."

"But the weakness is throughout the Veil," Matthew said with some urgency. "Not in one spot or another. How do you propose to strengthen something that exists everywhere?"

He's right, Izzy thought with fading hope. Matthew is right. It can't be done.

"I have to try," Thomas said. Hints of steel and diamond had replaced his creaky, old man's voice. "To do less is to admit failure before we start."

"Thomas stays then," Philip said, ending that particular argument. "And I doubt Katie will agree to stay, so she'll accompany me. What about the rest?"

"If Katie goes," James said, "I should go along. While you might not need a Healer, she certainly may."

"That won't work," Izzy said. She was tired of sitting on the sidelines. These men were powerful and old, but she still had her own destiny to follow. "You need to stay back and care for Bartholomew."

"You've been doing that for weeks now," James said. "You can still take care of him."

Izzy drew in a steadying breath. "Not if I'm with Philip and Katie."

Philip rounded on her, and Katie actually smiled.

Izzy raised her hand. "In police work, no one goes into a shoot-out without—"

"Backup," Gene said. "You intend to be his backup."

"Yes," she said, nodding. "Katie and I will be Philip's backup."

John raised his hand like a schoolboy. "Aren't you forgetting somebody?"

Izzy smiled crookedly at him. "Are you telling me you're willing to leave your brother behind just so you can write the story about a visit to Hell? I mean, didn't Dante already do that?"

John lowered his hand. There was an unexpected seriousness in his demeanor. "Don't mistake my love for my brother with dereliction of duty, young lady. I deserve better than that from you."

Upstairs, a door slammed shut, and Izzy heard footsteps.

Natalie was home.

"I'm sorry," Izzy said. "You do deserve better. But why would you go? What help could you be?"

"Because," John replied, "at least one of us should accompany Philip. If he dies, one of us will have to take up the standard and sally forth. I may only be a writer, but I am a very tough writer. Besides, I don't know if Thomas can bring back two Innocents without one of us to focus on."

"Three of us," Gene said. "I'm going too."

"And the brothers will not need to part," Matthew said, his voice so full of dread Izzy thought it would break into pieces.

John frowned at him. "Why not?"

Izzy watched Matthew look down at his hands. They were clenched so tightly the knuckles shone white.

A sudden dread rose up in her. A memory, something she was supposed to remember. Her mind chased after it, but the effort made her head hurt. It was like trying to find a hole in the wind: it kept eluding her.

Matthew lifted his head. "Because," he said, "I will accompany Philip."

***

Natalie led Sean into the kitchen.

"You want a glass of water, a soda maybe?" she asked him. "Or I can make coffee if you'd rather have that."

"I'm good," he said. His eyes darted around the room, flitting like a fox on a hunt. "Where's your mom?"

"Probably downstairs. Spending time with her company, no doubt."

"And you don't think she'll mind me being here?"

Good question, Natalie thought. And I'll probably know the answer soon enough.

"All she can do is ask you to leave." Her lips curled into a playful grin. "I mean, she hasn't shot anyone recently, so I'd say the odds are pretty low you'll be hurt."

The blood ran from Sean's skin, making his pale face look like unleavened dough. "Shoot me?"

She punched him lightly in the arm. "I'm just kidding with you. She's from a cop family, which means she owns a gun, but I don't think she's picked it up in at least a year."

"Gun?" Sean took a panicked step back. "You didn't tell me she had a gun!"

Natalie's smile faded. "Chill, Sean. My mom's not going to do anything." She went to the fridge and pulled out a cola. "Here," she said, holding the can out to him. "Drink this. I'll be right back."

Sean took the soda. "Where're you going?"

She headed for a door in the hallway. "If I tell my mom you're here, she's less likely to be surprised." She opened the door. Stairs led down to the basement. "Mom, you down there?"

"Yes," her mom called up. "I won't be much longer."

"No worries," Natalie said. "I—uh…I brought a friend over."

There was a moment of silence, then her mom said, "I don't remember you asking me."

She turned to Sean and winked. "We won't be here long. I just wanted to show him around."

"Make it quick." Her mom's tone conveyed a sense of frayed intolerance. "I'll be up soon. We need to talk."

Natalie shut the door. "I'll give you the nickel tour," she told Sean. "Then you'd better leave. She may not go for her gun, but her attitude can cut you deeply."

Sean set down the soda. He still looked pale as snow. "Can I use your bathroom first?"

"Sure, down the hall and to the right. Second door." Natalie walked him down the short hallway. "You don't have to be afraid. I won't let anything hurt you."

Sean halted. "Any*thing*?" he said. "Don't you mean any*one*?"

Natalie wanted to bite her tongue. "Yeah. Sure. Anyone."

He stared at her for a moment longer and then disappeared around the corner.

Natalie helped herself to Sean's cola. "Smooth," she muttered. "Real smooth."

She heard her mother's footsteps coming up the basement stairs and she put her gaffe out of her mind.

She had other issues to deal with.

**

His heart hammering, Sean flushed the toilet and washed his hands.

Gun. Natalie never said anything about a gun.

Neither did that creeper, Whitlock.

His little job suddenly became more dangerous.

Out of his jacket pocket he removed the dreamcatcher. Despite its apparent fragility, it hadn't bent or warped as he'd carried it around. He checked the bathroom for a place to hide it. The bathtub wouldn't do; too open. Nor would the toilet fill tank work. He didn't know if the dreamcatcher was waterproof. The vanity had three drawers on either side. He opened them at random. Each was filled with junk: hairdryer, deodorant, bottles of makeup, tampons, brushes, medication (a quick look showed nothing of interest), extra tubes of toothpaste. He might be able to lay the dreamcatcher flat over the detritus, but all of it looked like it could be used every day. The odds that someone would notice it seemed pretty high.

He was taking too long. Natalie would come looking for him, and he would lose his chance.

He listened at the door, heard nothing, and eased it open.

No one in the hallway. He could hear Natalie talking to someone, a woman. Her mother had come up from the basement.

Shit. He had to hurry.

From what he'd seen already, his best bet was the living room. Whitlock had wanted it there anyway. Fortunately, being the closest to the bathroom meant he wouldn't have to move far. Unfortunately, he would have to sneak down the same hallway that led to the kitchen. Natalie or her mom might catch him.

No matter. He had to risk it. Planting the dreamcatcher remained the quickest way to get his hands on that sweet guitar. Besides, the old creeper promised no one would get hurt.

You know it's not simply a dreamcatcher, his rational mind whispered. Remember how it affected you, how you almost lost yourself in its shifting glitters? If it can do that, what else can it do?

The guitar, he argued with that hated rational voice. Think of how I'll play with that baby in my hands. And what danger does a dreamcatcher really possess? The reward outweighs the risk.

Sean pushed his thoughts aside. He didn't have time for this bullshit.

Without realizing he had made his choice, he stepped into the hallway. Natalie's conversation with her mom became clearer.

Natalie: "I just wanted to show him where I live. Where's the harm in that?"

Mom: "You know the risks. What if he sees something he shouldn't, or overhears part of a conversation between Philip and the others? How are you going to explain that?"

Natalie: "You really think he could put things together with so little context? Come on, Mom."

Mom: "And what about the danger you've put him in? Have you considered that?"

Mrs. Marzecki's words caught Sean's attention like a hand on his throat. If he was in danger, he needed to finish what he came here to do and get the hell out.

He peeked around the corner. Natalie had her back to him. He couldn't see her mother.

Offering a prayer of thanks, he slipped around the corner, padded into the living room, and moved out of view of the hallway.

A large space, the living room contained a sofa, two chairs, and a low table. No pictures on the walls. None on the end tables. That's when he realized he hadn't seen any photographs in the house.

Pretty freaking weird.

Licking his lips, aware that he had at most a handful of seconds before he would be missed and Natalie would come looking for him, he searched for a place to hide the dreamcatcher.

Under the sofa? Behind one of the chairs? What if they vacuumed and found it?

No, it needed to be hidden well, in a place where no one would normally look.

His eyes bounced around the room, searching.

Then he heard Natalie say, "I wonder what's keeping Sean?"

Christ, do something! Who the fuck cares if they find it, as long as they don't find you planting it!

He picked one of the chairs, lifted its cushion, and shoved the dreamcatcher underneath.

He had just dropped the cushion back in place when he heard a voice like brittle iron say, "What are you doing?"

Sean whirled. A woman—obviously, Natalie's mom—stood at the entrance of the living room, fists planted on her hips. She had auburn hair, freckles around her nose and cheeks, and a mouth that was currently bent into a frown.

"Uh...hi. I'm Sean." He crossed the room, his hand extended. "Pleased to meet you."

The woman ignored his hand. "I asked you a question. What were you just doing?"

Sean fought the urge to bolt out the front door. This woman owned a gun, and he had no desire to get shot. But running would only make things worse; impossibly worse. Mrs. Marzecki might search the room and find the dreamcatcher. Forcing his jumbled emotions into some kind of order, he let a smile warm his face.

He pointed to the walls. "Why don't you have any pictures? I haven't seen one since I got here."

Mrs. Marzecki's gaze peeled him from top to toe as she took in his unruly hair, thick eye liner, battered clothing, black boots. Her disdain for him was obvious, and to Sean, who had received that same look time and again, it was familiar. That familiarity lent him a measure of courage he would not normally have possessed.

"I'm sorry," he added with a hint of asperity. "It's not like I'm an intruder. Natalie invited me."

"Intrude contains the word rude," she said. "As in, it's rude to wander someone's house without letting them know you're here. And to me, the two words amount to the same thing. Now, I'll ask you one last time: What were you just doing?"

Sean let his resentment rise to the surface. Better he looked offended than guilty. "Just because I look like this doesn't mean I'm a liar, or a crook." A thought occurred to him; an excuse. "I heard you and Nat talking in the kitchen. I didn't know what it was about and decided to come in here until you finished. My parents taught me to respect people's privacy. I got bored and started looking around. I didn't know I was committing a crime."

Natalie appeared behind her mother. "What's going on? Mom, what are you doing?"

Mrs. Marzecki held onto her anger for a moment longer, then unclenched her fists. Her stance softened. But her eyes never changed. They remained hard as agates.

This woman didn't trust him, not one bit.

"I found him 'looking around,'" she said, and turned to face her daughter. "Finish your tour. We have a lot to do."

Without saying goodbye, Nat's mom stalked off.

Sean released a breath he hadn't known he'd been holding. His whole body seemed to slump as the tension fled his muscles. Even his skin felt clammy with spent anxiety.

"Some lady, your mom," he said, not bothering to hide his irritation. "I should count myself lucky she wasn't carrying that gun."

"What did she say to you?"

"Nothing, really. She was just all-in-my-face suspicious. I didn't like it."

"Try not to be so hard on her. She's been through a lot. More than you can imagine. She's just being protective." Her voice grew heavy with memories. "Remember I said I was kidnapped once. I would have died if she hadn't found me. She has reason to be cautious. I just wish she didn't distrust everyone."

Sean grew cold. He'd forgotten about the kidnapping. What if Whitlock had lied to him about the dreamcatcher, how it wasn't dangerous? He could be causing this family more distress.

No. It was only a dreamcatcher, nothing more. A silly construct meant to decorate. What possible danger could it pose?

And then there was the guitar, and how badass it would sound plugged into his amp.

Conflicted, Sean considered telling Natalie about the dream-catcher. Her kidnapping story had touched him that much.

She frowned. "What else did my mom say? You look like you want to throw up."

"I think I better go," he said. "Your mom needs you."

A look of pain crossed her face, like she'd been slapped. "I was going to show you the house."

"I've seen enough for now," he said, and started for the front door. "Maybe I can see more next time."

"Will there be a next time?"

Her question stopped him. What if they find the dreamcatch-er? Mrs. Marzecki would know immediately who put it under the cushion. He would likely be barred from ever seeing Natalie again.

Or suppose the dreamcatcher did something horrible? What if Natalie and her mom die because of it? Is a guitar really worth that much?

He'd held onto the dream of being a rock star for so long he couldn't imagine doing anything else.

So yes, it was worth that much.

Besides, it was a damn dreamcatcher. It couldn't hurt anyone.

He gave her a wan smile. "I certainly hope so."

Without waiting for her response, he turned and left.

***

Izzy waited for her daughter and the fireworks that would sure-ly follow, but before Natalie made her entrance, Kevin wandered into the kitchen.

Her adopted son's wrists and ankles stuck out from the ends of his mismatched pajamas. He was growing so fast. He would soon need a whole new wardrobe.

He approached her, his rolling gaze taking in everything but her face. His von Kliner's syndrome, so much like autism it was hard to distinguish between the two, had ravaged his young mind. She knew from experience, though, that von Kliner's differed from autism: the latter rarely improved, while the former ebbed and flowed like an alien tide. And according to Owens, it could disappear entirely as Kevin grew older. The old man had had experience with von Kliner's syndrome; Darryl Webber's sister had suffered from it, and Darryl had killed her because of it. Darryl also kidnapped her daughter and was responsible for the deaths of so many, including that bastard Jack Sallinen.

She almost sighed. Jack Sallinen—Kevin's real father. By some ghastly process she didn't understand, he and Darryl Webber had combined to become another Fek, replacing the one she had killed. And, given what Philip and Katie had said, that new Fek was now dead.

A chill ran up her spine. If they were dead, and if Hell was a real place, would she encounter Jack Sallinen and Darryl Webber in Topheth? She prayed not. Despite all the harm they had caused, and the deaths for which they were held responsible, to witness their eternal torment might be enough to break her.

Izzy opened her arms. Kevin melted into her embrace. She could feel his heart beating against her chest.

Remember that feeling, she told herself. While you wander the horrors of Topheth in search of Owens's soul, remember Kevin's heartbeat. It will lead you home as surely as your own daughter's.

Kevin began squirming in her arms. She'd held him too long; his truncated endurance for physical contact had reached its limit. She released him.

"What do you want, honey?" she asked him.

He smacked his lips hungrily. "Smart pop!"

Smiling, she went to a cupboard and found a box of strawberry Pop Tarts and handed him two.

While he munched on his treat, she asked him, "Kevin, do you know I'm going away?"

He didn't respond.

She gently gripped his chin with one hand and forced him to look at her. "Sweetie, can you talk to me for a moment?"

Like a timid animal, his soulful eyes could only meet hers for a moment, then they moved on, rolling in their sockets, as if she wasn't there. Or wasn't important enough to notice.

"Kevin," she said, low and urgent. "Will we succeed? Will we come back alive?"

Like a supernatural divining rod, von Kliner's syndrome drew otherworldly power to those afflicted with it, a power strong enough to smother the expression of other powers, like Philip's skill at finding things, or Bartholomew's innate ability to cause pain. It was powerful enough to nullify any Forever Man's tendency to heal. In the boy's presence, they could die. That's why she had asked Kevin to stay in his room: like kryptonite to Superman, he was deadly to them.

In addition to his nullifying ability, Kevin's von Kliner's syndrome also expressed itself in a kind of clairvoyance. He possessed an uncanny knack for knowing the future. Unfortunately, it only expressed itself during her adopted son's lucid moments. While these episodes of lucidity had increased in frequency and duration as he aged, they still occurred rarely. She had only seen a handful of them in the last year.

Marbæs feared the inherent power of von Kliner's; it may be powerful enough to kill her. That fear prompted her to try and steal Kevin away from Kinsey and raise him herself. She wanted him on her side so that he couldn't be used as a weapon against her.

Some might argue that what she and Bartholomew were doing for Kevin wasn't much better than what Marbæs would have done, had she succeeded in Kinsey, but they would be wrong. She and Bartholomew never spoke of Marbæs in front of Kevin, never coached him about the dangers of the supernatural world.

Bartholomew insisted that the boy come into his powers on his own, that they not influence him one way or the other.

"He needs to be his own man," the old man had said often enough. "Possessed of his own opinions. Otherwise, he will be little more than a puppet, a tool to be used and cast aside when he is no longer useful. That's no way to live a life. He deserves more. We all deserve more."

Now she risked influencing him. She knew it wasn't right, but she was afraid. Terrified. And she wanted some assurances that she and the others would be okay.

However, this wasn't one of Kevin's lucid moments.

"Kevin!" Fear made her voice as sharp as a newly stropped razor. It cut through the air, demanding his attention. "Can you tell me, will we make it back from Topheth alive? Please, tell me I'll see you and Natalie again."

It was no use. The diffuse armor of his von Kliner's proved too strong for her fear. Ignoring her plea, he stuffed more of the pastry into his mouth.

"Smart pop!" he cried joyfully. Crumbs tumbled down the front of his pajamas. "Love them!"

She couldn't help it. Tears filled her eyes, and she hugged him. "And I love you," she whispered into his ear. "Never forget that."

"Love love!" he crowed. "Love you, love you, love you!"

She released him, perhaps for the last time. "Go to your room," she said, and gave him a push toward the door. "Your uncles will be coming up from the basement soon."

Nodding absently, he wandered away.

So much depended on him.

How could they be sure he would pick the right path?

Had she asked Judas Iscariot the same question, he would have laughed until he wept.

***

Natalie returned soon after Kevin departed. She stormed into the kitchen, thunderclouds for eyes.

"What did you say to him?" she demanded. "The poor guy couldn't get out of here quick enough."

Izzy's failure with Kevin had left her feeling raw. She didn't need this too. Old defenses rose to protect her vulnerability.

"Have you considered that Marbæs might have someone watching the house? That she might have sent creatures out there—monstrosities we haven't yet encountered—just waiting for an opportunity like this to present itself? Have you ever thought about any of that?" She didn't want to go on the attack, not when she could still feel the memory of Kevin's tender embrace in her heart, but Natalie's attitude didn't leave her much choice. It's a tough world, and she needed a tough daughter. "Bringing that boy here could raise suspicion. Why is he so important? Is he a simple love interest, or could he be more? Is he a potential ally? Does he possess powers of his own? Marbæs would burn with curiosity, a need to find out the truth. His ignorance wouldn't be much of a defense against her questions, but soon she'd realize he doesn't know anything. Then what? You think she'd let him go?" She snorted, a harsh sound that made her want to retch. "You may have cost that boy his life."

Izzy's concerns struck her impetuous daughter with the force of hammer blows. Natalie stumbled to a halt, her eyes wide with alarm.

"You don't really think...?"

"No, I don't," Izzy said. With all of the Forever Men gathered in one place, she couldn't imagine Marbæs passing up a chance to destroy one or more of them. That nothing had happened argued against her concern about the house being under surveillance. If Nat would only apply a little reason, she would have come to the same conclusion. "But what you did was still reckless. We've talked about the need for protocol, how important it is to follow the rules. It's as much for the protection of the Innocents as it is for us."

The clump of footsteps on the stairs. The others were coming up from the basement. Soon the house would be consumed with activity. Izzy didn't want to leave what could be her last serious interaction with Natalie on a sour note.

"I don't think you did him any real harm," she told Natalie. "And I apologize if I was brusque. Old habits and all."

Not quite mollified but with her composure restored, Natalie straightened. "He'll never be able to come back, will he?"

Izzy hesitated, then shook her head.

The muscles of Natalie's face shifted until she looked like she would cry. "When will I ever have a normal life?"

Now Izzy's heart ached, the last traces of Kevin's embrace stripped away by Natalie's pain. "I'm sorry, honey. I never wished this life on you."

"But I have it anyway, don't I?"

"We both do," she whispered.

The basement door opened. Gene Vincent emerged first, followed by Philip, Thomas, John, and Matthew. Apparently, James had stayed behind, probably to care for Bartholomew.

Gene wiped a shaky hand across his mouth. "I'm going to lay down for a few. I need to wrap my head around a few things." He turned to Natalie. "Hey, kiddo. Your mom clue you in to what's about to happen?"

Natalie shot Izzy a puzzled look, her ire seemingly forgotten. "What'd I miss?"

Izzy couldn't resist. "Remember how many times you told me to go to Hell? Well, you're going to get your wish."

Katie Bethel entered the kitchen last. Natalie took her friend by the hand. "You and I need to talk."

Frowning, Katie allowed herself to be led away.

Thomas, Matthew, John, and Philip each took seats around the kitchen table. Old as they were, they looked like they'd aged decades over the last hour.

Philip spoke first. He directed his words to Thomas. "How long before we can leave?"

Thomas bit his lip. A multitude of questions clouded his expression. "If I start work now? Two days. Three at the outside. I haven't tried anything like this before, so I don't know how this will test my abilities."

Philip considered his brother's words. "We need it done correctly more than quickly. Don't rush and make any mistakes. The consequences would be too severe."

Izzy thought Thomas might be offended by Philip's comments; Thomas was understandably sensitive when someone questioned his dedication. The Forever Man surprised her, though. He laughed as if Philip had told the best joke in history.

Wiping tears from his wrinkled cheeks, Thomas brought himself under some semblance of control. "You are a treasure, Philip. Did I ever tell you that?" When he spoke next, his tone had changed. Absent was the soft rumblings of an old man. Thomas now spoke with the unyielding authority of a legend. "Bartholomew is lucky to have you as his friend, his brother. We all are. I will do all I can do to return you to this world. I promise."

Philip grasped Thomas's hand and gave it an encouraging squeeze. "I know you will."

Reluctantly, as if the outcome of the world now rested on his shoulders, Thomas rose to his feet. "I'd best get started. You'll leave from the living room, so I'll work there. Do me a favor and keep everyone out, if possible. I need to concentrate."

Izzy watched the wrinkled old man depart.

John pulled out his pen. "You know, now would be a prime opportunity for Marbæs to do something, to interfere with our plans. Has anyone thought of that?"

"I have," Izzy said, amazed at how closely she had come to think like one of them. "Nat and I were just discussing it." She summarized her encounter with Natalie's friend, and why she didn't think Marbæs knew they were here. "I told her she needs to be more careful. Mistakes can be deadly in this house."

"The journey to Topheth will cause ripples throughout the world," Philip said. "The amount of energy we'll expend will surely be noticed. While I'm not worried about Marbæs right now, she'll soon figure out we're up to something. I'd give it a day at most before she knows where we are." His eyes cut to John. "You'll have to prepare. It won't take her long to figure out what we're doing, and preventing our return would guarantee our failure, or at least the deaths of a few of us. You might have a battle on your hands before we even find Bartholomew."

"Thomas won't have time to craft something for our defense." John's pen clicked away. To Izzy, it sounded like birds pecking at her already frayed patience. "That means James and I will have to come up with something."

"Natalie and Kevin," Matthew said. He had grown increasingly reticent throughout the morning. "We should consider moving them. A war zone is no place for children."

"Yes," Izzy said, more forcefully than she had intended. Matthew's statement had filled her with dread. "We can't risk them. Everything we've worked for these last few years hinges on Kevin. And Natalie...well, she's my daughter. She's the air I breathe. Without her, I wouldn't be able to live." She couldn't lose her daughter. Not after all they'd been through together. Not ever. "But where would they go?"

No one spoke. Izzy pleaded silently with the others: Don't risk my children, don't put them in harm's way while I'm gone, while I'm not here to protect them. Please don't.

"Nowhere," Philip said bitterly, as though he hated the word. "Moving them risks detection. We'd also have to leave someone there to protect them. Thomas has to stay with his device. James has to stay with Bartholomew." He turned to John. "I doubt we could persuade you to stay with them. You rarely part from your brother's side."

"You wound me, Philip." Indeed, John's expression looked truly hurt. "As you pointed out earlier, we are here because we chose to take on a mission of unbelievable importance. We sacrificed our humanity, our sense of mortality, to that cause. And you make it sound as if I'm hitching along for the ride; that I have no passion for what we're doing. Well, you're wrong." John dropped his pen onto the table and sat back. "If I thought it would help, I'd babysit them for decades and not complain. But moving them wouldn't do any good, and that's why you're right. They're safest here."

"Why?" Izzy's voice sounded rough, concern for her children making it hard to breathe. "Why would moving them be a mistake?"

"We can't be sure moving them isn't the ultimate goal of all this," John said. "Judas, and by extension, Marbæs, are far-thinking and extremely clever. Whatever Judas said to get Bartholomew to agree with this mad plot, it could have been a lie. Judas knows how we feel about Bartholomew. He knows we would attempt a rescue if given the chance. He can probably guess who will go and who will stay. That you would go, dear Elizabeth, is a given. He also knows how much you care about your children, both natural and adopted. He'll assume you'll want to keep them safe, and to do that, you would need to move them. It would be brilliant. He could snatch up Kevin while we're busy saving Bartholomew. The best way to thwart him is to do what he doesn't expect, which means doing what doesn't seem right. I agree with Philip. They need to stay here. Their presence changes nothing and provides Judas with no opportunity. It's the safest choice."

Izzy clenched her fists. Of all the Forever Men, John proved the most difficult. Probably because he was also the most brilliant. But that didn't mean he was always right.

"That presumes Judas knows we are here," she said. "And the fact that we haven't had an attack suggests the opposite. Think about it. Kevin is here. You and the others are at your most vulnerable. If Kevin is standing close enough, a bullet could kill you. But nothing has happened. I don't think Judas knows we're here. We can safely move Nat and Kevin."

She could feel Philip's and Matthew's eyes on her. Their scrutiny made her skin itch. But she kept her attention fixed on John. Her children's lives were at stake.

"That would be true," John said, picking up his pen, "if killing us is his goal."

Izzy frowned. "What do you mean? Marbæs has been trying for centuries to kill you."

"And she hasn't succeeded. She might have decided that particular approach isn't the best. Remember the events in Kinsey. She didn't send Webber there to kill Bartholomew. She sent him to kidnap Kevin. He was her target. All of this might be an elaborate scheme to get Kevin. With him under her influence, she could cause more harm than by ridding the world of us. And she risks fewer losses to her assets." John slid the pen into his pocket. "This is all speculation, of course. We don't know anything for sure. The only thing we do know is that taking unnecessary risks is a dangerous thing in this house. I heard that somewhere, you know."

"This isn't a joke," Izzy said from between her teeth.

"And I'm not considering it as one," John shot back. "What I'm considering are the various possibilities at play here. We have to choose carefully. Make a mistake and someone dies. I prefer it not be me."

"I thought you wanted an end," Philip said. "That you were tired of this life. You mention it often enough. Now you seem to be backtracking."

John's face flushed. "Wishing an end to an interminable existence is different from offering my life up in a useless gesture of resistance."

"Stop it, both of you," Matthew said. Though he sat in a chair, hands folded in front of him, his posture suggested rigid anger. "I tire of this talk about endings and death. We have decided on a course of action. All this back-and-forth will just delay us, and I, for one, would like to get it over with." He turned his attention to Izzy. "I understand your concern, but John is right. We can't risk moving your children. They'll have to stay here. I suggest keeping them downstairs, near Bartholomew. If this house is attacked, whoever comes will have to kill John, Thomas, and James before they can get to Natalie and Kevin. It's their best chance for survival."

Philip shook his head. "We can't have Kevin down there. Bartholomew needs his healing ability. The boy's presence would nullify it. We might end up killing Bartholomew off faster that way. We'll have to think of something else."

"Fine," Matthew said, clearly irritated. "They can stay upstairs. Either way, they would be the last targets of an attack. Maybe we can help them devise a means of escape. If they could climb out a window and make it safely to the ground, they could run away."

Izzy's eyes narrowed as she watched Matthew argue with John and Philip. His demeanor had definitely changed. At one moment he seemed concerned, next angry, followed by despondent, then back to concerned. She'd seen emotions cycle like that while interrogating suspects; it often played into her gut feelings about guilt and innocence. Now Matthew, the most phlegmatic of the Forever Men, acted like someone who had committed a crime.

She reached out and touched Matthew's hand. "Do you want to tell us what's going on?" she asked in the gentlest tone she could muster.

Matthew tensed at her words but quickly recovered. The fine muscles around his eyes relaxed. His lips stretched into a thin smile.

"Stress," he said. "A lot hinges on the choices we make here. The lives of Bartholomew and the Innocents are at stake. I want to make sure we're doing all we can to ensure our success."

He sounded sincere, but Izzy recognized a snow job when the flurries flew right in front of her face. Apparently, so did Philip and John.

"Now that Elizabeth mentions it," John said, "you have been acting odd."

Philip nodded in agreement. "It began after we decided to journey to Topheth."

Matthew maintained his disinterested expression, wearing it

like a mask. "You're reading too much into this. I'm fine. I'm just worried." He looked away and shrugged. "We are so used to success that we forget to fear failure."

Something about Matthew's words bothered Izzy. They didn't match his behavior. He acted guilty, not worried, as if he had done something wrong or said something offensive or—

Then she had it: her conversation yesterday with Kevin, when he'd had one of his lucid moments.

I feel sorry for you, for all of you. Most of all, I feel sorry for Matthew.

I feel sorry for Matthew.

"You've made some kind of decision, haven't you?" she said suddenly. "And that decision bothers you."

As if taken by surprise, Matthew's eyes grew wide. His aged skin paled to the color of chalk.

Before the Forever Man could respond, Philip leaned forward, his beard bristling. "What decision, Matthew? What are you planning on doing?"

"Yes," said John. "You are up to something. I can see it writ in tone and tenor, in glance and grace. Whatever you are planning is noble but it also frightens you. That is plain. You can deny it, but you cannot hide it."

While the Historian's words seemed out of time, Izzy knew from experience that John, when worried, often spoke like that.

The weight of that concern seemed to add to the burden of whatever Matthew had decided. His shoulders started to slump... but stopped. Unexpectedly, inexplicably, he drew from some inner wellspring of strength—or deceit—to once again compose himself.

His thin smile returned, not that it helped.

Izzy, Philip, and John waited for Matthew to reply. Three to one: he was outnumbered and he knew it. His smile disappeared. Instead of opening up, though, his demeanor hardened, as if he had become an old tree root, stubborn and inflexible. "If I *had* made a decision—" his tone clearly implied that he had not "—then it would be mine to keep or share as I wish. Since I have said nothing, you will have to assume that either I have made no decision, or I prefer to keep it private." He stood. His next words were directed at Izzy. "I will not be interrogated. I have done nothing wrong, and will not suffer that particular humiliation. I carry humiliation enough already."

Stiffly, Matthew turned and stalked away.

***

Preparations for the journey moved at a rapid pace.

Thomas labored to create the device that would convey them to Topheth, rarely sleeping and only pausing to eat a small meal or sip at his water bottle, and only when forced. Izzy wasn't sure what exactly he was doing—she didn't see anything that resembled a means of transportation—but Thomas showed signs of fatigue: sweat stained his shirt, his thin hair floated in wild tufts about his head, his wrinkled skin seemed to sag in ever looser folds from his thin frame. But he continued his efforts like a man determined to prove himself worthy.

How he knew to create this device also remained a mystery. He didn't work off a blueprint or drawing. He just...crafted. It would have to do.

After the confrontation in the kitchen, Matthew had retreated to his room. He took his meals there and rebuffed any attempt at conversation or company. For a man who claimed he hadn't made a decision, he certainly kept to himself.

Izzy made a mental note to watch the troubled Forever Man.

James and John met often, discussing ways to fend off attacks, should they come. They understood their limitations. The Healer and the Historian were not like Bartholomew, their Protector; they did not possess his innate ability to defend and harm. After exploring several options, they decided on a more mundane means of protection. They both left, rumbling loudly on their motorcycles. When they returned, each carried two handguns, a large caliber rifle, and enough ammunition to defend the house against a terrorist attack.

"The bullets will take care of ordinary threats," John had said when Izzy questioned him about the guns, "but if everything goes to hell, we'll retreat to the upstairs rooms. Kevin will be there. Anything supernatural will be neutralized and will get a round or ten through their now susceptible flesh."

Izzy didn't like the idea of the brothers using Kevin that way, but their plan made sense. Besides, she wouldn't be there to stop them even if she did object.

"Remember that a firefight will bring the police," she warned them. "Get my children out of there before that happens. A quick search would reveal who they are, and then everything falls apart."

Philip and Katie spent their time huddled together, planning their approach to finding and rescuing Bartholomew. Katie would carry the cube, while Philip used his ability to lead them to Bartholomew. Matthew would act as backup to Philip, Izzy and Gene as backups to Katie.

During a rare quiet spell, Izzy went in search of Gene. She found him in the room he shared with Kevin. The two were on the floor, Kevin coloring in a book Gene bought for him during a recent excursion for supplies. Gene smiled as he watched Kevin apply yellow and green streaks to a large egg sitting in a basket.

When Gene looked up, she gestured for him to follow her.

"I'll be right back," he told Kevin as he rose. "You keep coloring."

"Okay," Kevin chirped as he added thin blue lines to his drawing.

Out in the hallway, Izzy put a hand on Gene's chest. Watching him interact with Kevin, she realized (again, she supposed) how good a person he was; how kind he was. She didn't want to lose such a wonderful friend.

"We'll be leaving in the morning," she told him. "Thomas said he should be done by then."

Gene met her pronouncement with calm acceptance, even though the thought of traveling to Topheth clearly terrified him. "How should I prepare?"

"No one's ever been there before. We really don't know what to expect, so it's hard to know how to prepare."

"Food and water?"

She nodded. "Some. The hope is to quickly find Bartholomew."

"Once we find him, can we return right away or do we have to travel back to where we started?"

"Thomas can bring us back from anywhere. He just can't send us right to Bartholomew because no one knows where he is." She moved her hand from his chest to stroke his cheek. "You don't have to do this. The four of us can go."

Gene grabbed her hand, brought it to his lips, and kissed her palm. The gesture made her heart swell.

"I spent years apart from you," he said. "I won't do that again."

"I know, but this is different. We talk about returning, but there's no guarantee any of us will survive, let alone come back. We might die, which would be our best worst fate. What if we get trapped there and can't get back home? What if we don't die? What if we *can't* die? It would mean spending eternity in Hell. Think about that, how horrible it would be." She shook her head. "I'm going because I have to, because of who I've become. You just walked into this mess. You don't have to accept that level of responsibility."

"You invited me, remember. I'm going with you."

"That makes no sense. You're risking an eternity of torment. If it's really because of me, you need to rethink your priorities. No person is worth that much. Don't follow me out of some silly notion of love or dedication. Real people don't walk smiling into danger. They're afraid. They want to turn and run. What you're doing could be considered insane."

He released her hand. "When I do manage to fall sleep, which is rare anymore, my dreams are filled with nightmares, and I wake up drenched in sweat. I keep looking for monsters lurking in dark corners. I want to lock the doors and bar the windows. If anyone so much as sneezes, I'm ready to jump out of my skin. So yeah, I'm terrified. But I do understand what's at stake. I've listened to you and the others. I've seen the reports on television. I saw first-hand Celeste driven mad. Yes, I don't have your experiences, or the relationships you've made with Owens and Philip and the others. But I still care. You know, sometimes love is all we have left to keep us going, and we have to act on it. I am going. I'm scared shitless, but I'm going."

She had expected his response, and had formulated a counterargument. "Natalie and Kevin," she said. "If you and I and Katie end up lost, who will take care of them? We talked about backup going into Topheth. Well, I need you here as my backup for them. You're Natalie's godfather, and you're the last link Kevin has to Kinsey. I don't want them growing up alone, without someone from their old lives to guide and assist them. Would you consider staying, if only for their sake?"

He didn't immediately respond. His breathing remained even and steady, but the vein in his neck throbbed with new urgency. "Not fair," he said. "Not fair at all."

"I know, but will you do it? Will you stay behind for their sake?"

He took his time before answering, but when he did, his voice rang of conviction. "From all you've told me, if you fail, the world as we know it will gradually disintegrate. Horrible possessions. Violence. Mass deaths. It could mean the extinction of mankind. Nothing I could do from here would prevent that. But if I'm with you, and I'm the last person standing or sane or whatever, perhaps I can return the cube and revive Owens. I would be doing something to stop this madness from happening. I can keep Nat and Kevin from living in a world filled with real nightmares. So I'm going with you, and I'll do what I can to make sure we succeed. But if you're worried about Nat and Kevin, I'll give Natalie her dad's cell number. If we fail, it won't matter anyway. She might as well spend her remaining days with him. She can take Kevin with her, or she can try and find his brother. J.J. never made it to college. He works near Marquette operating a bulldozer. Does pretty well, I hear. Kevin can go back to his brother. They're the best choices we have."

Izzy's heart sank. "Don't do this, Gene. Don't throw away your life."

"I don't want Celeste's death to be meaningless, and I don't want to lose you."

Damn this man and his stubbornness. "Try and get some sleep," she told him. "Once we're gone, it may be some time before we get a chance to rest." She hesitated, then leaned in and kissed him. "I still think you're crazy."

He screwed his eyes together and stuck out his tongue.

She laughed. "Go. I'll wake you around five." She pushed him toward the bedroom, and as she did, her mood fell. "And I mean it. You don't have to go. Think hard, Gene. Once you're there, you'll have to see it through to the end."

He paused. He wasn't smiling. He didn't look playful at all. "I'm not sure why I feel so strongly about this. Maybe I'm looking for a way to reestablish a sense of nobility in the world. Too many people nowadays are takers, and we're all suffering for it. For my part, I'd like to be a giver, help a little, even if no one will know what I did." He shrugged. "Maybe that's the definition of crazy."

He turned away, leaving Izzy standing alone.

"Maybe it is," she whispered, and went to find Natalie.

Her daughter was holed up in her room, on her bed and staring at the screen of her laptop. Her eyes were like flecks of black glass, unemotional and unforgiving.

Izzy sighed. She understood her daughter's anger—their forced isolation from friends and family and future had taken a toll on everyone—but the damage this solitude had inflicted on a twenty-something who wanted nothing more than be a normal person was akin to torture.

I'll make it up to her one day, she thought. If I'm still alive, and if the world is still in one piece.

"We're leaving in the morning," she said.

"Whatever."

"What we're attempting is dangerous." She stepped further into the bedroom. "I might not come back."

Nat's expression hardened. "Save the melodrama, Mom. You'll be back. You always come back." Rising from the bed, she reached for her jacket. "I'm outta here."

Natalie tried to leave, but Izzy stopped her. "I said we're leaving in the morning. That means you stay here. No going out."

Natalie rounded on her, her expression livid. "Let go of me!"

Izzy pulled her close. "What did you and Katie talk about?"

"I said let go!"

"What did you say to her?"

"We didn't talk about anything!" Natalie shouted, her face red.

She looked afraid, almost panicked.

"You're a better liar than that." A chair sat in the corner of the room. Izzy guided her daughter to it, and Natalie sat. "Whatever you two discussed, it riled you up. I want to know what it was."

"I'm not ten," Natalie said. "I don't have to report to you on everything I say or do."

Izzy maneuvered her body between her daughter and the bedroom door. Fists on her hips, she said, "You will this time, because I'm not leaving until you do."

Natalie seemed to swell with anger. "This is bullshit and you know it."

"I do, but that changes nothing. I want to know what you and Katie discussed. I have the feeling it was important."

"If you think it was so important then go ask her!"

Izzy's reaction was pure instinct. Her hand shot out and struck Natalie across the face. The contact made her hand hurt, but her heart hurt more.

"No matter how you feel about me, I'm your mother. I deserve better than your shitty attitude. Are we clear on that?"

Her hand pressed to her face, Natalie said, "You never slapped me before."

"You never deserved it before."

Natalie seemed to consider her words. Lightly rubbing at her cheek, she leaned back in her chair and draped the jacket across her knees. Except for the rosy part of her cheek where she'd been slapped, the color had bled from her face.

Izzy knelt next to her. The two didn't say anything for a long time.

"You," Natalie eventually said. Her voice hitched as if she'd been crying, even though her eyes were dry. "We talked about you, Katie and me."

Izzy waited for her daughter to continue.

"You're always so composed, so sure of yourself," Natalie said. "You never seem to waver. Me, I'm always confused. I don't know how you do it, how you stay in control. It makes me angry, as odd as that sounds."

"You're angry because you're not like me?"

"Not exactly. I do want to be myself, my own person, but it wouldn't hurt to have a little of your toughness."

"And what did Katie say?"

"That she felt the same way, before Bartholomew entered her life. Her dad's suicide left her feeling lost, and her mom wasn't much help. Mrs. Bethel spent too much time drinking and not enough time parenting. She told me all that changed when she met Bartholomew."

Katie Bethel had changed. She now possessed a self-assurance far exceeding that of a normal twenty-two-year old. "But that came over time," Izzy said. "And she did it herself. She worked for it. There's no reason you can't do the same. When I get back—"

"Don't you mean *if* you get back?" Natalie's tone was like small pebbles scattered across the surface of a mirror.

Izzy stifled a desire to snap at her daughter. Why did children, even when they're not children anymore, have to make everything so difficult?

"If I get back, we'll work on this. Maybe I can help you, the way Bartholomew helped Katie. But until then, hold tight. John, James, and Thomas are remaining behind. You and Kevin will stay upstairs. She outlined the brothers' plan to keep them safe. "Work with them on an escape route, maybe find something you can use to climb out the window and down to the ground. And please, keep Kevin with you. I know he's been difficult but he really is just a little boy. He's going to need you—"

An overwhelming sadness rose up inside her and choked off her words.

She may never see her babies again.

The realization of what she was about to attempt, where she was about to go, fell on her with crushing force. A sob escaped from her throat, carrying with it her unspoken words of grief and loss.

Next to her, Natalie watched intently. Perhaps seeing her mother in a moment of weakness would help her gain a little perspective.

"I'm sorry," Izzy said when she could pull herself together. "I don't mean to push this on you, but you're the only person I've got.

The others...Philip, Thomas, the rest...well, they're beyond me in some ways. I need someone back here that I can count on. If you want to hate me for that, do if after we've rescued Bartholomew." She straightened her back. Gene told her they needed the old Izzy, and he'd been right. Putting as much iron in her voice that she could muster, she added: "Until then, suck it up, buttercup. People are risking a whole lot more than you to keep this world safe. The least you can do is keep Kevin safe."

"I hear you, Mom," she said. "I hear you."

***

Gene tried to get at least a little sleep. Too often he heard footsteps in the hallway, or the murmur of voices from downstairs. Despite these distractions and his own sense of unease, he managed a few hours of rest, and when Izzy woke him at five, he had fleeting memories of sewing shears and mutilated dogs and shadowy images filled with black menace.

He dressed quickly in the dark, not wanting to wake Kevin. Before he left, he gave the boy a light kiss on the cheek. He couldn't fathom why Kevin was so important—other than what Izzy had told him. Still, that an autistic child could carry such import made Gene marvel.

Everyone collected in the living room. Philip and Katie talked with Izzy, their expressions drawn tight. Thomas, his clothes wrinkled, his cheeks rough with whiskers, smoothed back what little hair he had and stretched. Matthew, dressed in jeans and a dark, long-sleeved shirt, handed Thomas a cup filled with steaming coffee. John and James stood off to one side, watching.

Gene approached the middle of the room, and what had to be Thomas's creation.

About three feet tall, it had clear, sleek spindles flowing from a central plinth like rays of twilight. To Gene, it resembled a glass tree. But it couldn't be made of glass. When he looked through it, what he saw wasn't the other side of the room. From within the spindles, tiny images flowed, dark, sublime, compelling. Fascinated, he peered more closely. A face, bruised, covered with gore and screaming. Bleak lands scored and blasted apart by terrible forces. Masses of huddled figures, naked, their skin blistered by the fires surrounding them. Fearsome beasts with wings and horns.

Gene's stomach lurched, and he stumbled back.

He was looking at Hell.

A hand gripped him, forced him around.

John stood there, smirking at him. "See something you didn't like?"

Gene knocked John's hand aside. "You're pretty brave for a man who's staying behind."

John's smirk fell away in chunks, as if it were being dismantled by Gene's accusation. "Callous is the man who throws guilt at those who have suffered the most," he said. "Do not judge me. You don't have the right. You have not earned the right." His eyes narrowed. "Perhaps if you survive Topheth, I will let you stand as my equal, but until then, remember your place."

"No." Gene had had enough of the supercilious Forever Man and his condescension. "If you are who you say you are, then you know we all stand equal. Isn't that what you told me: you gave your existence to an ideal because it meant so much to you? I guess you've forgotten, or eventually chose to ignore it out of pettiness or boredom. Either way, stop talking down to me. You haven't earned *that* right."

James stepped up and laid a hand on his brother's shoulder. "Enough," he said. "We all have our jobs, and this man chose his willingly. I think he's proven himself."

John's expression grew even haughtier, if that was possible. "He may have proven himself to you, but he hasn't to me." He turned and strode away.

"What's he got against me?" Gene wondered aloud.

"It's not you," James said, throwing a sorrowful look at his brother. "Memories fill his head until he can barely control them. They plague him day and night. He can't escape." He grew quiet. "My brother has not slept in over three hundred years."

The words stunned Gene.

My brother has not slept in over three hundred years.

Owens and his constant pain. John and his sleeplessness.

Do all the Forever Men suffer so?

"How does he live?" Gene asked. "I mean, how does he stay sane without sleep?"

"We don't suffer from the same aliments as you." James's mouth twisted. "At least, not anymore."

Gene felt like a man drowning in a sea of impossible sacrifices. "No wonder he wants an end to his life. No one should be asked so much, not even you six. It's...inhuman."

"John's the way he is," James continued, as if he hadn't heard Gene, "full of unspent energy and irritability, because he can't avail himself of sleep. No, his condition won't drive him insane, but he will suffer from sleeplessness's other effects. You don't have to like him, Mr. Vincent, and do not pity him. But at least understand him. Along with Bartholomew, his condition has caused the most suffering."

"I'm sorry. I didn't know." Gene's abhorrence to John's condition remained, but James's words had tempered it. "What about you? Do you suffer from any of these side effects?"

"Like Thomas and Philip, I experience fatigue after using my ability. And like them, I am allowed the grace of sleep. After a few hours, I feel fine."

"And Matthew? No one told me what he can do. And I don't remember seeing one of those tattoo things, like Owens has, the teardrop mark at the corner of his eye."

James sagged, as if a great weight had been placed on his shoulders. "We do not speak of Matthew's ability."

"Why not?" Gene asked, frowning.

"Of us all, he is the most troubled."

"I don't understand. Troubled about what?"

"Matthew," James said, "has no ability. He bears no mark like the rest of us, and never has." The Healer's voice became gruff with emotion. "Much to his dismay, he has lived all this time without purpose."

***

Philip gathered them around Thomas's mysterious creation.

"It's time to leave," he said, his tone grim but determined. "Is everyone prepared?"

Gene raised his hand. "We're traveling to Hell and may never return. How can anyone prepare for that?"

Philip gaze him a flat look. "No one would think less of you for staying behind."

"I know," Gene said, feeling like an ass for speaking up. But damn it, he might die. "Except all of you are taking the same chance, and I would think less of myself if I chickened out. And I guess that's all that matters."

"Gene and I talked about this," Izzy said, and laid a supportive hand on his shoulder. "He knows his own heart."

"Kinsey folk are tough," Katie added with a grin that looked a little forced. Like the rest, she carried a small pack of water and some protein bars. "He'll handle whatever Topheth throws at him."

"I'm sure he will," Philip said wryly. He gestured to the others. "James, John, stand near the doorway. Thomas, what do we need to do?"

"Each of you grasp a spindle," Thomas said, his eyes bright with excitement. "You don't have to hold too tightly. Just make sure you keep in contact with it."

Gene did as asked. The material—certainly not glass—felt eerily pliable in his hand. It was also very cold.

When everyone had taken hold of a spindle, Thomas said, "All you have to do is hold on. Don't break contact. You may feel odd, almost sick to your stomach, but that should pass quickly enough." He licked his lips. "It may help to close your eyes."

Gene pressed down on his spindle, bending it. "This doesn't look like it'll hold up to a journey. What happens if it breaks halfway there?"

Thomas frowned at him. "It isn't going anywhere. You are. I thought we'd made that clear."

"You're thinking of travel in the conventional sense," Izzy told him. "Topheth isn't a place in this dimension." She thought for a second. "Did you ever see the movie *The Time Machine*, the old one with Rod Taylor?"

"Sure."

"Remember how the world aged around H.G. Wells, but his time machine stayed in the same spot? This works on the same principal. Thomas's device won't move, but it will convey us where we want to go."

"And how do we know it will send us to the correct place?"

Thomas smiled. "Because it's already there."

"The visions you saw inside the *gellyd*." Philip pointed to Thomas's creation. "It's like looking through a tunnel. You're seeing where the other half of its existence lies. We know we're going to the right place because we can see it."

Gene's mouth suddenly went dry. "So part of this...this *gellyd* stays here, and the other half stays in Hell?"

"Topheth," Matthew said. "Hell encompasses many places. We intend to visit only one."

"Whatever," Gene said. "Can anything escape Topheth and return here using this *gellyd*?"

"Not unless I allow it," Thomas replied. "And I most definitely will not allow it."

Gene wasn't convinced. "How do you know that can't happen? You said it yourself—you've never done this before. What if there's a power or something, some demon or devil, that can overpower you? You might find yourselves in a fight for your lives."

"We're not defenseless," John said, speaking up for the first time. "We have our own skills, some of which you are unaware. And then there's the boy. He can nullify any supernatural threat and make these—" he patted the gun tucked into the waistband of his jeans "—more than effective."

"This debate serves no purpose," Philip said. "Whether Thomas is right or Gene, we must still make the attempt."

Izzy, standing behind Gene, again laid a hand on his shoulder. She didn't have to speak. He understood the gesture.

"I want to help Owens too," he said softly.

Philip stood straighter. "Thomas?"

The other Forever Man nodded. His eyes closed, Thomas began muttering, speaking words that Gene didn't understand but felt were ancient; words no one on earth had heard for a very long time. Nothing seemed to happen, then a light flared inside the strange crystal of the *gellyd*. Pale yellow, it started in the plinth and quickly spread to the spindles. The glow did nothing to relieve the *gellyd*'s bitter cold, but it did seem to warm the air around them.

Gene looked at the others. Of all the travelers, he was the only one with his eyes open.

He couldn't help it. He needed to see what happened. Going blind into danger made his terror worse.

Thomas's voice strengthened, his words sharp and biting. He threw his head back. Chords of muscle stood out in his neck.

The light swelled in brightness, as if it were a small sun. James and John raised their hands to shade their eyes. The early morning shadows were driven back. Gene could see every nook and crevice of the living room, the sharp angles where walls met ceiling—reality brought into ultra-high definition.

And then it began. At the edges of his vision, the world *rippled*. What he saw, what he knew to be real, began to crumble under the onslaught of Thomas's words and the ethereal power of the *gellyd*. It's power slowly encroached upon them, dissolving what he assumed was this dimension. And behind it...

Gene turned away. What he saw—

God help us.

Abruptly, he noticed another light, but not from the *gellyd*. This light came from a chair. No, it came from *beneath* the cushion of the chair. It shot out in rays like harsh lasers, red and unforgiving. Where they intersected with the crumbling reality of this dimension, sparks flew in every direction. The dissolution wavered. Cracks appeared in the bizarre unreality of thinning space-time.

Thomas, almost shouting now, cried out in pain. James and John sprang forward, guns drawn.

Now Philip was shouting. "Don't let go of the *gellyd*! *DON'T LET GO!*"

The unraveling of this dimension suddenly accelerated; fibers of space-time dissolved at a rapid pace into nothingness. Gene saw a vista of blasted land, great fissures from which gouts of fire flared. Masses of the damned crowded around horrifying beasts with twisted features and black ichor seeping from flayed skin.

Gene couldn't help himself. He looked away.

Hands clenched into fists, Thomas resumed his ancient chant. He threw words at the mounting chaos.

Then whatever hid under the cushion exploded, burning the chair to ashes and hitting James and John with the force of a hurricane. They were thrown helplessly against the wall.

As one, Philip, Katie, Matthew, and Izzy screamed—

—and then were gone.

Reality snapped back to normal. The ethereal light winked out like an offending candle snuffed by an angry breath.

Gene staggered, releasing the *gellyd*'s frigid spindle.

Thomas lay on the floor, unconscious. At the other end of the room, John and James struggled to their feet.

"I'm still here," Gene said, his voice trembling. "Why am I still here?"

CHAPTER TEN

Disoriented by the translation, blinded by the light of the *gellyd*, Izzy stumbled and fell.

The air felt hot. The ground felt hot. Her skin felt hot.

She pushed against hard sand or gravel and stood.

"Gene?" she said weakly. "Katie? Can you hear me?"

Nothing.

She shouted. "Philip! Matthew!"

A rancid smell like spoiling meat assaulted her senses. Her stomach, already queasy, revolted, and her meager breakfast splashed onto the charred ground. She ran a sleeve across her mouth.

"Okay, don't panic," she muttered, reaching out into the darkness, fingers searching. "Give yourself a minute." And pray your vision returns.

Time passed. "Is anyone there?" she called out.

Her appeal was met with terrifying silence.

Something had gone wrong.

Where were the others?

She started to shake. Panic threatened to take her, and her knees almost buckled.

Was she alone in Topheth?

No, no, no. I can't be alone!

She needed to calm down, to steady herself. She counted her breaths, gave herself something to focus on instead of her fear.

Gradually her galloping heart slowed, and she swallowed.

"Better," she said, the sound of her voice comforting her. "Much better."

As she brought her panic under control, she noticed a light, ruddy, like the glow of a massive bonfire, erupt in the distance. It stretched into the dark, starless sky and faded.

A short time later another light flared, this time from a different direction.

She held her hands in front of her face, saw the faint outline of her fingers. She wiggled them, just to be sure.

Yes, she could see.

Okay. That's a start.

It took almost a hundred breaths for her vision to return completely.

The blasted terrain gradually came into focus. Treeless, with nothing to interrupt her vision, it stretched unbroken in every direction. The ground appeared black, almost burnt, with yawning fissures that opened in spots like diseased flesh rent violently open.

Good thing she hadn't wandered. One false step...

She looked around, searching, and her heart sank.

There was no sign of the others.

She was indeed alone.

***

Izzy began walking. She didn't know what else to do.

Sweat trickled down the center of her back. Her hand strayed to her hip, where she used to wear her gun holster. But that was years ago, in a different age of her life.

In a different world...

How is it I'm breathing? she thought. Does Topheth have air?

Did Thomas's device change me as well as translate me, allow me to exist in this impossibility?

I'm lost in Topheth, separated from the others. I don't have access to the gellyd.

I'm not just lost; I'm trapped.

Panic crept up on her like an assassin, a dark, menacing threat she could neither see nor comprehend.

If she lost it, she'd die before she had a chance to save herself, before she had a chance to save the others.

But to do that, she needed to find them.

Were they back in her world, or had that strange, interfering force flung them all to different points?

She needed to find her friends.

Her panic lurched; finding people wasn't her specialty.

Philip. The Finder. For as long as she'd known him, in all the curious stories he'd told her, he'd been able to locate anything he'd set his mind to finding. By now, he'd surely have started searching for her.

All she had to do was stay put and wait.

A disturbing thought occurred to her: How expansive was Topheth? Hundreds of miles across? Thousands of miles? Hundreds of thousands? Does it even end?

It could be months before he found her, or one of the others. If they had truly been separated, it might take months more before they were reunited.

Months.

Too much time. She didn't have food or water enough to last.

Izzy steeled herself. She needed to do something, to think of something, to get them back together, and quickly.

But what?

Her heart quailed at the prospect. She scanned the horizon. Fires erupted here and there, sending tongues of flame high into the endless sky, only to be swallowed by the ever-present darkness. She could find no landmarks, nothing to provide her with a sense of direction. If she went in search of the others, she could end up wandering in circles.

The stench of decay smothered her, made it hard to breathe. And where were the children, the drums, the carnage that Philip had warned her about? Had she been sent somewhere else entirely?

None of that mattered; she didn't know the answer and had no way to find it out.

On an impulse she checked her watch. A curse slipped from between her dry, cracked lips. The hands didn't move. She had no way to tell time.

Just another problem for her to contend with.

Izzy set out to find her friends, watching her feet, planting one in front of the other in as straight a line as she could manage.

She walked for what seemed like hours, ears alert for any sound, eyes for any sight. Nothing seemed to change. The blasted landscape rolled under her like a massive wheel, the same black terrain passing beneath her feet time and again.

Stay positive. Don't give up. Think of your children. What you do, you do for them.

After a brief rest, she started counting her steps in an effort to measure the passage of time and distance.

About one a second. Sixty a minute. Thirty-six hundred an hour.

After traveling for roughly three hours, when she stumbled rather than walked, Izzy halted. Sweat had soaked through her clothes. Her stomach cramped with hunger. She pulled a protein bar from her pocket, took a bite, and saved the rest. She allowed herself one mouthful of water from her supply. The pain in her stomach eased, but exhaustion still made her limbs feel as if they were fashioned from concrete.

She would need to sleep soon.

She gritted her teeth. Two more hours. I can do two more hours before I face that problem.

Izzy continued her trek.

Fatigue eventually clouded her mind, and she lost count of her steps. Still, she pushed on.

I should have reached one of those fiery explosions by now, she thought numbly.

She walked until she couldn't put one foot in front of the other. Her knees folded and she sat.

Another bite of the protein bar; another mouthful of water.

She would have to sleep, to lay unguarded and vulnerable in this horror, where anyone or anything could sneak up and attack.

Again, she had no choice. She simply could not go on without rest. As she slid the water bottles from their slings, intending to keep them gripped in her hands while she slept, her ears picked up a new sound.

Footsteps.

Someone was approaching.

She quickly stood. Yes, she could hear footsteps, the distinctive crunch of trampled gravel. They seemed to be coming from behind her.

She spun, her eyes squinting against the inky darkness, and gasped. There! A figure, darker than the dark background! It appeared man-shaped, walking upright, and was no taller than her.

Remember where you are, she thought. Remember the danger.

While the dark figure still remained some distance away, she called out. "That's close enough."

Whatever it was stopped. She thought she heard a low gurgle come from it, like laughter but filled instead with hate. Then it crossed its arms and turned back and forth, as if hugging itself.

"Who are you?" Izzy said, her voice carrying in the deadly stillness. "What are you doing here?"

The dark figure didn't immediately answer. Instead, its turning, its shifting, increased in frequency; back and forth it rotated, moving rapidly, more rapidly, too rapidly. Its gurgle shifted to a cry, high pitched, like a rabbit caught in a painful snare.

The hairs on Izzy's arms rose, standing stiff in terror. She could feel something, a gathering of force. It ran along her nerves like a low-voltage current.

Adrenaline poured through her, and she turned to flee.

The dark figure suddenly shouted—it sounded like a word, but not one she recognized—and from it, she sensed a release, a discharge of whatever gathered energies she had felt.

Before she could take a step, something slammed into her back, propelling her from her feet and sending her pin-wheeling through the air. She landed, the gravel tearing at her skin, and instinctively rolled, dispersing the gathered force of her impact. A whiplash of pain shot down her arm. Ignoring her injuries, she rose to her feet.

The dark figure moved rapidly toward her, traveling at an inhuman speed. Izzy had no time to prepare a defense. Shrouded in what looked like hundreds of filthy rags fastened to its skin with cruel-looking hooks, the dark figure bounded into her, its long arms grappling, and they tumbled to the ground.

Izzy had been in her share of fights. She'd been trained in close combat techniques. Before the dark figure could gain an advantage, she shifted, pulling with one arm while pushing with the other, and gave a tremendous heave. The dark figure, momentarily unbalanced, loosed an angry shriek as she scrambled out from under it.

She regained her footing and backed away, hands raised in defense.

The dark figure stood. All that could be seen apart from the rags were two merciless black eyes and a mouth like a yawning pit, too wide and filled with broken teeth. That horrid mouth stretched wider, and it spoke.

"I can smell you, your purity. Your sanctity. The sweetness aches like a memory of...of..." The dark figure's corrupt rags shifted on their own, the multitude of hooks digging deeper into its flesh until it cried out. "*Why do you punish me so?*"

Izzy steadied her breathing. Her arm hurt from shoulder to wrist, and she wondered if she'd broken it in her fall. "I don't mean to hurt you," she told the creature. "I'm just trying to protect myself."

The dark figure sniffed. "Teasing bitch! You breathe. You bleed. Your heart beats!"

And I intend to keep it that way, she thought, and took a step back. "Who are you? Do you have a name?"

"A name? Perhaps once, long ago. But no more." A guttural sound like a sob escaped from its throat. "Never again."

"I don't mean to cause you pain."

The dark figure's rags again tightened, squeezing until a dark ichor oozed from between them. It howled in pain.

Izzy took another step back. "Do you know this place? Can you tell me where I am?"

A tongue of fire erupted nearby, closer than any Izzy had yet experienced. The dark figure didn't seem to notice. Its black eyes glittered with intense hatred.

"Pain and punishment, a land of unending repentance. But you know that, don't you?" Its fists clenched. "You are a lie, a memory, a false promise!"

"I don't want to be here any more than you want me here, but I don't know where to go. I—" She hesitated. She didn't want to give this...whatever it was...an advantage, but she might need its help. "I have friends nearby, or I think they're nearby. I'm trying to find them." A thought occurred to her. "How did you find me?"

"Hope," the figure said, weeping. "Nothing in this wretched place cradles such hope in its breast. You practically shine with it. I came to witness your false temptation. I came to taste of it." Its emotions abruptly shifted; its harsh lips curled back into a sneer. "I came to eliminate it."

Izzy's thoughts raced. She needed to get away from this monstrosity and the threat it represented, yet she also needed an ally, someone to help her navigate this horrible place.

"If you want me gone," she said, "then help me find my friends. Without them, I can't leave." She lowered her hands and stepped toward the dark figure. "My name is Elizabeth Morris."

The hooks binding the rags tunneled further into the figure's malign form. It writhed in fury and pain. "A life escaped! Have I not suffered enough?"

"My friends. Can you help me find them?" She edged closer. "Please."

"No! I am gone from that existence! You cannot harm me further!"

Izzy hesitated. Was she causing it to feel such pain? "You're hurting because of me?"

"No—yes," it rasped. "Of course. Love. Torture. The heart of each rests with the familiar."

Rests with the familiar?

Her skin grew cold, despite the oppressive heat. "Do I know you?"

A wicked-looking hook, the pitted metal coated with gore, rose from the figure's shoulder to its cheek, pulling a filthy rag like a funeral streamer behind it. It found an exposed patch of flesh and dug in until only the tip of the shaft remained visible. The rag contracted like a muscle, cruelly wrenching the figure's head around until it cried out. "You do not belong here!"

"No," she whispered. "I don't." Then, louder: "You said I shine, that the light drew you to me. Well, my friends should also shine." Two as brightly as stars, she supposed. "Maybe you can see them, too."

The figure wept, its bandaged head bent severely.

Izzy pressed on. "Can you lead me to them?"

"Back away," the figure cried. "Back away!"

Frowning, Izzy retreated. To her wonder, the rag attached to the figure's cheek went slack. The dark figure's head eased upward, and it stood straighter.

It fixed its baleful glare on her. "Keep your cruel secrets to yourself. Tell me nothing more. I know too much already."

"Fine. Great. I'll keep everything to myself." Not that she understood what was happening, or what to keep secret. "You want me gone. I want to leave. The only way to accomplish that is to find my friends. Can you do that?"

"Killing you is as good as being rid of you, but I cannot approach. I cannot deal that blow. You are too much, too close. I cannot exceed my suffering." The figure sobbed. "It has always been so."

Those words, that voice. Izzy couldn't shake the feeling she knew this desperate figure; this damned person, for that's who it must be.

She then recalled the first attack: the invisible force that had propelled her through the air.

"You don't have to be near me to attack," she said. "You did something earlier. It hurt me. Don't think I've forgotten that."

The figure seemed to gather itself. Its sobbing faded. With a visible effort, it unclenched its fists. For the first time since Izzy had seen it, the figure looked almost human.

A sad, wretched shell of a human, but nonetheless a human.

"Not again," the figure said. This time, its voice sounded less harsh, less feral—and more like a...man. "I cannot do that again, not for a while, and not to you. You are now unassailable."

Izzy stifled a sigh of exasperation. She didn't have time to puzzle out the mysteries of this condemned figure, or of this hellish domain. She had a mission to complete. Others depended on her.

"My friends," she said. "Can you help me find them?"

The figure bared his teeth. In some weird flash of intuition, Izzy realized he was smiling at her.

"Already you exceed me," the figure said. "Were I to stand in the presence of others like you, I would never recover. You ask too much."

"You found me. You can find them. I'm sure of it."

"You have eyes. You are not blind. Search for them yourself. I have made a mistake." The figure turned away.

"Wait. Don't leave." Izzy advanced on the figure. Immediately, the figure's rags shifted, drew tighter. Cruel hooks dug into his flesh.

"Stay away! Do not approach!"

Izzy jerked backwards. The dark figure's writhing eased as the rags unclenched.

Her mouth dropped open in surprise. She'd finally made the connection. Realization made the hairs on her arms rise.

Her proximity caused the hooks to dig into the dark figure.

Something about her triggered his torment.

This can't be a coincidence. His pain was linked to her, at least in part. She had some sort of connection with him. "I knew you once, didn't I?"

The figure groaned. "Have I not suffered enough?"

"Perhaps you have. And for that, I am truly sorry. But my friends are here somewhere, and I'll never find them alone. I don't have the same...the same vision you do. I can't see what you see. I need your help." A thought occurred to her, sad and yet promising. "You're in this place for a reason. You're being punished for something you did. I don't know if it would make a difference, but helping me might shorten that suffering. Doing a good deed might help balance out whatever horrible act sent you here." She paused. "If we were once friends, I would take some small gratitude in helping end your torment."

"Fool! You talk of endings, as if I could simply walk away from *this*." He clutched at the rags that bound him. "It is a sweet dream but a false one, and it will only add to my suffering. Nothing here ends. I am irredeemable. Go and seek your friends. My doom lies elsewhere."

The dark figure walked away with the shambling gate of a broken soul. Izzy followed, careful not to move too close. The darkness seemed to gather until all she could see were herself and this wretched man.

"Do not follow," the figure said without looking back. "I will not lead where you wish to go."

"My choices are limited—either follow you or give up and wait to die. I'm not ready to die, not in this place."

"I witnessed your light. Death would not keep you here."

"It's still failing, and I have something important I need to finish."

The dark figure chuckled. "You were always stubborn."

The words washed over Izzy's spine like a splash of cold water. "So I do know you."

"You never knew me," the figure returned bitterly. "As if knowing would have helped. My pain was evident, yet no one saw it. No one cared enough to notice." The dark figure paused, cocked his head to look over his shoulder at her. "I am forgotten detritus adrift in this sea of offal. You would be wise to remember that."

Izzy scrambled to recall the people in her life who had suffered and died, who would have been bad enough to be condemned to Hell.

One name leapt ahead of the others.

Jack Sallinen. The greedy banker who had orchestrated her daughter's kidnapping. The man who had invited that sociopath, Darryl Webber, into their town and their lives. A man tacitly complicit in the deaths of four of Kinsey's citizens.

But, no. This man didn't sound like Jack, didn't move like Jack, didn't present himself like Jack.

Who else had she known broken enough to be condemned to pain and punishment? Possibly someone she had arrested, a child abuser or wife beater? An addict who had killed to score another hit of heroin?

Again, no. She doubted a criminal would possess enough intimate knowledge of her. The dark figured spoke as if he had known her, had been familiar with her personally.

She did have a close circle of friends, though. People with whom she was constantly associated. If this dark figure had known her...

"The friends I seek," she said, "it's possible you might know one of them, too. I brought two with me from Kinsey. Gene Vincent. He owns a bar named the Lula. And a young woman, Katie Bethel. Did you know either of them?"

The dark figure uttered a sharp hiss like a curse. "You brought a child to Topheth? Are you mad?"

"She's not a child any—"

Izzy's heart leapt up into her throat, cutting off the rest of her words. She'd made the connection at last.

"Adam?" she said. "Adam Bethel?"

The dark figure flinched. "Don't call me that. I have no name here."

Izzy gazed at him in sorrow. Adam Bethel was Katie's father, a sad man who had suffered from severe mood swings. He killed himself years ago, when Katie was only a child; a selfish act that had apparently condemned him.

"Oh, Adam. I'm so sorry."

Adam Bethel spun to face her, a snarl on his black lips. "Now you're sorry, after the damage has been done?"

"We didn't know. You never told anyone how bad it had gotten."

Several hooks curled into his body, but this time Adam didn't react. His focus—his impotent fury—was directed completely at her. "You don't know what it was like, struggling to get out of bed every day, forcing myself to smile and pretend my life wasn't a hopeless mess. Living with a wife who couldn't care less what happened to me, or a daughter who demanded I be more than I was. I fought every day, *every single day*, until it finally wore me down. Still no one noticed. And you dare lay blame for this on me?"

"Who else is there to blame?" Izzy felt pity for the man but, as he had always done in life, Adam Bethel blamed everyone else for his troubles. "You killed yourself. You made that decision, when there were other options open to you. The responsibility falls on you, not on those around you. I would have thought you'd learned that by now."

"Only a fiend finds fault with the victim. The blame has to lie elsewhere."

"If that's true," Izzy said quietly, "then why are you here?"

"Stop it!"

"Maybe if you'd accepted responsibility—"

"Leave! I am done with you!"

"—your punishment might end."

Adam Bethel stiffened. "Did you not hear me? I am unredeemable."

Perpetual self-loathing and denial: Adam Bethel wore both like the rags that covered his body, so much so that he couldn't see the obvious. Perhaps that was the true nature of condemnation.

"And you will remain unredeemable as long as you believe it." She couldn't waste any more of her time. Adam Bethel had been a pitiful man in life; he hadn't changed in death. She would get no help from him. "You were right about one thing, though. We are done. I'll find my friends—I'll find your daughter—by myself. I'd wish you well, but that seems pointless. No one could be well existing like this for an eternity."

Adam's black eyes narrowed. "How long, Izzy? How long have I been here?"

She hesitated, not wanting to tell him. But in the end, she decided to answer. He created this punishment, and whatever she said was unlikely to make it worse. "A little over ten years."

"That's all?" he whispered. "It feels like centuries."

"I have to go, Adam. I don't know how long it's going to take to find my friends, and I'm afraid of staying here too long." She forced a smile. "I hope you find redemption someday. You were never an evil man, just sad and hopeless."

A particularly large hook on his chest wound its way into his flesh. Adam Bethel grimaced. "Don't tell Katie about me. Or Jenny. Let them think my suffering is at an end. I don't want them to worry."

"I—I won't." She didn't have the heart to tell him his wife, Jenny, died years ago, murdered by a twisted creature composed of fur and snake scales and razor teeth.

Adam nodded, a curt yet surprisingly grateful gesture. Then his face grew slack. The corners of his mouth drooped. He looked like a man who had come to grips with his faithlessness.

He turned and pointed. "One of those you seek, he lies that way. His spirit lights the skies like a beacon." He turned back to face her. "Be careful. I will not be the only one who sees."

Gratitude flooded through her. She laid a water bottle on the ground like an arrow pointing in the direction Adam had indicated. When she started to thank him, though, he stopped her with a harsh gesture.

"Don't," he said. "Your pity is like an auger digging in my soul. I cannot take any more. Do what you came to do, leave this place, and never return."

Before she could respond, he set out, his gait as broken as his spirit.

Izzy watched his departure until she could no longer distinguish his rag-bound shape from the ever-present darkness.

She shifted her gaze to the region Adam had indicated. She picked up the water bottle, sipped a mouthful of water.

And then she set out.

***

Izzy walked for what seemed like hours, ate another bite of protein bar, permitted herself another sip of water, and, reluctantly, slept.

How much time had passed? How many days? Her pace was necessarily slow and deliberate, as she focused her energies on staying on course.

After her fourth rest, a fitful sleep that left her feeling more haggard and worn than before she'd stopped, she began to suspect Adam Bethel had betrayed her, that he had sent her on a false path, though she couldn't imagine what benefit he would have gained from such a ruse.

Regardless of the motivations Adam Bethel held in his narcissistic heart, she had to continue. After another bite of protein bar and a sip of water, she set out.

The fire eruptions had disappeared a while ago; murky darkness filled her long hours. All she had for company was the sound of her footfalls scraping against the broken ground.

Counting her steps, she'd walked for three hours when she stopped, lifted the water bottle to her lips, and paused.

Something had broken the depressing monotony of her search.

A tremor. Faint, but definitely palpable. It rose through the soles of her shoes. She knelt. Placed her hand on the ground.

The tremor intensified. Gravel skittered and danced beneath her fingers. A deep rumbling, not unlike thunder but not like it either, sounded off in the distance.

Standing, Izzy slid the water bottle into its harness. She slowly turned in a circle, trying to determine from which direction this new sound came, but the darkness was too complete; she couldn't tell one direction from the next. The rumbling was just...there.

And it was getting closer. The rumbling vibrated her bones.

Only, now that she could hear it more clearly, she realized it wasn't rumbling.

It was a throaty, sonorous groaning. The unmistakable sound of a living thing, or what passed for living here.

Her mouth went dry. She prepared to flee, to run in a vain hope of finding Philip or Thomas—one of them might prove powerful enough to protect her—but she abruptly halted.

Her water bottle. She'd forgotten to lay it down to mark her direction. And she had turned, trying to locate the source of the groaning, twisting this way and that.

She didn't know one direction from another.

She'd lost her bearings. She might end up running back in the way she'd come.

The groaning filled the air. It reverberated off the shattered ground. A grim emotion could be heard in that sound, a ferocity so terrible it made her stomach turn.

Screw it, Izzy thought, and bolted into the nothing. She might die here, but she didn't have make it easy.

The groaning turned to a cry of fury, then an enormous crash, like a mountain toppling. The ground buckled. Izzy spun her arms, tried to keep her balance. The earth heaved again. This time the violence overcame her, the contortions of the terrain too forceful,

166

and she fell. Blood seeped into her shirt, her pants.

The ground vibrated constantly. Mighty explosions like granite breaking assaulted her. Whatever had come for her, it was almost here.

Izzy heaved herself off the ground and ran. Her heart thudded in her ears. The ground bucked again. She managed to keep her feet, but she couldn't run fast enough. That horrible groaning battled with the sounds of her racing heart as she pushed herself harder and harder, her shoes skidding wildly on the unsteady ground, her breath coming in short gasps. She needed to get away. She couldn't die here.

The terrain sloped downward. Before she could wonder why, her feet left solid ground and she fell. Momentum carried her forward. Her body slammed against something solid. Desperate, her arms shot upward, found a ledge. Her fingers strove for purchase, her fingernails digging into loose dirt. The ground crumbled under her right hand, fell away. Suddenly she hung suspended by one arm.

And then that ground gave way.

"No," she muttered. "No. I refuse to die here."

She swung her right arm up, fingers splayed, groping, until they found purchase in the gritty dirt. With a shout of joy, she hauled herself upward. The rough wall scraped her cheek as she slowly but inexorably pulled herself out of whatever pit or crevasse she had fallen into. She couldn't see the top, but she sensed it was close. Some different quality in the air told her it was close.

Just a little more.

Just a little.

With a final effort she heaved herself up, and out.

Yes! Izzy swung her legs to aid her balance, threw her arm forward, dug her elbow into the ground, threw her other arm onto the ground and pulled.

The dirt suddenly shifted, then crumbled like powdered sugar beneath her arms. Izzy felt herself shift, then slide, the weight of her lower body pulling her, drawing her downward. A scream tore from her throat. Panicked, she scrambled for purchase, arms outthrust, fingers hooked into claws, but they raked through the dirt as smoothly as if it were dust.

Izzy thought she heard shouting but realized it was her own cries of terror.

Her body skidded further down. Her fingers lost their grip.

"No! Oh God, no!" she screamed, and slipped into the crevasse.

CHAPTER ELEVEN

"I don't care what you think," Gene Vincent said, his hands clenched into fists, "you have to send me there. You have to make the attempt."

Thomas glared at him, his normally rheumy eyes sharp with anger. "We don't understand what happened, the mechanics of it, or if it could happen again. If I tried to send you, I can't be sure where you would end up. You could end up lost."

"I don't care. I won't leave Izzy—"

John raised his hand. It held the charred circular object they'd found under the cushion of a chair. "How do you suppose this got here?"

"I don't even know what it is," Gene said.

"Neither do we," John said. "Which makes it mighty strange. There aren't many things on this world we haven't encountered at one time or another."

Gene wanted to spit. He'd been left behind, blocked from going with the others, presumably by whatever they had found. Someone had sabotaged their plans, but who could have antici-pated—

"Judas," James said from his spot on the sofa. After he had made sure Gene hadn't been harmed by the aborted translation, the Healer had isolated himself from the others. Now he spoke up, his expression tight with worry. "It had to be him. I can't think of anyone else with the power to create that thing." He pointed to the object his brother held.

"Which, of course, means Marbæs," John said.

"They anticipated what we would do," Thomas said. "What we were planning. And they set a trap."

The sounds of footsteps came from upstairs. Natalie stepped into the living room. "Uncle Gene, what's going on?"

Gene somehow managed to keep the anger out of his voice. "Our plan didn't go as planned."

Natalie frowned. "You mean Mom already left? I thought you were going with her?"

"I was supposed to." Gene took the charred object from John and held it toward her. "Have you seen this before?"

"No. Why, what is it?"

Gene jabbed a finger at the chair and the scorched cushion resting on the floor beside it. "You didn't put this on that chair, under that cushion?"

Natalie's frown deepened. "I told you. I've never seen it before. Did something happen to my mom? Is she okay?"

"I don't know," Thomas said. "I was working the translation when something happened. A flash of light, and then smoke. When everything cleared, Gene remained and the others had gone. That object your godfather is holding—we think it caused the disruption. We just don't know how it got here." He gave her a sad shrug. "We don't know what happened to your mother, or Katie, or our brothers. I can't see them in the *gellyd*."

Natalie took a step forward. "But you'll be able to find them, right? You'll be able to bring them back?"

"He's going to try." John stood and took Natalie's hands in his. "And then we'll bring them back. We won't abandon your mother, or anyone else."

"Damn straight they won't," Gene said. He'd had enough discussion. The time for action had arrived. "Thomas won't sleep until he finds them. Then he's going to send me in, so I can help them escape."

"And do what?" John said. "They already have Philip and Matthew. Elizabeth is no slouch. Neither is Katie. What exactly do you think you can do that they can't?"

Gene whirled to face him. "I can be another body, another voice, another idea generator. I can help carry someone who's hurt, or stand guard. I can join the damn fight. I can—"

"You can be with the woman you love," John said with surprising compassion. "I understand, Gene. I get it. You may have forgotten, but my brothers and I are here, today, two thousand years into our lives, because of love. A tremendous, abiding love, at first for one man, and then for all people. If anyone understands the desperation that love engenders, it's us." His voice hardened. "But we're also realistic. There's nothing you can do for them. What you *can* do is help *us*. Elizabeth and the others will return. In what condition, we don't know, but they will likely need our help, and we can't prepare for them if we're standing around arguing with you, now can we?"

Gene bit back a sharp reply. He'd never warmed to John, and his first response was to deny John's words. But he'd also gone through enough shit in his years to learn the benefits of listening. These people had centuries of experience with many different situations. Gene even recalled how Owens had spent time as a tank commander in World War Two. With a conscious effort, he brought his anger under control. To help Izzy, to help the woman he loved, he needed a clear head, not a troubled heart.

The woman he loved.

Had his feelings been that clear, or was John simply that perceptive?

"Fine," he said. "I'll help. What do you need me to do?"

John turned his attention to Natalie. "Where is your brother?"

"Upstairs," she said. "In his room."

"Good. Make sure he stays there. We're too vulnerable with him nearby."

James moved to stand next to John. "And you're sure you've never seen that burned thing?"

Natalie took it from Gene, turned it over in her hands. "I don't know," she said, and handed it back. "It kind of looks like a dream-catcher, doesn't it? All those circles within circles. But it must be made of metal. Yarn or thread would have burned to ash."

"But you've never seen it before?" Gene asked.

Natalie shook her head.

"So, Natalie isn't involved," James said, looking at his brother. "And neither are we. Gene obviously hasn't seen it before, and I can't imagine Izzy or Katie working against us. That leaves Kevin, or someone else."

"Kevin never leaves the house alone," Natalie said. "Either my mom or I would have noticed if someone gave him that."

Thomas, who had been examining his *gellyd*, looked up. "Natalie, didn't you have a visitor recently?"

"Sean. I brought him here yesterday to see the house."

"Your mom mentioned him," Gene said. "She caught him here, in the living room. She thought he looked nervous, like she'd caught him where he shouldn't be."

"Who's Sean?" James asked.

Natalie bit her lip. "A guy I met at the mall."

John's expression hardened. "How long ago?"

"A week," she said. "Maybe two."

"And you brought him here?" Thomas said, joining the questioning. "When you've only just met him?"

"But I tested him," Natalie said. She turned to face Thomas. "I sprayed him with that stuff you gave me. Nothing happened. He's human."

"Marbæs uses humans more than creatures," John said. "Think of her goal. She wants Innocents to despair, to turn on one another. For her, condemning an Innocent is more satisfying than using a creature that has never lived and has no soul. She wants to trick him into betraying his humanity. And even better? Using an Innocent to trick one of us." He paused. "Do you know where he lives?"

Natalie pressed her fingertips to her temples and closed her eyes. "He has nothing to do with this. He's my friend."

"John and I would like to make sure," James said. "A quick visit, check up on the boy, and we're gone. Provided he really hasn't any involvement in this."

"You're wrong," Natalie said. "He wouldn't do anything to hurt me."

Gene gently grasped Natalie's wrists and pulled her hands from her head. Her eyes sprang open. "Wha—?"

"Listen to me," he said, dredging up a tone he hadn't used with her since her childhood. "Your mom is in trouble. So are Philip and Matthew and Katie. We need your help, not your attitude. This guy needs checking out. If you're right and he has nothing to do with this, then we'll apologize for doubting you. Until then, you'll do what James and John say. Tell them where he lives."

"Let go!" Natalie tried to wrench her arms free.

Gene tightened his grip. "*Tell them.*"

"You're hurting me!"

"Tell them."

"I don't know, all right?" she shouted. "I don't know where he lives."

John suddenly darted in and snatched Natalie's cell phone from her back pocket. He tapped the screen several times. The phone unlocked.

"No!" Natalie's face went bright red. "You have no right!"

"I have every right," John said. "People I love are in danger." He found her contacts and flipped through them. "Ah, here we go. Last name's Leyton."

"Does it list an address?" James asked.

"No," John said. "Just a phone number."

"May I?" James asked, holding out his hand.

John handed over the phone. "What do you have in mind?"

Thomas approached from across the room. "Yes, what are you planning?"

"My brother isn't the only creative mind in the family," James said, and hit the dial button.

"Please don't," Natalie said, tears on her cheeks. "You'll ruin everything."

James held up a warning finger. "Hello, Sean?" he said. "No, I'm Natalie's uncle. Do you happen to know where she is?" Pause. "Yes, I understand I'm using her phone. It's here but she isn't, and I'm getting worried. Have you seen her?" Pause. "Not since yesterday? Damn." Pause. "This morning. We had breakfast, then a fire broke out in the living room. We found a strange, metallic thing charred to almost nothing. I think it started the fire, though I can't find a power source." Pause. "Yes, it was bad. Her brother got caught up in it, suffered burns to his face and hands. Right now he's at the hospital with his mom. I got the impression Natalie blamed herself for the fire. I thought she'd gone up to her room, but when I went to check on her, she was gone." Pause. "No, she's not there. We checked with her mom. Is there any chance she might show up at your place? She's been talking about you recently, so I figured she might seek out a friendly face." Pause. "You sure she doesn't know? That girl's bright. She might have picked up something from an off-hand comment you made. If it's within walking distance—" Pause. "That far? Quite a long walk, but the girl is stubborn. Look, I'm going to search for her. If she does show up, please call me on this phone. I'm starting to get scared."

John handed the phone back to Natalie. "Get your coat on. We're going for a drive."

***

Natalie drove her godfather's car through the neighborhood of Westhaven, with John in the seat next to her and James in the back. They had traveled most of the streets when Natalie stopped the car.

"There," she said, pointing. "That's his car."

A beat-up sedan with a Metallica sticker on the rear bumper sat in the driveway of a modest colonial with tall columns flanking the front door and a satellite dish on the roof. A light shone in a downstairs window. The upstairs windows were dark.

Natalie parked down the street from the house. "I'll talk to Sean. You two will just scare him."

"And say what?" John asked. "Hey, Sean. Did you hide a gizmo beneath the cushion of my mom's chair? Oh, and how did you come by it?'"

"John has a point," James said. "He may have already sabotaged us once. If he thinks you suspect him, he may shut down. I'd like to know who set him up for this, and if he has anything else planned."

Natalie pocketed her keys. "What do you suggest?"

"Bring him here," John said. "I'd like to talk to the boy myself."

"You're not going to hurt him?"

"You're worrying more about his safety than your mother's?"

"We don't hurt people," James added. "Unless there's no other choice."

"There's always a choice," Natalie said, and opened the car door.

***

Minutes later, she slid into the driver's seat. "He's not home."

"Did you find out where he is?" James asked.

"Your call might have set him off. According to his mom, he left the house about an hour ago."

"Without his car?" John said. "Not likely. I'd wager he's still in the house."

"His mom has no reason to lie," Natalie said.

"If she thought her son was in danger, she might." John rolled down his window. "You hear that?"

Natalie's heart sank. "Sirens."

"Time to go," James said. "We've worn out our welcome."

With the barrage of sirens pummeling them, Natalie pulled away from the curb, accelerated down the street, and took the first right.

"Not too fast," John said. "Don't draw attention to yourself."

At the next cross street, she turned left and headed for the main road out of the neighborhood.

"I see flashing lights," James said, his voice remarkably calm. "They know where we are."

Natalie mashed on the accelerator.

A police cruiser pulled into the street ahead of them. She took a side street, just missing a car parked near the intersection.

"Slow down." John put a hand on her arm. "You're going too fast."

"They'll catch us!"

"There might be children around."

She eased up on the gas. "What do I do?"

"Car chases are dangerous," James said. "The best thing would be to stop. Let's talk to the police."

"After we ran from them? Are you crazy?"

"Talk can mean many things." John smiled. "Find an out-of-the-way place and pull over."

***

Natalie chose an alley behind a nearby strip mall and parked next to a large metal dumpster.

A police cruiser, bubble lights flashing, pulled in behind her. Two more parked behind the first.

"Do exactly what they say," John said. "I don't want anyone getting hurt."

"That's comforting," Natalie muttered.

Five officers gathered at the mouth of the alley, guns drawn. Two approached the car. "You in the car," one said. "Put your hands outside the windows and keep them there."

Natalie did as they asked. So did James and John.

"Are you armed?" the officer said.

"No, sir," John said.

"Are the doors unlocked?"

"Yes, sir."

The officers pulled them from the car. One officer, a younger man with short cropped hair, pushed Natalie over the front of the car. "Keep your hands flat on the hood," he said.

The officer on the other side of the car suddenly grunted and slid to the ground.

James rounded the car to join her. He disarmed the young officer as if he were a child and jammed the gun to the man's temple.

"Natalie," James said. "Ground."

She dropped flat on her stomach.

"I'm Sargent Halpert," said an officer at the mouth of the alley. He had a shaved head and a no-nonsense attitude. "Put the gun down."

"This gun," James said, "is my only negotiating chip."

"Other cars will be here soon," Halpert said. "You'll be surrounded. There's no room for—"

Movement from behind the dumpster. Four men shambled into view. Blood covered their clothes. One held a crowbar, one clenched a switchblade in his fist. The other two carried small caliber pistols. They never hesitated. The man with the switchblade fell on Natalie, while the man holding the crowbar swung at James. The lunatics armed with guns fired. John cried out, as did another man.

Natalie rolled, twisted. The blade skittered off the concrete. She drove her knuckles into her attacker's throat. The man gagged, coughed. She brought her elbow hard into his chin. He shook off the blow, stabbed. She cried out as the blade sunk into her shoulder.

The man attacking James collapsed. The crowbar flashed, and the man on top of Natalie screamed. He rolled off her, holding his now broken wrist, the one that had held the switchblade.

Gunfire erupted in the alley. One of the pistol-wielding maniacs staggered, returned fire, fell. People cried out. People died.

James dropped to his knees, grabbed Switchblade Man by his shirt. "Do you know me?"

"Let me go!"

"*Do you know me?*"

The man suddenly recoiled. His eyes bulged. "No! It can't be! IT CAN'T BE!" Then he screamed and collapsed.

The shootout had drawn attention. The wrong kind.

More blood-soaked crazies approached from the far end of the alley.

"What's going on?" Natalie bit back a scream as James pulled the switchblade from her shoulder. "Why are these people attacking?"

"It's the Veil." James helped her up. "The spirits of the dead are returning. They're taking over the living."

The gunfire stopped. The four who had attacked them were down. So were four of the cops. The remaining officer stumbled back to his cruiser.

They hurried to the other side of the car. John lay on the ground, blood pouring from two wounds in his chest. His eyes were closed.

"Help me get him into the car," James said.

***

Back at the house, James, Gene, and Thomas carried John to his bed. Natalie followed. The irascible Forever Man hadn't regained consciousness.

James removed his brother's blood-soaked shirt, revealing two bullet wounds, one low and left on his abdomen and the other, the worst, a gaping hole high on his chest, right of his heart.

"Leave us." James covered John's chest wound with trembling hands. "This is going to take a while."

"Come on." Thomas motioned for Natalie to follow him. "We need to bandage you up."

The three left James to work on his brother.

Using a first aid kit kept in the bathroom, Thomas bound Natalie's wound. Then they gathered in the living room.

"Shouldn't we take her to a hospital?" Gene said. "That cut's going to need stitches."

Thomas shook his head. "James will tend to her later. Tell me what happened."

Natalie related the events as best she could. She hadn't witnessed most of the gunfight, but the results spoke for themselves.

"This was Marbæs's plan all along," Thomas said. "She wanted the Veil weakened."

"What can we do to stop it?" Gene said.

"James did something." Natalie's shoulder ached, but she did her best to ignore it. "He confronted the man who attacked me, or whatever was inside him. It seemed to work. I guess he banished it."

Thomas approached the *gellyd*. "That's as good a word as any, I suppose. But how do you banish an army of possessed? From what we've seen, there are too many affected to deal with effectively."

"My mom's trying to save Bartholomew," Natalie said. "But what will that change? One more of you can't make a difference against so many."

"Rescuing Bartholomew won't change anything," Thomas said, gazing into his creation. "But he and Philip work well together. They have solved some of our worst problems. Maybe together they can come up with a solution." His brows drew together, then he stiffened. "I've found them! They're alive!"

Natalie's heartbeat quickened. "Can you bring them back?"

"Just give me—" The blood drained from Thomas's face. "They're not all there."

"What do you mean?" Gene said. "Who's missing?"

A pounding came from the front door. A voice yelled: "Natalie!" She threw a worried look at her uncle. "It's Sean."

"Ignore him," Gene said. Then, to Thomas: "*Who is missing?*"

"You have to bring them back." Kevin stood in the entryway to the living room. He still wore his pajamas from this morning, and his hair hadn't been combed. But his eyes...they were clear and focused. "You have to do it now."

Thomas nodded, and bent his concentration on the *gellyd*.

"Go back to your room," Natalie said. "This isn't the time for your 'magic boy' stuff."

Kevin flinched. His fingers dug into the meaty part of his thigh. "You don't get to make fun of me, Natalie. Not this time."

"You can't talk to me—"

"Stop it, both of you." Gene gripped Kevin by the shoulders. "You know Thomas can't bring them back if you're here, which means you're here for a reason."

"I just—" Kevin's lips trembled. "I can't. I just can't..." The boy suddenly threw his arms around Gene's neck, kissed him on the cheek. "Thank you," he whispered. Then he left, running back upstairs. The door to his bedroom slammed shut.

Gene touched his cheek. "What was that about?"

"Natalie, open the door! Please!" Sean's voice broke on the last word.

"Shit," Gene said. "Nat, get rid of your boyfriend. Thomas, who's missing?"

Natalie swallowed her frustration. Yanking open the door, she was ready to tell Sean off. Two things kept her from blowing up.

One was that Sean wasn't alone. A man stood behind him. She recognized his swarthy features.

Judas Iscariot.

The second was the bright flash of light behind her, the sound of people falling to the floor. Coughing, sputtering, and then a voice filled with sorrow.

"I'm so sorry. We failed."

PART THREE: BETRAYAL AND HOPE

CHAPTER TWELVE

Screaming, Izzy clawed for purchase. Her fingers dug at the crevasse's wall but could not find a niche or indentation, nothing she could use to stop her descent.

Her body slid further into the opening.

She was going to die.

The horrible groaning thundered above her. It sounded close, almost on top of her.

Something hard clamped around her wrist and jerked her out of the crevasse. What held her wasn't even vaguely human: slug-like, with a long body of mottled black skin, a wedge-shaped head, a cluster of orbs that might have been eyes, and two long append-ages that ended in claws not unlike a lobster's.

It roared and shook her. Pain shot up her already wounded arm. The creature dragged her through the air. Another shattering groan, this one loud enough to hurt her ears. She gagged at the stench of putrid flesh that washed over her.

Then it grabbed her other wrist and began to pull.

Izzy's back arched. A searing agony exploded in her shoulders. Her arms were being torn from their sockets.

"*NO!*"

Izzy's head snapped up. She hadn't shouted; she could barely breathe over the pain.

Then she felt it. A power gathering nearby, running like a low-voltage current along her nerves.

Whatever held her roared. It pulled on Izzy's arms. Her flesh and muscle held, though they wouldn't for long.

She heard a shout. She suddenly fell, her wrists no longer held. The impact with the ground knocked the breath out of her.

"Leave now!"

Izzy recognized the voice: Adam Bethel.

"I can't," she said. "I'm hurt."

Adam didn't respond. Instead, she felt his power gather again, and release. The monster bellowed, its roar shaking the ground. A kind of rank fluid oozed from a wound in its side. Adam attacked again. This proved too much, and the creature retreated, bleeding more freely.

Adam approached her. "Are you okay?"

"My arm, it hurts. I think it's dislocated."

"Can you stand?"

She got to her feet, held her wounded arm against her chest. "You came back for me."

Adam Bethel didn't respond.

"Thank you," she said.

"Keep your gratitude," he said. "I didn't do this for you."

"Then why did you come back?"

He gestured. "Follow me."

They hadn't traveled for long before she saw lights flaring in the distance. The fire eruptions.

She had returned to where she started. "That's impossible," she said. "I walked for hours, maybe days. I can't have come all the way back."

"If the terrain were the same all the time, we would find comfort in that predictability. Direction and distance don't matter. Location has no meaning when nothing remains the same, when everything changes. Misery is more than just pain. Perpetual confusion hurts too."

"We have to be going *somewhere*."

He didn't hesitate. "I'm getting you out of here."

"That's not the Adam Bethel I remember."

"I care little for what you think. Who I am now bears little resemblance to who I was back then."

Izzy's hopes surged. "You're really taking me to my friends?"

His body, wrapped in rags and with cruel hooks twisted into his flesh, suddenly hunched over. A spasm of pain crossed his face. "Do not speak. It hurts too much."

Then she remembered. The hooks, they dug into his flesh at any mention of help or kindness—the eternal punishment for his sin of selfishness.

They continued to walk. Before they reached the fire eruptions, Adam Bethel turned. They now walked parallel with them.

As they travelled, Izzy mulled over the riddle of Adam Bethel. A weak and self-absorbed man, he rarely took the time to help anyone but himself. Yet he'd found her, had saved her, and soon he would reunite her with Philip and the others. He acted like a completely different man.

Then she recalled their conversation about redemption. He called himself unredeemable, but…perhaps…he wasn't completely gone. What would have gotten to him so much—

Then she had it. "Katie," she said. "You poor man, you're doing this for your daughter."

Hooks curled into his flesh, deeper this time, and he groaned. "I do this for no one but myself."

"You still love her, don't you?"

"Leave me alone. What I'm trying to do is difficult enough."

"What's so hard about walking?"

His lips parted into a snarl. "You always thought you knew more than everyone else."

She noticed a pattern. Like a petulant child, whenever contradicted, Adam Bethel became angry. Well, she knew how to handle that. Her estranged husband had a similar attitude.

"I'm sorry. I didn't mean to insult you."

He didn't respond, but she sensed her words had mollified him.

"What *are* you trying to do?" she said.

"I told you, find your friends."

"No, I mean what are you doing right now? What's so difficult?"

"If I answer, will you shut up?"

"I promise."

"While it's true that nothing here is consistent, that doesn't mean it can't be controlled to some extent. The easy way to find your friends would mean walking for days or years before we ran into them. I have plenty of time. You don't. Two of your friends shine like beacons, but with hope instead of light. I can sense them. So I am altering distance so we reach them quicker."

Izzy marveled at what Adam had said. "Can anyone here do that?"

He nodded. "Some better than others."

"Last question. Will it take long?"

"Who cares. Time, like distance, holds no meaning here."

"What does that mean?"

"What it means," Adam Bethel said, his voice harsh and filled with anger, "is that when you go back—if you make it back—hours could have passed, or years, even centuries. Time has no meaning here."

Centuries? She could return to a world that no longer existed as she knew it; to Natalie and Kevin, both long dead and in their graves.

Despair sapped her will, and she stumbled. Small stones and pebbles scattered beneath her feet.

"We're almost there," Adam said, and halted. "Over that small ridge. Can you see them?"

Izzy forced herself to look. "I don't see anybody."

"Not on the ground, idiot. Above it."

"Above—?" Then she saw it: a faint glow like a spray of stars against Topheth's bleak sky. They swirled upward, caught on eddies of something she couldn't detect. "How did I miss that?"

"Because you did not know what to look for." Adam Bethel winced as more hooks sunk into his flesh. "Go. Leave. Do not come back. You won't find me." He turned to leave.

"Wait? Is Katie there?"

He hesitated, then nodded.

"Is she alive?"

"Yes."

"Adam?"

"I told you to leave."

"Adam, look at me."

Slowly, reluctantly, he met her gaze. "What?"

"Don't you want to see your daughter?"

"You want her last memory of me to be this?" He thrust his arms out, displaying his bandages and hooks. "What good would that do her?"

"Better than the memory she has now," she shot back. "You with your head blown off by that shotgun!"

Adam Bethel lowered his arms. "I had it planned out. Jenny would come home from work. She'd find me before Katie got home from school. Katie wasn't supposed to even see me. It's not my fault."

"For fuck's sake, Adam. You killed yourself, you hurt your wife and daughter more than you could imagine, and you're still avoiding responsibility. Katie is over that ridge. She hasn't seen you in years. You might want to use this opportunity to heal some of the pain you caused her. Take responsibility for a change."

"You don't understand." Whether in response to her words or to his own inner struggle, the hooks corkscrewed into him. Rags pulled at the side of his head, dragging it painfully downward. He let out a cry of anguish that nearly broke her heart. "She can't see me like this!"

"She's stronger than you think. You'd be proud of what she's accomplished. And those...those *things*." Izzy pointed to the hooks embedded in his skin. "They're a punishment. I see that. But maybe you're being given a chance. Have you thought of that? You made mistakes in life. What if you could make up for some of them now? What do you think would happen to your... punishment?"

"The pain never ends," Adam Bethel cried. "Why can't you understand that?"

"It may—if you have the courage to face it. Look, this is a

place of punishment. You're suffering. I get that. But there has to be a point to it. Who cares if you're punished when there's no opportunity to learn from it? Have you thought of that? And to learn is to better yourself. Maybe you've never been brave enough to try."

"You haven't existed here. You haven't seen the things I have. There is no hope."

Izzy pointed to the ridge. "You said there is hope over there. You can see it. Suppose you're right and there is no hope in this place. We brought it with us. Two of my friends, they're special. More special than anyone you've ever met. They might be the hope you need—the help you need. Come with me. Talk to Katie. Face up to what you did. Be a dad for a change."

Some of the madness fled from Adam Bethel's eyes. "Special?"

"Trust me, Adam. Talk to your daughter."

She couldn't spend more time convincing him. Either he would follow or he wouldn't, so she set off for the ridge.

Soft footsteps followed her.

The distance to the ridge ended up being farther than she thought, but she eventually crested it. Down in a shallow valley on the other side, three figures stood. Two, both men, glowed with a soft illumination. The third was female.

Not bothering to check if Adam Bethel followed her, Izzy set off to meet up with her friends.

***

The ridge rose at a sharp angle and she was panting by the time she crested it.

As she descended into the valley, the others turned to face her. Philip smiled. Matthew nodded. Katie handed Thomas's cube to Philip and hugged her.

"Philip and Matthew just found me," she said. "We were going to look for you next, but Philip said you were nearby."

Izzy hugged her back. She hadn't understood until now how fond she had grown of the spirited girl. "It's okay. I don't know what happened, how we got separated, but we're together again."

"How did you find us?"

"That's complicated. Does anybody know what happened?"

"Something intervened," Philip said. "It separated the four of us."

"Four?" Izzy said. "There were five of us. We need to find Gene."

"That's the problem," Matthew said. The Forever Man looked grimmer than usual, his face pale and drawn. "We don't think he's here."

"I can't sense him," Philip said. "For some reason, he never arrived in Topheth."

"How sure are you of this?" Izzy said. "I don't want to go back if it means risking leaving him here."

"Well, I've never been here before," Philip said, "but there's no reason to think I can't find things here the way I do in other places. I could sense you and Katie and Matthew." He hesitated. "And I sense the man who led you here."

Katie frowned. "You found someone to help you in this awful place?"

"Yes," Izzy said, reluctant to say more right now. She wasn't sure Adam Bethel would have the courage to show himself, and she didn't want to cause Katie unnecessary grief. "Did he leave?" she asked Philip.

"He's still—" Philip said. "No, wait. He's moving. He's headed this way."

Matthew drew himself taller. "Is he a danger?"

"I don't believe so," Izzy said. "He's afraid, and very confused, but I don't think he'll harm anyone." The memory of Adam Bethel's confrontation with the beast clawed at the back of her mind. "Though he does possess the capacity to inflict pain, or even kill."

"Izzy, Katie," Philip said. "Stand behind Matthew and me."

Izzy drew Katie by the hand. Once behind the two Forever Men, she stopped. She didn't release Katie's hand.

Out of the gloom, appearing slowly like a figment of nightmare come to life, Adam Bethel approached. He stooped even more than before, his body drawn tight in upon itself by the rags and hooks. Spit slicked a corner of his mouth. Even bandaged as he was, fear showed clearly in his black eyes.

"That's close enough," Philip called out. "Come no nearer."

Adam Bethel halted. He licked his lips, then nodded at Izzy. "I came. I didn't want to, but I did. You have no idea how hard this is for me; how much it hurts."

Katie's hand clamped down on Izzy's. The blood had drained from her face. "I know that voice. I know who that is."

"Give him a chance," Izzy whispered. "He's suffered so much."

"No," Katie said stiffly. "I won't have anything to do with him."

"Who is he?" Philip said.

The gloom seemed to gather around Katie. Her nostrils flared in anger. "He's my father."

***

Neither Forever Man looked surprised. Philip would know of her father, given their friendship, and nothing seemed to startle Matthew.

"Can I approach?" Adam Bethel mewled like a cat caught in the grip of a pit bull. "Please?"

Katie started to answer, but Izzy cut her off. "I believe in my heart he's being given a chance. If he doesn't do this, he'll wander this horrible place for eternity knowing he didn't do anything to help you. Move past your anger. Do you really want the responsibility for condemning him?"

"You know what he did," Katie said. "He killed himself. He left me and Mom to deal with the wreckage he caused." She swallowed. Hearing her father's voice hurt so damn much. "I was only a child. How was I supposed to understand, or cope? And now you want me to greet him like a long-lost friend? No. You ask too much. Any responsibility falls on him. I accept no blame for his actions."

To Katie's surprise, Matthew spoke. His words lashed out like whip strikes. "Have you learned nothing over the years? All that we do, all that we are, is based on forgiveness. One man taught us the power of compassion, the power of love. We are so much more than what we think. Our ability to love one another is what makes us human. Here is a man who made a mistake; a terrible one. Yes, he hurt you. Yes, he left you behind to deal with the grief and the guilt. But do you see what he has become? What this place has done to him?"

Katie faltered. A shadow flitted across her features; a cloud of confusion passing before a sun of rage. She released Izzy's hand and approached her father.

Adam Bethel seemed to shrink from her presence. Hooks tunneled into his flesh, causing black blood to seep into the rags. "No closer, please. I can barely stand the pain as it is."

"You left me," Katie said. "You killed yourself, and you left me with Mom. A kid, alone with an alcoholic. Do you know what that did to me? Do you have any idea the pain you caused?"

Her father held out his arms. Rags covered his body, his head. Ugly metal hooks pierced him in many places. "What do you think this is? I pay for the pain I caused you and your mom with every tortured moment of my existence. I will feel that pain for the rest of eternity." He folded his arms around his chest. "I was too weak. I should have been a better father, a better husband. I know these things now. But I cannot undo what I did. I'm bound by my decision forever."

Katie's cheeks grew hot. "You weren't weak—you were selfish. Calling it weakness sets up a straw man, someone else to blame. You were strong enough to take your own life. That means you were strong enough to face your failures. You chose not to. I won't let you get away with minimizing your responsibility."

"No, that's not true. I—" The hooks curled into him and he cried out. "Yes! You're right! I'm sorry, but you're right. I could've tried harder. But the depression. It was like a weight on my heart, it hurt so bad. I don't think you understand."

"I understand there is always a choice." She wiped at the tears running down her cheeks. "Did you ever love me?"

Adam Bethel either coughed or barked—a harsh sound that sent shivers up Katie's spine—followed by a series of softer moans. But when she listened closer she realized they weren't moans.

Her dad was crying.

Someone stepped up behind her.

"Go to him," Philip whispered. "Show me what you've learned."

"You taught me how to kill," she said, "but who do you think gave me a reason to kill, to try and stop the evils of the world? Why do you think I followed Bartholomew, why I joined with all of you? It's because of what you represent. You have purpose, a drive to help the weak. Innocents, you call them, and for the most part they are. But my father showed me the darker side of life, how pain and misery and guilt can pile on to such an extent that someone can take his own life. When I fight alongside you or Bartholomew, I fight to keep another person from killing himself." She lowered her voice. "I failed with Miles. I won't fail again."

"Miles Knight sacrificed himself to save people." Philip's words were harsh against her back. "What he did was noble, not an act of cowardice. You demean yourself if you think otherwise."

"There's nothing noble about this man," Katie said. "Don't compare him to Miles."

Adam Bethel took a step forward. "Who is this Miles? Your husband?"

He could have been, she thought. As selfish as he was when they'd met, he grew into one of the bravest men in history.

"He was a friend," she said softly. "I loved him."

Philip put a hand on her shoulder. "You talk of sacrifice and nobility. You're right, they are connected. But you're missing one part. Probably the most essential part."

"What's that?"

"Forgiveness," Philip said, and pushed her forward.

Katie could feel the eyes of the others on her as she approached her father, the man she had despised for most of her life. The man who had turned her into an assassin.

"You could have left just now," she told him. "Instead, you came here. Why?"

Her father's black eyes fixed on her. The tone of his voice changed. He no longer spoke like a beaten man, one tortured beyond sanity. He spoke now like a parent, like the father she'd always wanted. "You were never a stupid child. Use your head. Think."

She considered his words. "You're doing it for yourself. You want to escape this condemnation, so you're doing what you think will help aid your escape. You haven't changed. The only motive you have is selfishness."

"It could be," her father said, nodding. He looked like a servant agreeing with his master. "But you'd be wrong."

"Fine. Enlighten me."

"You're so young," her father said. "You know little of the world, let alone *this* world. There is no hope of escape; punishment is eternal. Selfishness gets me nowhere. Nothing I do will stop these hooks. I will forever bear them, and the memories their pain inflicts. What I do, Katie, I do for you. I have one last chance to be a father, to do something a father could be proud of, and then that moment will pass, never to arrive again. I've made so many mistakes, missed so many things. Yes, I blamed my depression, because I was depressed. But I should have blamed myself." He paused. "Or maybe I did blame myself. Maybe that's why I never felt better, why the therapy or the medication never seemed to help. I could never get out from under that burden of guilt. Maybe I knew it was me all along."

Adam Bethel stood a little straighter. "It makes sense, not that it matters. I'm a condemned man. But I can do something beneficial before you go. I can give you a chance to confront the man who hurt you, who hurt your mom. I heard you just now. You've become an assassin of sorts. You said I turned you into one. I can't let that go on, Katie. You are too good of a person. You can't destroy me; redemption is never that easy. But you can take that anger out on me, deal directly with the man who caused it. Then maybe you won't feel that compulsion to harm. Go ahead. Do what you need to do. I want my baby girl to be happy again, and I want to be the one to give her that chance. That's what a real dad would do."

Katie felt a constriction in her chest. She had held this man in contempt for so long, hearing him speak like a caring parent had set her off balance. He had offered her a chance she had long dreamt about, and now that she had the opportunity, she found herself hesitating. This man—her father—had suffered so much. He would suffer more, for longer than she could even imagine.

Izzy believed she should give him a chance. So did Matthew: *All we do, all we are, is based on forgiveness.*

Katie touched her father's cheek. "You are the one who suffered most. Yes, I hated you, for what you did and for leaving me behind.

But I see that I was being selfish too. I'd turned those feelings inward, and they did harm. You and I are alike, but in different ways, if that makes sense. So no, I'm not going to take anything out on you. All I'm going to say is I'm sorry, and I love you, and I hate that you will be paying this price. Thank you, Dad. This will take a while, but I think I can finally let my anger go. You did what a dad is supposed to do, which also makes me sad. I won't be able to know you as a father, only as a man who is being punished."

She lowered her arm and stepped back.

"I'm proud of you," Philip said. "I'll make sure Bartholomew knows of this."

Katie didn't have words sufficient for a reply, so she said nothing.

***

Izzy felt her heart swell with pride. The little girl who had hurt for so long, who had been left broken by a man she desperately wanted to love, had found it in herself to forgive.

Philip approached Adam Bethel. His white beard bristled with determination. "Do you know me?"

"Yes," Adam Bethel said, cringing as Philip stopped before him. "You are the Promise."

Izzy's brow furrowed. She hadn't heard Philip called *that* before.

"And do you know what that means?" Philip said.

Adam Bethel nodded. "The Promise is the end of suffering, but I never believed in it. False hope is part of my suffering; without the false hope of the Promise, my torment would not be complete."

"And now? You stand in the presence of the Promise. Do you still not believe?"

"I have to believe," Adam Bethel said. "You and the other one"—he indicated Matthew—"I saw your Promise from far off. It drew me here." He issued a low growl. "Others will see it. They will come. You are in danger as long as you remain. You have my daughter. Please, take her from this place. I thought my torment complete, but if she were to die here, it would ruin me. She does not deserve this fate. I'm begging you. Depart."

Izzy glanced at Katie. Tears streamed down the girl's cheeks.

"Perhaps you have learned," Philip said, drawing Izzy's attention back to the exchange happening in front of her. "Perhaps your penance is done."

Adam Bethel looked unbelievingly at Philip. "You mean to invoke the Promise?"

"Yes," Philip said. "You have shown repentance. You are now the man you were intended to be. To keep you here would serve no further purpose." Then he smiled. "I know your daughter. She is an exceptional woman. I do this not just for you, but for her." He raised his hands, clearly preparing to do something, and paused. He looked over his shoulder at Matthew. "Would you like to do this?"

"No," Matthew said. "Katie is your friend more than mine. The honor is yours."

Philip turned back to Adam Bethel. He began to sing. Izzy didn't recognize the words, but the melody spoke to her; it made her think of love and happiness and laughing. To experience such joy in a place like Topheth left her feeling unreal.

As Philip sang, as his words and intonations filled the air, Adam Bethel changed. The cruel hooks uncoiled and left his flesh. The rags that had bound him for so long unraveled in gore-sodden streamers and fell to the ground. His exposed skin, full of seeping wounds, healed. His flesh filled out, his bent frame straightened. But the changes to his face caught Izzy's breath: Adam Bethel's black eyes cleared, revealing the warm brown irises she remembered.

"Thank you," Adam Bethel said, his voice clear and strong. "Thank you so much."

"You no longer belong here," Philip said. "It's time for you to go home."

Adam Bethel raised his hand. "Wait. Katie, come here."

Katie approach her father. The girl's movements were slow, deliberate, almost hesitant. She stopped about a foot from her father, her head bent, her eyes fixed on the ground.

"Katie," Adam Bethel said. "Look at me."

Katie raised her head. She was weeping. "You're going away again."

"I've learned—I've grown—and I'm tired of the pain. I want relief. You understand that, don't you?"

"Will we always be apart?"

"Not anymore," Adam Bethel said. "Because of you, not anymore. I've seen who you've become, and I'm so very proud. I know most of the hard work was done by your mother, but I like to think I played some small part."

"You did," Katie said, and hugged him. "I love you."

"I love you, too."

"Katie," Philip said. "Step back."

She hugged her father tighter. "Can't I have more time."

Adam Bethel extricated himself from his daughter's embrace. "You don't have more time. You have to leave. I wasn't kidding about the danger." He stepped back, his eyes bright, and turned to Philip. "Do it," he said. "Send me home."

Philip bowed, a slight bend at the waist. "You are once again an Innocent. Go to your Promise."

What happened next Izzy had seen before, weeks ago on a grassy meadow in Dearborn, Michigan, when Miles Knight had placed the Crown of Thorns on his head: Adam Bethel faded. This body, so recently healed, became opaque, then translucent, until all that remained of him were clear lines of light at the edges of his lanky frame, until even those faded.

And he was gone.

CHAPTER THIRTEEN

They traveled for hours.

Philip led the way. Katie and Izzy followed close behind, talking about what had happened. Matthew brought up the rear, wrapped in his own thoughts.

Philip suddenly halted. "We're getting close. Bartholomew is nearby."

Katie lifted the wooden cube. "What am I supposed to do with this? How will we get his spirit into it?"

"Thomas fashioned it for such a purpose," Philip said with a shrug. "If Matthew or I concentrate, Bartholomew's spirit should simply travel into it."

Katie said, "That sounds too easy."

"We have to trust in Thomas," Philip said, and began walking.

They traveled for what seemed like hours more. The perpetual darkness numbed Izzy to the passage of time and distance. When Philip pulled up short again, Izzy almost ran into him.

"What is it?" Izzy said.

"There's something ahead," Philip said. "Matthew?"

The other Forever Man joined them. "I sense it too."

"Sense what?" Katie asked.

"Bartholomew, for one," Philip said. "And something else. It's barring the way."

"We can't go around it?" Izzy said.

"Too big," Matthew said, his voice filled with awe. "It spans so much area."

"What is it?" Izzy repeated. "What do you sense?"

"A building," Philip said. "I've never encountered something this massive. If we could see to the horizon, we wouldn't be able to see it end-to-end. It's that big."

No one spoke, then Katie said, "Is the building empty?"

Philip snorted. "You're the one who said this sounded too easy. What do you think?"

It took another two hours for them to reach the edifice; "building" simply didn't convey the size.

The surface seemed irregular: it bowed out in some spots, while other sections looked smooth. When they were close enough, Izzy realized the edifice had been constructed of bones. Millions upon millions of human bones. The wall facing them stretched as far as they could see, and it rose into the dark sky until it disappeared from view. Gouges and cuts on the bones suggested something had clawed at the wall, or gnawed on it.

"I don't see a door," Katie said. She held Thomas's cube tightly in her arms. "How are we supposed to get in?"

Izzy touched the wall. She couldn't see how the bones were fixed together, other than by the crushing weight of such a large construction. "This is disgusting."

"They're the bones of the condemned." Matthew scratched at his right forearm, as if the skin under his sleeve itched. "All these people, over thousands and thousands of years. You're right, it is disgusting."

"Disgusting or not," Philip said, "we have to find a way in." He touched the wall with both hands and bowed his head. "That way," he said moments later, leading them to the left. "I sense an opening. It's not far."

Katie found it before the others: a ragged hole like a mouth in the face of the wall. Broken bones hung from the top like teeth.

"Something in there smells horrible," Izzy said. She had investigated crime scenes involving dead bodies where the stench of putrefaction had made her almost puke. Whatever was inside this horror smelled worse.

"Doesn't matter," Philip said. "Bartholomew is that way. Either we go through, or we go home."

"No one is going home just yet," Izzy said. "Philip, you lead the way. Katie, stick with Matthew." The Forever Man gave her an uncomfortable look. "Do you have a better idea, Matthew?"

Matthew shook his head. "Your plan is fine."

Izzy looked at where he was scratching. "Is there something wrong with your arm?"

"It just itches," he replied. "Keep going. We're almost done with this."

The opening turned out to be a tunnel leading downward and ending in a wide room. The ruddy glow from the upper region was stronger here. Bones continued to form the walls. They arched above them, forming grotesque buttresses. The place reminded Izzy of a church, albeit a corrupt one.

"What is making that smell?" Katie said, a hand covering her mouth and nose.

"The dead," Philip said. "I think they collect here."

"Will they try to stop us?" Izzy said.

"If you were condemned to spend eternity in this awful place, and suddenly four living people appeared, evoking memories of life, would you ignore them?"

"Adam told me you and Matthew would attract them," Izzy said. "He said you glow."

Philip started forward. "We may attract them, but I doubt they will attack us. They aren't like what we encountered above. These are poor wretches with nowhere to go and nothing to look forward to."

"If there are enough of them," Matthew said, following close behind his brother, "the sheer numbers could stop us."

They found a hallway at the other end of the room that ended in a four-way intersection.

"Look at the walls," Katie whispered.

The bones here looked...fresher. Scraps of meat and gore hung from them. One skull still had an eye in its socket. Izzy half expected it to move when they passed.

"Bartholomew is that way." Philip pointed to the right-hand corridor. The putrid smell came strongest from that direction. "I believe the dead have gathered around him. He may not have a living, breathing body, but his spirit would glow as brightly to them as Matthew's and mine. We might have to fight our way through."

"Then let's get going," Izzy said, her chest tight with fear. She would do anything for Bartholomew, but fighting a sea of the dead? "I want this done before we need another rest."

Philip headed down the right-hand corridor. Soon the walls took on a glistening sheen, and a sharp, coppery scent filled the air. Blood. Blood coated the walls.

Up ahead, the corridor widened, then fell away into darkness. They stood in a space so vast Izzy's mind had trouble comprehending how something this huge could exist. She could not see the top, the sides, or the other end.

And filling the space were the bodies of the dead. Naked, some with rotted flesh, others with missing limbs, they milled aimlessly about, bumping into one another. Several looked up and howled.

"Bartholomew is there," Philip said, pointing beyond the mass of the dead. "On the other side of these poor souls."

"If they are attracted to Bartholomew," Matthew said, "then they will also be attracted to us. We'll draw them in like moths to a flame."

"We'll never get across," Izzy said, dismayed. "There are too many."

"We have to," Katie said. "I'll go alone if I have to. I won't go back without Bartholomew."

"We're not splitting up," Izzy said. "Philip, you're the biggest. You push, we'll follow."

Philip surged into the bodies. Izzy grabbed Katie's hand and followed. Matthew strode close behind them.

Together, they forced their way through the dead. Hands groped for them. Bodies shambled closer, hindering their progress. The stench hit them like a physical blow.

And still the dead came.

"They're massing ahead," Philip said. "Already a barrier is forming."

"Not a barrier," Matthew said. "A ring. They've surrounded us. They're trying to get close."

Izzy squeezed Katie's hand. "Can we make it through?"

"We have to," Philip said. "There's no way out now."

Their advance proved difficult. Philip managed to push aside a few bodies; more of the condemned quickly replaced them. Izzy shoved and Katie shouldered, to little avail. There were too many. Soon the dead had forced the four interlopers closer together. Izzy could barely move her arms.

"They don't need to attack," Katie said. "Their numbers alone will crush us."

Philip threw himself into the crowd and a few dead fell back, but his efforts were short-lived. Too many bodies hindered them. The dead pressed harder, closer. Hands reached out to clutch at them. One pulled at Izzy's hair. Another grappled with Katie, almost knocking the cube from her hands. But most of the dead reached for Philip and Matthew. They clawed and scratched, eager to get close to the Forever Men.

Izzy pushed away a woman who had a gash across her throat. "We're surrounded. And there are more coming."

"We can't turn back." Katie shouted over the clamor of the dead. "We have to keep going."

"You don't understand," Philip said, panting from his exertions. "There are too many. We can't move."

"We'll stand behind you," Izzy told Philip. "The three of us will push from behind. You just keep going." She glanced over her shoulder. "Matthew, I want you to—"

The Forever Man had stopped his advance. He stood several paces behind them, a circle of dead clamoring for him, his arms raised, the sleeves of his shirt rolled back.

"I am the Promise!" Matthew called out. "I have come to you! Hear me! I am the Promise!"

The dead halted their clamoring. As one, they turned to face Matthew.

"Philip!" Izzy cried, grabbing him by the shoulder. "Matthew! Look at him!"

Philip turned. His eyes widened. "Matthew! No!"

Matthew, his arms raised, continued to shout at the dead.

That's when Izzy noted something new on Matthew: on his right forearm, which had been unblemished, a mark had appeared. Similar to the other Forever Men, it resembled a tattoo. Where Bartholomew had a teardrop shape under his left eye, and Philip had a crescent moon on his right hand, Matthew's new mark resembled a stylized star. It radiated like hope from a point on his skin.

Then on Matthew's left forearm, another mark gradually appeared, identical to the one on his right forearm.

Matthew, who, much to his personal pain and embarrassment, had never borne the mark of the Forever Men, now possessed two.

Matthew turned his attention to Philip. "The answer is balance. The Crown sent a man where no living man had ever gone. That act threw everything out of the balance. That one act weakened the Veil, and allowed the dead to return to the world of the living. To stop the possessions, we need to repair the Veil. Don't you see? We need to restore the balance. To do that, someone needs to stay here, a living person. One who will live forever." He swallowed hard. "You always had a purpose. I never had one. I never felt like a brother to the rest of you. Now I have my purpose. I am supposed to stay. As long as I do, the balance will be restored. The madness will end."

Philip tried to push past Izzy. His face had contorted; his eyes were livid with rebuke, his cheeks flush with denial. "You will not do this," he said. "We can find another way to fix the Veil."

"This was your decision," Izzy said to Matthew. "You planned to do this before we left. That's why you were so upset."

Matthew nodded. The dead shuffled toward him. He backed away and the dead allowed his retreat.

"Don't stop me," he said, his tone pleading. "Let me be who I was meant to be."

Philip surged forward. "I won't leave you!"

Still Matthew retreated and the dead followed. His next words were directed at Izzy. "I do this for your children, and the children of the Innocents. I do this for everyone, for we are all children at heart. If I don't, everyone could die. Please, don't let Marbæs destroy the world."

Izzy felt torn. She wanted to save her friend, to prevent this sacrifice. But she also knew he was correct: without restoring the Veil's balance, her world—her children's world—would turn into a nightmare.

In the span of one heartbeat to the next, she made her decision. She stepped in front of Philip, blocking his advance.

"Turn around," she said. "Don't make his sacrifice meaningless."

Philip spluttered. "What? You can't possibly mean—"

"You and the others were put here to save Innocents," she said, her voice shaking. "You have done that but he hasn't, and that knowledge has hurt him deeply."

The agony tearing at Philip was almost palpable. "Yes, but—"

"He has a chance to save more Innocents than any of you could in all your years. Let him have his purpose. Let him be who he was intended to be." Her voice firmed. "The marks on his forearms, they prove he's right. He's found his purpose. Or are you going to start questioning the man who gave him the job?"

The strain in Philip reached some sort of climax. He threw his head back and howled. "Matthew!"

"I hear you," Matthew said, his voice clear above the din of the dead. "I hear you, and I tell you that I love you. I love you and the others. But I also tell you to leave. Go save Bartholomew. He will be needed in the years to come. My only use is here." He moved away at a faster pace. The dead hurried after him. "I make one request, though. When the final confrontation with Marbæs comes, as we all know it will..." He blinked back tears. "When that day comes, promise me that you will hold me in your hearts. If you do, I will know, somehow. I will know what happens. Now go! Save Bartholomew. Tell him of my deed. I think he will be proud."

Before any of them could react, Matthew turned and strode away. "I am the Promise. Follow me!"

The entire mass of dead followed.

When the way was clear, Izzy said, "Let's go. We also made a promise, and I intend to keep it."

203

***

Izzy followed Philip and Katie across the blasted terrain. She relied on the Forever Man's preternatural sense of direction; the fractured landscape looked similarly bleak in every direction, and Philip had the skill to fix in his mind a destination or object. His role as the Finder had become indispensable to the party.

Katie slowed, allowing Philip to move ahead and Izzy to catch up with her. The girl hugged Thomas's cube to her chest as if it were a precious infant. Perhaps it was; if they were successful, Bartholomew's soul would return to his body, which could be seen as a peculiar form of rebirth.

"I feel terrible," Katie said, her face drawn and haggard. "There must be something we can do for Matthew, some way to get him back?"

Izzy suddenly recalled a conversation with Kevin, not a week ago, during one of his few lucid moments. They had been standing in the kitchen, waiting for dinner.

"*I feel sorry for you,*" her son had said. "*For all of you. Most of all, I feel sorry for Matthew.*"

He hadn't been able to say why, his moment of clarity slowly crumbling under the weight of his von Kliner's syndrome. The autistic-like disorder afforded him a sort of prescience; a glimpse into the future, or, she supposed, a possible future. This time, it seemed correct.

But he had also told her one other thing: "*You have to go away. It's the only way to save Bartholomew...only, the answer you're looking for isn't where you think it is.*"

She glanced at the cube Katie carried: the answer to their problem. Did Kevin mean it wasn't going to work, that they had travelled this far for nothing? Had Matthew sacrificed himself to an empty cause?

She thought about it. No, Matthew's sacrifice would repair the Veil; if he was correct, it would stop the dead from crossing, stop the possessions, stop the eventual downfall of humanity.

It would stop Marbæs from winning. But Marbæs was a creature of time, and she possessed incredible cunning. She would have known, or at least suspected, a way existed to fix the Veil, and that the Forever Men would attempt it. Yet, she did nothing to prevent them.

Did she want the Veil fixed? If she did, she would have to gain something greater, something far more valuable. Marbæs played this game on several levels, like a chess master; sacrifice one piece to capture the king and win the game.

What would be more valuable than destroying humanity, the end goal of all her plotting?

Unless Marbæs thought humanity could not be destroyed.

Was there something else out there, some power of which Izzy or the Forever Men were unaware, something Marbæs feared even more than Bartholomew and his brothers?

She grew cold at the thought.

"Izzy?" Katie nudged her ribs with an elbow. "You with us?"

"What Matthew did," Izzy said slowly, "he was destined to do. He waited long for a purpose, and now he has one. It may be a terrible purpose, but it will save billions. I'm sick at the thought of him existing here forever, balanced against the stresses placed on the Veil. But it needed to happen. Who are we to take what was given to him?" She pointed to Thomas's cube. "Keep that safe, but also be careful. It may not be what we think it is."

Katie frowned. "Thomas made it. Surely he'd know if it was a fake."

"Not a fake, just not necessarily the solution. All I'm saying is, keep your eyes open."

They had walked for maybe an hour more, given the number of steps Izzy counted, when Philip abruptly stopped. Before them, the vast space narrowed to a point in the distance. The sudden construction looked like a black stone throat. A nauseating green light shone in the distance.

"Bartholomew is there," Philip said. The strain he felt could be seen in the lines of his face, the shadows like bruises around his eyes. He hadn't spoken about Matthew's sacrifice. Izzy doubted he would, not until they finished saving Bartholomew. "I can feel him now. He's in pain, great pain. More than the pain he feels every day. It's a pain of the soul."

"What do you think is happening?" Izzy asked.

"I don't know," Philip replied. "But I'm afraid."

Shifting the cube into one arm, Katie place a hand on Philip's shoulder. The gesture seemed to almost break the man. He swallowed roughly.

"This is the last part of the journey, the dark rescue of our friend," he said. "Pray it is enough."

***

The passageway, like most in this damned place, was longer than it appeared. They were exhausted by the time they reached the narrowest portion.

Izzy wanted to call for a rest. They needed time to recover their strength. Philip, however, wanted to continue.

"We're almost done," he said. "We need to keep going."

"We're not like you," Izzy said. "We don't have the same stamina. Katie and I will need at least an hour or two of rest."

Philip cocked an eyebrow at her. "You haven't noticed, have you?"

Izzy looked blandly at him.

Katie stepped forward. "Noticed what?"

"When was the last time you ate, or drank water?" Philip asked. "When was the last time you actually slept?"

"I don't know," Izzy said, thinking back. "A day, maybe?"

"Longer," Philip said. "More like three. And you keep going without sustenance. It's this place." He gestured around him. "It has a gradual effect on you. It changes you. Soon, if you don't leave, you will not need food, water, anything. And you might not be *able* to leave."

"Matthew," Izzy whispered. "That's how he will maintain the Veil, how he will live here for eternity."

Katie let out a horrified gasp. "Dear God."

"He made his decision," Philip said. "He accepted his fate. In the end, his dedication proved greater than all of ours combined. We hope for death one day, for a release from our duties, but he will never stop being a Forever Man."

Nearby, the green light pulsed, reflecting sickly against the glistening basalt walls of the cavern.

"Okay," she said. "We don't stop. It won't do any good to reach Bartholomew and then be unable to return him to our world. Philip, take us to him."

Katie smiled, though it looked wan and uneasy. Philip simply nodded.

Together, they approached the light, and their friend.

The smell hit Izzy first: a canker of decay in the air that turned her stomach. She gagged, brought a hand to her mouth. Katie pressed her lips into a thin line of determination, though her eyes watered from the smell. Philip seemed to ignore the stench.

As they advanced, the foul odor grew until Izzy had to stop. "What is that smell? I can barely breathe."

"Topheth is made of different levels," Philip said. "We are about to enter one of its lower ones."

Katie turned and vomited, though nothing came out of her. She dry-heaved until she regained control of her stomach.

"That's awful," she said, wiping her mouth with her sleeve. "Absolutely awful."

"Expect it to get worse," Philip said, and advanced into the throat of Topheth.

The ground turned rugged. Wide cracks ran in various directions, the green light seeping from the gaps. They stepped around them, and jumped the wider spans. But none were wide enough to prevent their approach.

"Shouldn't this place be guarded?" Izzy said. "If Bartholomew is so important, why aren't we being stopped, or at least challenged?"

"Marbæs can only do so much," Philip said. "Topheth is beyond her control, so she can't set up traps or throw hordes of condemned at us. And it's not just her. Judas has a part in this, one I haven't been able to fathom. He sent Bartholomew here, apparently with Bartholomew's permission. There has to be a reason the old man would agree to this madness." He scrubbed his face with his hands. "This place is deadly enough to stop us. So far, we have been fortunate."

They reached the narrowest point of the throat. Before them, the ground fell away, and the walls of the cavern receded into the distance. A craggy path led downward.

Philip pointed. "He's down there."

The stench, so awful now Izzy could barely breathe, acted like a physical barrier. She didn't think she could push her way through it. "How far?" she asked, gasping.

"Not far," Philip said, "yet far enough."

Katie hugged the cube. "Let's get this over with," she said, and stepped onto the path.

Philip stopped her. "I go first. You're next. Izzy, you follow last." His tone left no room for argument.

With the burly Forever Man in the lead, they descended. Izzy had to push herself. The air felt heavy with pain. A sourness filled her as she descended. Something awful lay down there. Such sorrow. Such misery. It tore at her heart.

Soon the path halted, and they reached a flat stone plane. Off to her right Izzy saw a structure. Low, black, with a door and no windows. A light, this one reddish, flickered from inside.

The ghastly stench seemed to flow from inside that structure.

"There," Philip said, indicating the structure. He spoke in a thin voice. The putrescent odor had finally gotten to him, and he tried to conserve his breath. "Bartholomew is in there."

Katie rushed forward. Philip tried to catch her, but the girl was too fast.

"Bartholomew!" she cried.

"Katie!" Philip shouted and bolted after her.

"Dammit," Izzy said and followed.

Katie reached the structure first and stopped. Izzy, close behind, realized why: the corrupt smell and the sense of anguish had risen to such a level that it felt like hitting a brick wall. The torment that must be going on in there...

Philip arrived and grabbed Katie by the shoulder. The man simmered with rage. "You wait for me!" he shouted. "Do you understand?"

Katie looked defiantly up at her friend. "He's my friend, too!"

"Everybody calm down." Izzy didn't need them losing their cool. "We're finally here. Let's go see what we can do."

When neither Philip nor Katie responded, Izzy shoved them both. "Listen to me. We made it here together, we finish this together. Don't let Topheth get to you. We are in this as one. Got it?"

Her push seemed to work; the anger faded from their expressions, though each retained an air of wariness.

"Good," Izzy said. "Keep your heads. We're not out of danger yet." *The answer you're looking for isn't where you think it is.* Could they have been wrong all along? "We enter together."

And so they did.

⁕⁕⁕

The red flickering came from two braziers flanking a plain wooden chair. In the chair sat Bartholomew, or at least a ghostly representation of him; he lacked the solidness of a real person. He faced away from Izzy, his gaze locked on the image being played out in front of him.

On the opposite side of the room, where a wall should have been, Izzy saw a swiftly flowing river with a sandy bank and tall trees. A woman lay on the ground, her blue dress torn, blood seeping from her mouth. A man stood next to her. She recognized him.

The Cybell.

A creature of Marbæs, the Cybell had helped Reverend Destiny in his efforts to instigate a global war to end humanity. Bartholomew had destroyed the fiend. But here the Cybell was, short, swarthy, his mouth warped in an evil grin.

"Oh, no," Philip whispered, a look of dismay on his face. "Oh Bartholomew, no."

Izzy watched as the Cybell pulled a cruel blade from his robes. With careful, almost gleeful precision, the creature set about stripping the flesh from the prone woman's body. He peeled ribbons of skin from her as she screamed, though Izzy couldn't hear the woman's cries. The Cybell worked efficiently. He soon had the woman flayed, his hands coated with her blood.

Then, with preternatural strength, he lifted the woman. Once again he reached into his robe, this time producing three long metal spikes. He then moved to one of the trees, placed her body, head down, against it, and drove the spikes into her using his sheer might.

He stepped back, the woman impaled on the tree.

Still the woman screamed.

The image flickered and, like a video set on a loop, the grisly scene reset.

Once again the Cybell drew his knife and set to work on the woman.

Izzy had heard the story. She knew the woman's identity.

Inanna, Bartholomew's wife. And his torment: bearing witness to her murder, over and over again.

"You poor man," she whispered.

Philip strode forward. The angles of his body—the bend of his arms, the rigidness of his legs—practically screamed fury. His oldest friend was in pain, and he meant to end it. Katie followed close behind.

Izzy joined them. Together, they faced their friend.

Bartholomew didn't seem to notice them. He stared at the carnage being reenacted before him, his mouth locked in a scream of revulsion. He eyes, no longer their fair blue color but now pale gray, bulged from their sockets. His ghostly fingers gripped the arms of his chair.

"Bartholomew," Philip shouted. "Bartholomew!"

The old man didn't respond.

"Katie," Izzy said. "Bring the cube over to him. We need to get him out of here before he loses his mind." If he hasn't already, she thought.

Katie brought Thomas's burnished wooden cube forward until it almost touched the old man's cheek.

Nothing happened.

"What else should I do?" Katie asked, almost panicked at her failure. "*What else should I do?*"

"I'm not sure," Philip said, concern for his friend plain on his haggard face. "Thomas never mentioned needing a trigger to get it to work."

Izzy waved a hand in front of Bartholomew's face. The old man didn't react. He couldn't see them.

"It can't be something on his part," she said. "He doesn't know we're here."

Philip reached out to touch his friend and his hand passed through Bartholomew's body. He frowned, then brightened. "Put the cube inside him. Maybe they need to touch."

Katie gently pushed the cube inside of Bartholomew's ghostly head. When nothing happened, Philip said, "Closer to the heart. That's where his soul would be."

Nodding, Katie lowered the cube. When it reached the level of Bartholomew's heart, bright white light burst from Thomas's cube, and Katie cried out.

Izzy grabbed the girl's arm. "Katie!"

Katie screamed and screamed and suddenly let go of the cube. It tumbled to the ground and broke into useless fragments.

"No!" Katie grabbed her head. "No! You son of a bitch, NO!"

Izzy quickly hugged the girl. "What happened? Katie, tell us what happened."

Weeping uncontrollably, Katie said, "Judas. I saw him again, like I did when Philip and I found the cube. He...he was laughing at me. He was laughing because he did something to the cube so it wouldn't work. I don't know how I know, but I do. The cube won't work. He laughed because we came all this way for nothing. We can't save Bartholomew."

Philip picked up fragments of the cube, stared at them, and threw them to the ground. "If I ever see him again, I'll kill him. If it takes me a thousand years, I'll kill him."

"No," Izzy said. "Bartholomew wouldn't have agreed to this if he couldn't be saved. There has to be another way. We have to do something else."

"What?" Katie cried. "Do what? Thomas's cube was all we had!"

"I don't know!" Izzy shouted. "All right, I don't know. But there has to be something." She refused to give up on the old man. She turned to Philip. "Do you have any ideas?"

The rage at Bartholomew's torment had fled Philip. His face sagged with defeat, and he closed his eyes. "The *gellyd* is nearby. I can feel it. I need my brothers. We have to go back, consult with them, and try again. Maybe being here once will help me find it again. Maybe we won't have to do all this over again."

Izzy stiffened. Retreat was as bad as defeat. And with Matthew's sacrifice, returning without Bartholomew somehow made his sacrifice far less worthy.

But perhaps Philip was right. They were exhausted and out of ideas. Though it pained her, his idea gave them their best chance for success.

Swallowing back the bile rising in her throat, she said, "Okay. We go back. But we will return. We won't give up on Bartholomew."

Her words seemed to strike Katie physically. The girl had spent her last few years with the old man, learning from him, bonding with him. She took a ragged step back. "You want to go back? Leave him here like this?"

"If you have any ideas," Izzy said, "now's the time to tell us."

Katie's mouth opened but no words came out. Her face crumpled. "All right. We go back. But we return as soon as we can. He can't go on like this." She approached Bartholomew. Fresh tears streamed from her eyes. "We'll be back soon. I promise." Reaching down, she wrapped her arms around the spectral Bartholomew. As she came into contact with his ghostly form, she once again cried out—

—and Bartholomew vanished.

As he did, Izzy suddenly felt a pulling, like someone had placed his hand around her spine and drew her away. The walls of the room faded.

And then she did too.

CHAPTER FOURTEEN

Gene stared as Izzy, Katie, and Philip suddenly appeared in the living room and tumbled to the floor.

"I'm so sorry," Izzy said, panting from the effort of talking. "We failed."

Philip struggled to his feet. He moved slowly, like a man who had given up on himself. "I don't know what to say," he muttered.

Gene noticed Katie lying on the floor. She wasn't moving. He knelt beside her, checked for a pulse. She was alive, but how seriously injured?

Izzy got to her knees, her curly hair hanging in damp strands across her forehead. Her eyes had taken on a haunted look. Gene wondered what horrors she had witnessed during her journey in Topheth.

"We didn't save him," she said. "Thomas's cube...Judas tampered with it. Bartholomew—" She shook her head. "We lost him. We almost had him, but then he disappeared. And Katie—something happened to her. She grabbed her head and screamed and fainted or something."

At the mention of Judas, the well-dressed man accompanying

Natalie's friend Sean Leyton stepped through the door, his lips set in a tight grimace.

"Of course I did," he said. "My nature demanded it."

Philip whirled, his face white with rage. Before he could advance on the traitor, Thomas put a hand on his shoulder.

"He's here for a reason," Thomas said. "Let's hear him out."

Philip shook off Thomas's hand. "He's betrayed us too many times. I don't trust a word he says."

Judas gave a half shrug. "You know nothing of my existence, and your judgments are determined only by your biases. Nothing I can say will change that, so why make the attempt?"

Sean Leyton stepped into the house, distrust plain on his youthful face. "You didn't tell me you knew these guys," he said to Judas.

"You were on a need-to-know basis, young man," Judas replied. "You didn't need to know that. In fact, you don't need to know much else."

Sean's cheeks reddened. "You make it sound like I'm no longer needed."

Judas pulled a handgun from inside his jacket. The barrel was long, too long, and Gene realized the man had fixed a suppressor onto the end of the barrel. Judas aimed it at Sean, and fired twice, *pfft pfft*. Sean issued a breathy *whoomph*, blinked stupidly at the bloody holes in his chest, and collapsed.

"No," Judas said calmly. "You are definitely 'no longer needed.'" Before anyone could react, he grabbed Natalie, locked his arm around her neck, and pressed the barrel of the gun to her head. "No one move, please. I'd rather this not get messier than necessary."

Gene rose as Izzy lurched forward with Philip. Both held murder in their eyes. Gene thought that Judas had just made a serious strategic error.

Thomas interposed himself between his friends and Judas. "Let's hear him out," he repeated, then his expression grew stern. "Though murdering an Innocent is never acceptable."

Gene heard footsteps upstairs and a door open.

"I heard shouting," James called out. "What's going on?"

"Come down here," Judas returned. "Bring your brother, if he's there."

A moment of silence, then: "I know that voice."

"You do indeed," Judas said. "I have a gun pointed at young Natalie. If you want her to live, you will do as I say."

Another set of footsteps. "Oh please," John said. Gene heard weakness in the man's voice, "You can't come up with something better than an old cliché like that?" His tone became mocking. "'I've got a gun to her head. Do as I say or else.' You were never an original thinker, Judas."

Judas's grip on Natalie tightened. "Come down here now. I want us together for this final act."

When Izzy took a step toward Judas, Gene told her, "Don't. He'll kill Natalie."

Izzy whirled on him, her face a shining mask of anger. Gene could see she had been tormented on her recent journey and had experienced too much failure. She itched for retribution, for some reason to keep going. Her drive had to be severe for her to consider an inadvisable move like attacking a man with a gun to her daughter's head.

"Think it through," Gene said. "Don't react on impulse. You're smarter than that."

Izzy hesitated. Some of her anger fled. As she turned to face Judas, James and John entered the room. John looked pale, and he had slung an arm over his brother's shoulder for support. They moved to stand with Philip and Thomas.

"Where's the boy?" Judas said. "Where's Kevin? And Matthew? I want them here, too."

"We know Marbæs desires either Kevin or his death," John said. "We won't turn him over to you, and we won't let you kill him." He sneered at his former brother. "You'll have to go back empty handed. I hope she takes your head for your failure."

"As for Matthew," Philip said. "He's gone."

Gene saw a glimpse of something—eagerness, perhaps, or relief?—flash in Judas's eyes. "Gone?" Judas asked. "Gone where?"

"He found his purpose in Topheth," Philip said. "An awful purpose."

John, James, and Thomas looked quizzically at Philip, but the Forever Man didn't elaborate. Judas, however, seemed to understand. He lost some of his tension. "He did it then. What Bartholomew and I had planned, Matthew fulfilled. He restored the balance to the Veil. I knew he was a brave man, but he surpassed even my own estimations."

Philip's expression hardened. "You expect me to believe you helped fix the thing you had a hand in breaking?"

"With Bartholomew's assistance," Judas said.

"Why?" Philip asked.

"I told you, it's my nature: to help and to hinder. I can do no less." Judas's eyes grew cold. "Now, on to other matters. Where is the boy, Kevin?" When no one answered, he turned to Izzy. The gun's barrel looked huge next to Natalie's head. "You fought to save her once. Will you see her die now?"

Izzy tensed like a coiled spring. "Harm her and I will kill you."

"Better people than you have tried," Judas returned.

"You know the risk the boy poses," Thomas said, his brows furrowed together.

James and John caught Thomas's implications almost immediately. "Yes," James said, and John added: "He could be your undoing."

Gene looked from person to person to person. "What does Kevin Sallinen have to do with any of this?"

"It's his von Kliner's syndrome," Izzy said. "Something about it nullifies supernatural abilities. In his presence, these people return to being merely human. It's hard to kill a Forever Man, but with Kevin around, it can happen. That's why Marbæs wants him so badly. It's why Judas has come for him now."

"You assume too much," Judas said. "I do not associate with Marbæs unless required. I find her...unpleasant. As for the boy, I haven't come to take him. I simply want him to stay out of my way. That's why I want to know where he is."

No one answered Judas, because no one had to. Kevin Sallinen entered the room. He had come silently down the stairs.

"Here I am," Kevin said. He stopped next to Izzy and slipped his hand into hers. "Sing a song of six pence, a pocket full of rye.

This bad man isn't so bad, though someone's still gonna die."

***

Izzy felt Kevin's hand squeeze hers, and she squeezed back. She would find a way to protect both her children, natural and assumed.

Except Judas said he didn't want Kevin.

Why then was he here?

On the floor, Katie groaned and opened her eyes. Izzy gasped.

Katie's irises had changed color, from their natural brown to a brilliant sky blue.

The same color as Bartholomew's.

Katie looked at Judas. "Did we do it? Did we restore the balance?" Her eyes widened with shock, and she brought her hands up to her face, turning them back and forth. "What happened? Why am I here like *this*?"

Judas nodded. "Indeed, we did mend the Veil, my friend. Which makes what I do next all the more painful." He released Natalie and pushed her away. "Take the boy and leave. Go upstairs. Do not come back down." When Natalie hesitated, Judas pointed the gun at her. "GO!"

Natalie, her eyes wide with fear, backed away from Judas. "He killed Sean. He killed him!" When she reached Izzy, she said, "What should I do?"

Good question, Izzy thought. She didn't want to simply give in to Judas; she hated handing the bastard that much power. But she also didn't want to risk her daughter or Kevin.

"Take Kevin and go," Izzy said, her eyes never leaving Judas. "Don't come down until I tell you." She released Kevin's hand. "Go with Natalie," she told him. "Go with Nat."

Kevin looked confused. "No go. Stay with Mom."

"Sweetie," Izzy said. "I don't have time for this. Do as I say. Go with Natalie."

Tears sprung to Kevin's eyes. "No!" He threw his arms around her waist. "Stay with Mom!"

Izzy gave her daughter a pleading look. Natalie nodded and

grabbed Kevin, prying him from her mother. "This isn't our show."

Kevin resisted, but his movements were uncoordinated. Natalie held him by the arms and dragged him out of the room. Kevin cried incoherently. He kicked Natalie in the shin. Natalie grimaced but continued to drag Kevin to the stairs, and then pushed him up them. Soon they were in his bedroom, the door shut.

During the drama of Kevin's removal, Katie had struggled to her feet. She pointed a finger at Judas. "Why did you do this? Why am I not in my body?"

Judas brought the gun to bear on Katie. "I am not unlike the Veil; I have a certain balance I must maintain. I've helped. Now I must hinder. Goodbye, my old friend."

Several things happened simultaneously. Judas's finger squeezed against the gun's trigger. Izzy, seeing what Judas was about to do, jumped in front of Katie. Philip and James charged Judas. John pushed Katie away from danger, while Thomas, his old eyes wide with surprise, took an ungainly step backward.

Then Gene suddenly lurched in front of Izzy. Before he did, she caught a glimpse of his expression. She'd seen it on him before: when she had gotten engaged to Stanley, when he had left for Chicago and she thought she would never see him again. Outside the cave in Kinsey, before they'd confronted the people who had kidnapped her daughter.

He looked like a broken-hearted man saying goodbye.

The gun went off with muted lethality. Gene cried out, his hands flying to his chest. Izzy screamed out his name. Philip and James fell onto Judas like hyenas and attacked him. Philip knocked the gun from the traitor's hand, while James pummeled Judas's face with his fists.

Izzy caught Gene as he fell. She eased him to the ground. What had he done? *What had he done?*

Gene's eyes were closed, his face pale. Izzy stared dumbly at the blood circling the wound in his chest. It wasn't spreading. Why wasn't it spreading?

"Gene," she whispered, stroking his cheek. "Gene, say something." When he didn't respond, she called out, "James! Help me!"

James, his forearm across Judas's throat, turned to look at her.

When he saw Gene, saw the blood on the man's shirt, a pained expression crossed his face. But the Forever Man hesitated. Izzy knew what was going through his mind; if he went to help Gene, Judas might overpower Philip and escape, but if he continued to restrain Judas, Gene might die.

James didn't hesitate for long; he was the Healer. He knew his role.

Releasing Judas, he hurried over to Gene. He closed his eyes and pressed his hands over the wound in Gene's chest.

"Please," Izzy said. "Please save him."

Judas also didn't hesitate. When James released him, he swung a fist at Philip, hit his former brother in the head. The blow stunned Philip. Judas hit him again, and again.

Thomas, his composure restored, advanced on Judas. Katie, her unnatural blue eyes flashing, followed close behind.

As James worked on Gene, Izzy watched Judas punch Philip hard enough to make the other man stagger. Judas rose, blood dripping from the corner of his mouth. He gave Katie a pained smile. "Don't forget the boy," he said, and bolted out the door.

Philip moved to chase him, but Katie stopped him.

"No," she said. "Leave him. You cannot kill him, and chasing him would draw too much attention. We have other matters to attend to."

Philip's brow wrinkled in confusion. "Bartholomew?"

Katie nodded. "I don't know how it happened, but I'm inside Katie."

"Where is the girl?" Philip asked.

Katie tapped her temple with a finger. "In here, with me."

Izzy forced her attention back to James and his efforts to save Gene. The Healer had pressed his hands over the wounds in Gene's chest, but nothing seemed to change. Gene's face remained frighteningly pale, his head lolled to the side. He didn't seem to be breathing.

Izzy traced Gene's cheek with her finger. His skin felt cool.

"I know why you did it," she whispered. "You always wanted to protect me, and now you finally had your chance. But I wish you hadn't." Her vision blurred with tears. "Don't leave me. Not when we've only just gotten back together. Don't you dare leave me."

James muttered under his breath, shifted his hands, then sighed and hung his head. "I'm sorry. I did everything I could. The bullet must have hit his heart. There are some injuries I cannot fix."

Izzy's stomach turned. She always prided herself on her strength, her ability to remain cool in a crisis. But this...this was too much. When would people stop dying for her?

Allowing herself this much grace, she put her head into her hands and wept.

***

They gathered in the basement.

Katie stood near the bed where Bartholomew's body lay, with Philip and John on either side of her. James and Thomas watched from the other side of the bed.

Izzy stood at the foot of the bed, her thoughts muddled by grief.

"I need to do something with Gene's body," she said. The words sounded alien to her: Gene's body. He had been a part of her life for three decades and now he was gone forever.

Her gaze drifted to the men surrounding the bed.

Well, maybe not forever.

"If I can find a way back into my body," Katie/Bartholomew said, "I will go with you. This isn't something you should do alone."

"Where am I going?" Izzy couldn't quite follow the old man's words. Too many thoughts cluttered in her head, like bees buzzing in her skull. It kept her from thinking clearly.

"Back to Kinsey. That was his home. That's where he should be buried."

"Why did you do it?" John said, a hint of anger in his voice. "Why make a deal with Judas? You know he can't be trusted."

Katie/Bartholomew shrugged, a distinctly Katie gesture. "We both understood what damaging the Veil would mean to the world. Possessions. Rising violence. Massive loss of life. Even an escalation of the stresses on the Veil to the point where it might rupture fully. This was Marbæs's real plan when she put the Crown piece into play."

"You let Judas send your soul to Topheth," Philip said, "so the Veil could be fixed?"

"My duty is to protect," Katie/Bartholomew said. "I could only save a few Innocents single-handedly. I needed to do something greater, something that would save the most in one single act. When Judas proposed this solution, I saw the wisdom in it. I had little choice, really."

Thomas cleared his throat. "You knew we would come after you, but how did you know Matthew would sacrifice himself to restore the Veil's balance?"

"I didn't," Katie/Bartholomew answered softly. "All I had was my hope and trust in my brothers." She raised her head. Anguish made her look older, more Bartholomew's age than hers. "What I went through was terrible. I felt like I would lose my mind at any moment, but that never happened. What is torment when insanity makes you unaware of it? What Matthew is going through, what he will endure until time's end, makes my sacrifice insignificant. My admiration for him goes beyond words."

Izzy pushed through her jumbled emotions to consider what Bartholomew said. "I don't get it. Judas helped weaken the Veil, then helped restore its balance. His plan gave us a way to recover you, but then he sabotaged it by altering Thomas's cube. And he didn't stop there; he provided a way to return your soul to this world but gave us no way to return it to your body. He's a walking contradiction."

"He's always been that way," James added. "We just never knew the depths of his duplicity."

Katie/Bartholomew turned to face John. "Are you still angry?"

"Yes," John said, his expression tight. "No matter, though. I'll get over it. But your analysis is missing a critical piece."

They all looked questioningly at him.

"He tried to shoot Katie," John replied. "But he waited until she spoke, until he knew Bartholomew's soul was inside her."

Izzy's eyes widened. "He tried to kill Bartholomew."

John nodded. "He couldn't kill Bartholomew in his own body, so he maneuvered events in such a way that he could kill him while his soul inhabited an Innocent."

"That's ridiculous," Thomas said with an uncharacteristic snort. "While Kevin was in the room, he could have killed all of us. But he sent the boy away. Explain that?"

"I don't have all the answers," John said, "only most of them. Who knows what Judas's real intent was."

"But he failed," James said. "And Bartholomew is still stuck in Katie's body."

"He didn't necessarily fail," John said. "If we can't find a way to return Bartholomew to his body, he will remain inside Katie. She will age and eventually she will die, and so will Bartholomew. It was a win-win for him. It's brilliant. Twisted, but brilliant."

"Judas said something before he left," Izzy said. "Remember the boy. Judas told us to remember the boy."

"'Don't forget the boy,'" John corrected her. "And he was looking at Katie when he said it."

"He was talking to you, Bartholomew," James said. "He was telling you something."

"He must have meant Kevin," Izzy said. "He's the only boy here."

Katie/Bartholomew frowned, and then her eyes lit up. "Go get him," she said excitedly. "Go get Kevin and bring him down here."

"I'll be right back," Philip said, and left.

"What are you thinking?" John asked.

"I'm thinking Judas gave us a final out," Katie/Bartholomew replied.

Philip soon returned with Kevin. Natalie trailed close behind.

The flesh around Kevin's eyes was red and puffy. He had been crying.

Izzy hugged him. "It's all right, sweetie."

Kevin hugged her back. "I'm sad, Mom."

"I know you are," she said, stroking his hair. "I know."

"Bring him over here," Katie/Bartholomew said, her voice trembling. "Have him stand next to me."

Holding Kevin's hand, Izzy brought the boy to the bed. The Forever Men looked uneasily at him. His special ability was anathema to them. But they trusted their brother and resisted the urge to move away.

Izzy watched as, at first, nothing happened. Kevin had no apparent effect on anything.

Then Katie stiffened. Her eyes rolled back into her head until only the whites showed. Her jaw clenched and her knees buckled. Philip, standing next to her, grabbed her and held her.

James hurried around the bed, but before he could get to Katie, she managed to stand. Her face had lost that aged look. Her eyes were once again brown. "He's gone," she whispered. "Bartholomew is gone."

"No, I'm not," came a voice from the bed.

Everyone turned. Bartholomew's eyes opened, his brilliant blue irises shining in the light. He smiled weakly.

"Kevin's von Kliner's," Owens said. "It nullified whatever power Judas used to keep me in Katie's body. That's what he meant when he said, 'Don't forget the boy.'"

Reaching out, Owens ruffled the hair on Kevin's head. "You did well, young man. Thank you."

Kevin giggled. "The man's not so bad, but the mean lady will make *him* sad."

"I suppose so," Owens said. "Marbæs will likely have words for Judas, and worse. Because of him, she's back at square one."

Izzy supposed she would.

James put a hand on Bartholomew's shoulder. "We'll get you out of bed in a while. You require exercise. Your body needs to recover its strength."

Bartholomew nodded. "We still have work ahead of us. Marbæs must be stopped, permanently." He gripped Kevin's hand. "And you, young man, will play a key role in bringing her down."

Kevin's eyes widened. "Game! Game!" he crowed. "We play a game!"

"What game, honey?" Izzy asked, though she dreaded the answer.

Kevin's hand slipped into Philip's. With surprising calmness Kevin said, "Seek and Destroy."

CHAPTER FIFTEEN

Judas Iscariot fell heavily to the floor. Bruises covered his flesh. Blood seeped from his many wounds.

"Why did you do it?" Marbæs said. She kicked him in the chest, breaking two more ribs. But it wasn't the physical pain that hurt most, it was the assault on his mind that drove him to the brink. She tore at every fiber of his being, shredding his sense of self until he thought he would unravel and float away. "Why did you help them?"

He didn't answer her; nothing he could say would save him. The world had branded him a traitor, but the world didn't know that he was the real balance, the waypoint between what Marbæs needed to succeed and what his former brothers needed to defeat her. Without him, neither would prevail. Thus, he endured his torment.

"Answer me!" Marbæs raged.

Gathering his strength, Judas finally gave his answer, the only epitaph he had left of any real value, and one he'd only recently learned to like: "Go fuck yourself."

Then he began to scream, and his screams didn't stop for a long, long time.

THE END

Brian W. Matthews has written several books and short stories. His novels include *Forever Man, Revelation, The Conveyance,* and *Dark Rescue.*

Brian lives in southeast Michigan with his wife, three daughters, and a cat named Gigi.

www.ingramcontent.com/pod-product-compliance
Lightning Source LLC
Chambersburg PA
CBHW020205270626
47157CB00028B/1416